WHARGOUL

DAVE BROCKIE

deadite
press

deadite press

DEADITE PRESS
205 NE BRYANT
PORTLAND, OR 97211
www.DEADITEPRESS.com

AN ERASERHEAD PRESS COMPANY
www.ERASERHEADPRESS.com

ISBN: 1-936383-36-5

Printed in the USA.

1
REDEEMER

I walk into the restaurant that is about to be bombed. It is a Polish diner, well known for its cabbage rolls. Choosing a seat with a solid wall behind me, I sit down just as the bomb detonates. The walls burst, the roof drops, my pants explode. People become bloody foam. Staring into my cup, I ignore their shrieks as my booth is heavily spackled with crimson clods. But my coffee is brown . . . and I am brown . . .

Eating my food slowly, I derive little from it but texture. It's bland, and it bores me, dulling my senses. I cram slice after slice of heavy bread into my mouth, chewing it with the occasional aid of my coffee, forgetting where I put the bomb or why I even brought it here.

The Poles babble insanely, and I scowl, realizing I have totally forgotten their language. I cannot tell them how very sorry I am for my appalling behavior in Warsaw, during the ghetto assaults. Every Wednesday I come here and eat heavy bread for hours, waiting. But the bomb has not gone off.

I've been many men, and once a woman. I have been the sodden earth beneath the wheels of legion. I have fought wars, fucked whores, known love and hate until they were indistinguishable. I have never really died, though I have been the maggot that ate my corpse. Learning much, I have forgotten most of it. I made myself forget many of the more horrific details, but I know that I am not only a child and woman killer, but a devourer of all forms of life, making me into, I believe, the most prolific active serial-mass murderer in the world.

Let this book be a record of my crimes.

I am Whargoul.

I have spent my life as a soldier, doing things I would rather forget. But still it comes back—random blotches of foulness and light, and I find myself sobbing uncontrollably as the waitress returns with my check, puzzled at the tears which slash my cheek. It takes great effort to retain control as a gang rape is thrust into my brain, triggered by the sweaty face above the fry vat. Shaking with tremor, I pay and turn to leave, hearing the pathetic cries of the woman and the tearing of her clothing, mauled by half the company as her village was burned.

I bumble out, bell clanging madly as half-chewed bread spills out of my contorted face. Outside the street is crowded with machines and humans, all emitting stench. New York is stinking hot, and the garbage men have gone on strike. Great piles of rotting trash slowly join puddles, turning the vast and once proud city into a colossal landfill. The people look bloated and annoyed as they litter, spit, and bitch loudly.

My presence here, amongst my victims, is a psychic intrusion. If only they were more empathic they would sense my thoughts, turn as one and stomp the life out of me. But they are ignorant, perhaps even de-evolving, believing themselves the masters of their Earth when in fact they barely qualify as prey.

I realize that I am on my tiptoes, arms out rigid, fingers clawed, looking like a stricken scarecrow. Wearing a look of utter hopelessness and growing terror, I bulge at the garbage-carpet and release a spit-flecked grunt. I bolt, bobbing and shrieking, running for my life from a blast that never comes.

I am hunted in the ruins of a great city. A creature much like myself is trying to destroy me. I am trying to destroy a creature much like myself. I have to do all manner of outrageous things. Things I never would have done but for the fact that I was hungry. And hunger gnaws at my mind, makes me writhe . . . hunger is a slow, lingering death for many. For me it is an abyss. It will drive me mad before it will kill me. But it can't kill me. I've tried that.

So I am just mad.

Stalingrad. Years ago. We are at the Square of the Fallen; Batz, Eurich, and myself.

We twitch with hunger and anticipation as dusk creeps over the ruined city. Tonight they (not we) are betting everything (and they have nothing left but their lives) on a last-ditch attempt at getting food. It has been days without a scrap. Batz is shitting out his water. He has dysentery and it is getting worse. His guts are liquefying and coming out his ass. The dugout reeks of his waste but we dare not move. By laying quiet we become a heap of rubble in a city of rubble, and do our best to ignore random shells. And tonight, when the planes of the Luftwaffe reach the halfway point of their perilous journey—when they drop their precious cargo with the Square before us as their aiming point, we shall be there, scanning the sky through the beacon of flares, searching for the canisters bringing bread, meat, and the promise of life.

They also bring out the Russians, and the Russians bring death. That is my food.

We wait in our lair, listening to Batz's ass mumble. Listening to the city die. The fighting has been going on here for months, and its grim end result is utter devastation. The square before us is ravaged, littered with broken stone and blackened stumps which once bordered the fair vistas of a city park. All that remains is a vast, desolate space, a killing ground. In the center of the lump-dotted landscape is a statue of a group of dancing children, black with soot and some headless but still standing—laughing at us. Few buildings bordered the square as most were knocked flat, and the ones that stand can provide little cover. They are grinning maws, their scars the broken teeth in a smashed skull, and they beckon only death, in the snouts of weapons trained and the actions of men with murder on their minds.

We have been cut-off for three days, and have to assume that we are surrounded. Though I wear no visible rank, my comrades accept my leadership without question. All attempts to reach our own lines have failed, so tonight hunger has compelled us to change our tactics.

"Look!" Eurich blurts, stupidly. I hiss at him as I see the dog, thirty meters away, sniffing at a pile of debris. The creature moves quickly, purposefully. He is too well fed to be a stray and undoubtedly his master is watching his movements with care.

The creature is searching. Searching for us. We are transfixed, breathless. Batz raises his rifle but I clamp an iron claw down on the barrel. A shell explodes nearby but we barely notice. The dog is coming closer, homing on the column of stink rising from Batz's ass. Its tongue lolls as he begins to trot towards our position.

"I could eat you," mutters Eurich.

It stops at ten meters and looks directly into my eyes.

Miles away the shell leaves the tube, soaring with blind purpose. The city on the river curls beneath it, until it leaps to greet the falling projectile.

The blast howls over us, and we bite the earth. For a moment we are gone. A loud buzzing brings me back. It is my brain. I squint through the heat that parts to reveal a smoking crater where the dog had just stood. Batz glares at me with his filthy, miserable face, spattered with bits of dead dog.

"Well there goes all our luck. I was counting on dog stew," he gasps.

"Lick your face," I say, grinning like a dirty skull.

It is a fine tradition that makes me a monstrosity. It is a noble cause that drives me to slay.

My mission is a sacred edict to commit mass murder. It will put things to right. It will establish order. These are the lies they tell. To be soldiers we must believe this, in order to rape and kill as one without fear of punishment. And we must never believe we are the blind led by the evil.

My masters must feed. They must feed on human corpses. Remember this when you are asked to worship their next warlord. See his shining face on TV, now promoting a book of his crimes. Think of his mouth packed to bursting with the flesh of the children that he must consume to continue his existence.

I live in a bad part of town, no matter what color you are. I have lairs all over the city but home for me is Harlem, New York, 2001. The city has been dying for years and my neighborhood is on the cutting edge. The buildings around my domicile are mostly deserted and many are in ruin. In a three-block radius, jammed against the railroad tracks, there are only around 15 legally inhabited buildings. Two highways and the railway, effectively isolating the "hood," hem in the area. A liquor store and a market where you can trade food stamps for guns dominate the passage out. The locals are generally desperate and chemically charged. They are also well armed and observant of weakness. Police patrol the edges of the area. All of these things made it dangerous to travel in daylight.

My building is a two-level garage of very durable construction, with crumbling wooden structures to either side. In front is a block-wide vacant lot littered with debris, behind is a mass of tangled foliage that drops steeply to the tracks. Anyone surveying the area would see a mass of shabby, untenable structures, but upon closer inspection would discover my building is sound, though all the doors and windows are boarded. Prying these loose (it had happened) would reveal bricks beneath. It would take nothing short of a battering ram to enter my property, and even if you succeeded, I would be waiting for you, and if I weren't, my pet would be. You have to know the hidden way, a tunnel connected to the bottom of the lift shaft. It emerges in the weeds out back, at the end of one of my burrows. This area is littered with trash and bones, which have been split and gnawed, sucked for the marrow. The burrows through the brush are a maze, and I delight in hunting bums through them. And so far, no one has discovered the ancient manhole cover, which is the first gate on the way to my lair.

***

1942. Now it is fully dark, a moonless night that fades the ruined buildings to dull smudges. A plane flies over, spewing flares that slowly float to earth. The light washes the faces of the dead, creating accusatory shadows which jab towards me. The sky is fused with the dust of today's bombardment, and even with my eyes, it is hard to see much. But I can hear the stomachs growling around me.

Tonight should be fun. I will continue my research and hopefully fill my "belly" at the same time.

Somewhere up there is a plane filled with supplies. Perhaps the pilot can even now see the smoldering city on the horizon, like a rift to hell opening through the crust of the Earth. I gaze into oblivion and imagine I'm looking into his eyes, trying to draw him to us.

We hear the drone of the engines. We look as one to the sky. Behind us searchlights snap on, stabbing the night. The stage is set—the judges of hell await amusement.

The noise grows—there are perhaps several aircraft closing on this spot. The Russian lights now join the spectacle, searching for the interloper, and the flak begins to rise. Burning darts cleave their way aloft, and as the pilot draws near he worries for the fire is intense. He can see the shimmering tract of the great river, and the city clutching it like a diseased lesion. He scans, face bathed in the glow of the instrument panel . . . there! The call of a thousand dying men brings his machine to the Square of the Damned.

Orders are barked; bundles are prepared. The moment is at hand. A cargo door is opened, revealing the frigid void. From below we gape up at blackness, torn by light, ripped asunder by the now-deafening flak—can he make it?

No, we see the pulsing daggers find his machine, even as the packages begin to tumble. The shredding lead makes short work of the JU-52's wing, reaching the fuel tanks, erupting them in a crimson blossom that heralds its destruction. It screams, then crumples, and begins to die.

Yet the canisters live. The chutes billow and fall crazily, they scatter, and careen through the evil light and in that breathless moment we know—we shall go! We shall go!

The noise is appalling as the plane sears a scarlet crescent against the sky. People stop killing each other for a moment to behold the falling angel. Within, the pilot flaps vainly against the tide that engulfs him. From where we lie in filth, Batz even now softly moaning, we plot the fall of the closest parachute. It will land close-by, and our lips draw back in lunatic delight.

Machine-gun fire rocks away—artillery pounds the square—smoke envelopes our position and within this smoke we rise. Eurich turns to me, so young, so wasted, eyes gleaming with starvation.

"Come on! Let's go die!"

He laughs and leaps away, into the acrid fog. We follow and immediately lose each other in the choking shit which moans about us, corpses whispering as they burn. I move forward, practically blind, one clawed hand clutching my weapon, the other groping the air. Stumbling over rubble, I sense the smoke dissolving and rush forward, low and fast. There are heavy sounds behind me, terrible sounds. The ground heaves with the constant detonations and then the smoke is gone, the arena beckons and I see the canister, parachute riddled with holes, crash into the center of the square moments before its deliverer, the flaming plane, meets earth, in the form of a squat stone building containing men of the NKVD (elite Russian troops), who in less than three seconds are erased in a ruinous hail of shattered block, searing metal and flaming gasoline.

I feel the wash of their deaths, much as you may breathe in moisture on a humid day.

I run for my life towards certain death. Batz and Eurich are to my right, both howling, and I let them pass, for there are others to be dealt with. To my left is a gaunt, wolf-like figure, clad in gray rags that were once the uniform of a soldier of the German Wehrmacht. An unwanted intruder masquerading as an ally, stumbling in my wake. And then before us, we see brown forms bobbing through the night.

Russians, making for the prize.

I fire while running, casings spinning forward, skipping my bullets off the pavement into explosions of fragmented lead, stone, and flesh. The gun roars with hate, and men go down. I am killing. I turn to the left, spraying. I am clubbing with my entrenching tool. Our new "friend" has his skull smashed open, and I plunge at the wound. He dies beneath my flapping tongue. I turn, panting, face slick with blood, unable to take the time to feed properly. I see Batz and Eurich grabbing at the shattered canister of salvation, oblivious of the advancing Russians, who gasp their surprise as I am suddenly amongst them, belching lead into their bodies, tearing apart their faces.

A confusing jumble of heat and stones. Batz is quickly torn in half. The blast deafens me and sets my hair on fire. Batz is screaming through a blood bubble, and Eurich just stands there. I re-load in slow motion. Always against the dirt which clutches everything in the war zone, there is blood cutting through in greasy rivulets, channeled through chunks of gore, and leading to the mangled shell of Batz, ripped like a pillow sack as me and the Russian collide. I drive my knee into his chest, putting my weight high and locking his leg with mine in a nauseatingly intimate manner, made palatable by the sheer pedestrian level of our contact. His gun fires, burning my leg, and he goes down beneath my combat weight, which bursts his throat.

Eurich still stands, though his helmet is gone. I wonder why the mortar that killed Batz doesn't fire again, and why Eurich stands, giggling.

"Toilet paper," he says, holding a roll aloft. A tail of white unrolls in the cordite breeze.

"Well, at least we can wipe our asses tonight!" I yell.

They sent a load of toilet paper. And I was hoping for grenades!

Eurich glares back. He doesn't know if he should loot a corpse or run. His needs, so different than mine, make him so weak. The mortar fires again and we flee, side-stepping the ruin that once was Batz. Eurich is now sobbing, wobbling with exhaustion as we flee a hideous cacophony of Russian lead, which begins to hose the square. We retreat back through the rubble, back to our hole and for a long time we just lie there gasping at the dirt wall. Finally I get up and look around, then sit back down opposite Eurich.

We have not a drop of water, not a crumb of food. But I have to feed tonight, so my friend must die.

Eurich's glittering eyes bore into mine, already hardening with the resolve to last another day. He is a desperate animal, cheeks sinking, lips cracked. Death would be a great favor to him. He is shuddering, rocked from within, as if a great cold had settled upon his form.

Well, after all, it was ten below zero out there!

He emits a long, low moan, closing his eyes and slumping back. I regard him closely, wondering about this bag of flesh, about the last three days, about the fact that I almost don't want to kill him. Then my needs take over.

Eurich looks up as I take him in my grasp, moving him like you would a doll. I hear him sob. Like a flapping bat I twitter about the wound he takes, stiffening. I'm slobbering my thanks as I produce a rasp of cartilage upon my tongue, with which I lick off his skin and tear into the flesh, pushing his face into the dirt to muffle his screams. I burrow into the back of his neck, which emits a gout of thick, hot, blood. Beneath the muscle is what I'm after—the brain stem.

It's sloppy but quick. Well, not really . . .

As usual, there is no summation to Eurich's life. There is no last word, no denouement. He just dies. His life passes into mine. I grow stronger.

Later, crouched over my prey, I strip off my German uniform and throw it over Eurich's corpse. The game is over. Still his bulging eyes peer out over the edge of the bloody cloth.

Looking at his face makes me uncomfortable. Or just his eyes, so I shut his eyes. Naked from the waist up, I make my way back to the Russian lines. You see, I have spent so much time killing Germans that I now desire to know a little more about them. I already know how they die, but what did they scream while they die? I seem to know their language, and I am beginning to like them more than I did the Russians I have been fighting with. After all, none of my commanders can control me, and one is trying to kill me. As I slip through the fading night, I once again consider switching sides. I believe I can pull it off.

It is that beautiful time on the battlefield when most people try to catch some sleep, right before the dawn. Of course, attacks still occur and I often hunt. But tonight I am happy to slip past the guard and return to my vault beneath the battered factory. Piled with weapons and body parts, it is my home, though scaly flesh-mongers felt free to steal from me. I shoo them away and the loathsome creatures scuttle off into the walls. I slump in the corner, popping my joints and reflecting on what I have learned.

The Germans are in bad shape. Lack of food is the biggest problem for them. First they eat the dogs, then they had eaten the horses and mules, and finally they eat the rats that had grown fat feasting on the detritus of war. When the rats were gone, they begin to eat each other. Bands of starving soldiers ruled the night, lurking, armed with clubs and shovels. They were cut off, surrounded, already sacrificed by their leader. It was perfectly natural for them to resort to cannibalism. I pitied them in the way you would a cow.

But their fate is not to be mine. I am their death in flesh. I process the matter of their souls and feel my strength return. Later, in the death camps, I will know more of these things, the harvesting of souls. And we will go there together.

New York. Not the nice part, the theme park, the glittering lie. The shit-hole.

I roam the streets, gazing at the ruined lives, and I wonder why. How can they live like this? The city is beyond management, out of control, rotting from within. People contemplate garbage as their children scream, restless eyes scanning crowded pavement as they pray for peace, perfect peace, and not a burgundy Chevy full of homicide. There was a heavy gunfight on the block last night, and the cops never came.

The people who live here are black. Much like millions of others, they are slowly being destroyed. I am black, but merely for appearance's sake. But I am aware of their position and empathize with their hatred. Uprooted, enslaved, they too have been sent sprawling, fatherless, into a world they didn't make. They are much like myself. And in this world I have lived and moved amongst them and can feel their growing hatred. But I find it difficult to interact with them. I don't know their slang or their customs, even though I am as black as any of them.

I don't like meeting people, I like eating people.

But tonight is special. I am out, and have to be careful of the cops. One of my biggest fears is being imprisoned. I'd live forever in solitary. After about sixty years they would start to wonder what the fuck was up with prisoner 137, the one that calls himself Whargoul. Yeah—the one that wouldn't die. Then the experiments would start. They would slice me into sandwich meat and put me in a museum. But no. The world will be dead before then.

I fly by the cubicles filled with other people's lives. Acutely aware of their contents, I don't think about it. I'm in the Riviera, my current favorite car. I motor, savoring the wind until it brings the sound of shrill cries—children screaming. The cries rend my ears, my face pulsing like boiling rubber. The engine throbs, traffic surges anew, and there is nothing to do but move forward, towards the sightless corner where the screams come from. There are others behind me. They want to see. There are bulky men in uniform, trying to control the crowd, draping children about a smashed structure of steel and glass. How close the dark is to the light. Hoses wash blood into the sewer and I turn my face away, appalled. The children are being machined into food, which is distributed to the crowd.

I'M THE FUCKIN' WHARGOUL
I'M—THE GHOST IN MINAS MORGUL
I DESTROYED YOUR LIFE
I RAPED YOUR WIFE
I AM WHARGOUL
I AM UNCOOL

I wrote those words to make myself feel strong, to exult in the evil of my actions. But it didn't help. I had become a beast with a conscience, addicted to and sickened by what gave me my ghastly life. Acts of mad murder, sexual gluttony, my life was a tapestry was both. Some humans know the utter mastery of the bloody blowing of chunks. Murder. Physical and mental orgasm, attainable godhead. Oh, but the price. Anyone but a monster would be horrified. But you know that the world is full of monsters.

Have you ever felt a human die? Feel the thing best called a soul slip to the ether? I feel them die. I feed off their deaths. Countless beings have died beneath my blows, my orders, my uranium-tipped bullets. Bullets that tear through steel and stone, flesh and bone. On the "Highway of Death," and the day of the dog. You do remember the Highway? I mean, everyone is so proud of what we did—but do you know what we really did?

The Gulf War. Biological weapons, oil fires, massed mechanized carnage in the name of a devil with the face of a man. Still, Stalingrad made Desert Storm look like a weenie-roast. And that's what we did. We roasted 'em up and we ate 'em alive.

The highway runs north from Kuwait City, all the way to Baghdad. It is the main invasion route for the legions of Saddam, and after the Allies liberated the city it became the principle route of retreat. The highway is jammed with every conceivable type of vehicle jammed with every conceivable type of merchandise, including human beings. They could have surrendered but the temptation to loot out-weighed the instinct for survival. Planes attack the head and tail of the column, immobilizing it. And then the real killing begins.

I am flying an A-10 Warthog. Really a nasty piece of work. Heavily armed and armored, it is *the* ground-attack aircraft. At least that's what they called it on the Discovery Channel. It really is a hellish device, an infernal machine that has no place on your Earth. Inspired by devils into the minds of the privileged "clevers," as they call the humans who bargain with such beings. It is designed to rip apart flesh, spilling your soul into the maw of the harvester—me.

My wing comes in low from the sea. I have just stolen this plane from an air base by rudely inhabiting the body of an American pilot. We tear past the dazzling breakers towards the fire, which engulfs the horizon. There is lots of radio chatter. Orders come in and are promptly ignored as the feast beacon calls. This won't be like sucking brain stems—I can kill thousands!

Death, a natural process. Whargoul, the fate accelerator. I recall undead lords I served. My grip curls into the stick and our three ships bolt like moths to a bug-lamp. The bugs without wings scuttle on the surface of the earth, milling about in terror and confusion. They wish they could fly.

Instruments whirl, minds boggle, turbo-charged metal claws for purchase at the fickle wind. I am this ship, this pilot. Since my awakening in the desert, my power has soared. I do not need my controls to deliver the payload into a squabble of vehicles. Men die. Women die!

Shit! They are even stealing the fucking whores!

I throw my machine at the sky. The earth moans in a six-G swoop and again I come about, turning on my electric Gattling cannon and spraying them with uranium-depleted core ammo, the spent casings of which will later bring skin cancer to the victors. A truck, hung with colorful blankets, flares and erupts—quick flash apocalypse, all for naught. Details, obscure, obscene. Configurations of metal tracing 50 years of Soviet tank design—shooting at me!

For a 30-year old tank (T-72) with its turret cranked hard right, while barreling through the clogged artery (yes, barreling, giving no heed to lesser vehicles, losing speed only to crush and roll over things. This is the way of the tank), to fire and hit my plane, moving at over 500 M.P.H. (U.S. style), with its main gun (122 mm, Soviet-style) . . . well, it's a million-to-one shot.

And he got it.

Now, years after the fact, I go back and replay, freezing frames of flame in torturous slow-mo. The event occurred with instantaneous force and glory. Such is the result when plane meets shell. I was up and out, glass disintegrating before the sound blew out my ears. Engulfed in burning jet fuel, I spun through space in my "titanium bathtub" (supposed to protect you) as the wasted column praised their god. My falling sun smeared into the highway, and a greater secondary explosion occurs, hurling my ignited form a mile away. The speed of my passage could not kill the flame and I collided with the yearning earth.

And yes, I do feel pain.

Much later I became aware of the soft sounds and sensations creeping in from the fringes of my being. There was a bubbling, liquid sound. I was reforming, and was still incapable of movement. I felt wet and numb, unable to see and glad of it. Gradually I could discern a far-off sustained roar, like great engines. It was very cold around me but great heat was emanating from within my regenerating carcass. Even in this early stage of the resurrection process I was curious as to my new being, and the space that it occupied. There was a swaying movement, translating to the orientation of up and down. I was lying on my back in a confined space, suspended in a frigid expanse of atmosphere. Sluggish alarm drifted through me but at that point I was powerless. I became one with the blackness again, passing from the world as I continued to re-form. Once again, I had survived.

That was in 1991. The year I came to America.

I was home, shooting junk. My last foray into the world of the living had been a good one, despite my encounter with the baby-killing machine. I had scored several small bags of different flavors of heroin, my substitute for morphine. I liked to sedate myself heavily and pass out in a black leather chair. It made me docile, even jolly, plus it took away my appetite. Lusting for the blood of the innocent was starting to lose its appeal. For the first time since the splendor of France, so many years ago, I did not have a war to fight. I was bored, and perhaps afraid to grapple with the curse of my future. So I stayed home and shot junk, and remembered . . .

My first life had begun in Stalingrad, 50 years ago. I have memories of other lives before then, but they are ancient and fused with murk. I think I had been dead a long time. Maybe they didn't need me, or maybe they had just forgotten about me. But Stalingrad brought me back. The "greatest" battle in the biggest war ever fought was too much of a summons for any self-respecting ghoul to ignore. I assume we returned from the dead in droves. I know because I have met some of my relatives.

I came from the river, drifting from the womb to the surface, trailing discarded scraps of placenta. I didn't know what I was. I didn't know I was supposed to know. But I do remember that slow ride to the surface as the only truly peaceful feeling I had ever known. Birth.

A Russian patrol found me washed up on the banks of the Volga, blue, swollen and frozen stiff. I was naked, and I later found that the only reason they had taken any notice of my corpse was because of my giant prick, which was hard as a rock and pointing straight up. Apparently it was so funny that they carted me back to headquarters to take a photograph. By the time we got there, I had thawed out enough to move. Boy, were they surprised!

But they didn't think it was funny anymore. They threw me in a cell underneath the NKVD prison. They thought I was a spy. If only I had been, then I would have known what I was. As it was, I didn't have a clue. I was just a hairless, naked guy with a flat, broad, face and a prick that had finally thawed out.

I sat in the hole for days and listened to the guards talking down the hall. I didn't say a word or move a muscle, even when they brought me thin gruel, which I never ate, so they stopped bringing that. I did start to grow hair. And as the days went by I heard the battle coming closer.

I came to recognize the dry rattle of the machine-gun, the banshee scream of the rocket launchers, as if they were something I was already familiar with. Like the words of my guards—I understood them perfectly. I heard my captors fret about the growing prospect of being sent to the line. Creatures known as "The Germans" were close to the city center, and threatened the district that housed the prison. The inmates were to be moved out of the city. I didn't want to leave.

That night, planes flew over and dropped bombs on us. One hit the prison and blew the roof in. My cell collapsed into the street in a jumble of smashed men and stone. After the dust had cleared I remained sitting in the middle of it all until survivors started to stumble out of the wreckage. Some prisoners slipped away—some were shot. I saw one of my guards had also survived, and he made his way towards me. Suddenly I leapt up.

"Comrade!" I yell, moving to embrace him.

" Huh!?" he says, stepping back, raising his submachine gun. "Hey, hold it!"

I look about, apparently baffled. "Where am I?" I say, "Comrade, please tell me . . . my unit—where is my unit?" I speak in perfect Russian, if slightly slurred.

"Now wait you," growls the guard, leveling his gun at my chest, "What unit?"

I grow more composed and step back, raising my arms. "Of course Comrade," I say loudly. "I could be lying. I respectfully request the presence of a political commissar to take my full report. The bomb blast seems to have restored my memories, and I have information vital to the high command!"

He seems unconvinced but then an officer walks up, having heard my shouting. Before he can speak I snap to a perfect salute.

"Request permission to report, sir!" I practically scream.

He visibly flinches. "For God's sake shut up, man! Are you deaf?"

"A little sir, the bomb and all . . ."

"What information were you speaking of? Where does this man come from?" he says.

"They brought him in last week. Said they'd found him by the river, near Rynok. A deserter or spy they said, but they never came back for him. Killed, no doubt. Anyway, he came in naked so we gave him a uniform. He hasn't said a word the whole time. Looks Mongolian, if you ask me."

"Yes, that's right, I'm Mongolian," I blurt out.

"Silence!" barks the officer. "All right, quickly give your report."

"Sir! I am Private Yorgi Stalyonavich of the 57th Rifle Division, 43rd Army. I was engaged in the defense of Rynok and killed many Huns. During the fighting I found a leather map case on a dead Nazi. I could tell it was important so I hid it in the sewer before the fascist scum overwhelmed our position. Then something big blew up and knocked me into the water. That's the last thing I remember."

"He's lying, sir," says my captor. " He's a deserter who should be shot."

"Sir, my commander is Captain Gulchuk. I beg you to return with me to my unit so he may verify my words!"

It's a good lie, pieced together from bits of information I'd been hearing all week. The growing drone of more approaching planes speeds his decision.

"All right Private," he says, casting a nervous look at the sky. "You certainly don't look German. You can ride with my unit to the Northern District. Come with me."

Luck, lies, and unseen designs had steered me well. I was in the

Russian army, holding on to the battered remnants of Stalingrad. And I was happy.

I wake again, definitely in a box. I move my hands to my face and feel smooth skin, breathe deeply with my newly formed lungs. I'm back.

It's happened before and you can't kill it. And every time, it gets stronger. Who knows where it came from, but its not done evolving.

It's me! But something bad had happened, something that made me unclean. And now I hear the low piping tones of an organ, playing a sonorous dirge . . .

U.S. Air Force Captain John Crinkle had enjoyed an illustrious career until I caught up to him. His only combat action before the gulf had been in Grenada, where his squadron had attacked and annihilated a colony of monkeys. There were medals all around. I don't like killing animals. How can humans claim they are superior to "beasts" that routinely see in the dark, run 70 M.P.H., and fly?

Once he dropped that cluster bomb he was hooked for life on the deadliest of highs—combat. That nauseous-on-adrenaline feeling was too good to resist, as if landing 20-ton jets on pitching carrier decks wasn't exciting enough. Drug-free (didn't even drink coffee), Crinkle was a junkie with a weapon. His jet-boy dreams turned into a full-on career, and he threw himself into his NATO training, relishing the "collapse" of the Soviet Union. Other grim tableaus were enacted, we wanted a war, and Crinkle ended up in Desert Storm.

I got him when he was out jogging in the pre-dawn mist. He was so gung-ho that he would trot far past the sentries, Colt .45 slapping the small of his muscular back. I came out of the deepest desert, my "awakening" behind me, gorged on the souls of 20,000 men. Formless, black and crackling, I moved like ball lightning towards my next encounter with fate, and he saw me coming.

He actually stopped, drew his weapon, and emptied the entire clip into me. Or rather through me. After two bullets he should have realized that the legends were true. Hot lead cannot reckon with necrotic madness, and I bore down onto him, into him, violating and invading his being, crashing into it, pushing through the pest and gristle, finding the heart and claiming it as my own.

Yet the crust was intact. I had captured good material and calmed myself within it. And when John Crinkle jogged back past the sentries it was just another day in the air war against our buddy Saddam's crummiest cannon fodder legions. I should have known—earlier that day I'd been one of them.

I collected my men, skipped breakfast (strange for the Captain) and was on my way to a rendezvous with a tank shell. Two hours later I was a blob of burning meat beside "the highway of death." Four days later a U.S. Graves Registration team scraped me up. One week later I was attending my own funeral.

But in what form? I touch my face, and the features are unfamiliar. A feeling of amorphous rage builds within me and I lash out against the coffin lid, smashing my fist through the thick wood. I immediately feel the terror around me and it makes me stronger. Grunting, I rip the lid off and sit up, taking quick note of my surroundings. The coffin sits on an altar in the midst of a medium-sized church. My funeral is well-attended by a lot of white people who are, to say the least, surprised to see a total stranger jump out of the coffin, which is supposed to contain a lump of burnt meat—"Really Mrs. Crinkle, there is no need for you to see your son." I barely notice my new skin is black as I am instantly sick from the fluids they have pumped me full of, and I shatter the box in a flurry of wood chips and vomit. The coffin awkwardly teeters and then crashes to the floor, spilling me down the stairs. It's all a blur as I lurch towards the aisle, the people screaming and parting, bumbling over each other in a mad panic to get away from the burbling maniac who has just ruined their funeral. Trailing splinters, I reel across the carpet, bellowing obscenities. A red-faced fool blocks my path—in an instant he is grasped by face and groin, groaning into my palm as his genitals are crushed. The stampede becomes frantic as men stomp their wives into the floor in their haste to escape.

I stand, shrieking, holding the man aloft. I snap his spine with an audible crack and hurl his broken body at the pews, bouncing him across the rows and into the retreating horde.

"WHARGOUL! WHARGOUL!" I slobber at soul-shrinking volume, wheeling up the aisle, pausing to shatter the front doors in a blow that surprises even me. I am lashed by rain—the mid-day street is evening-dark with a sudden thunderstorm. My body racked with nausea, I run into the street, bouncing through traffic. If any followed, they were greeted by a black storm that came from nowhere.

There had been a time, I was sure, when my being had inhabited a dismal swamp. Being of the devil, I was highly courted, and bound in covenant to my undead lord. I was granted power in accord with results, and rode a skeletal steed encased in once-fine mail, corroded by the tomb from which it had been wrested. My body was out of proportion with my spirit, which had been sold. When war beckoned, I followed, and found myself at the gates of the enemy castle.

'Repent!" I screamed, worms writhing across my face.

As mine was a mission of diplomacy, I was shown quarters. Here my body began to vaporize, emitting atrocious odors. My guards could not approach me as I stumbled about the room, still trying to talk to my hosts about a proposed alliance (a lie). When the flesh could no longer support itself, I crumpled to the floor, spirit shrieking back to oblivion.

Almost a dream, that. Except for the imprint of experience, like sun on your face, or dead flesh in your mouth. Horrible feelings you remember without guilt, knowing they were dreams. But then knowing they were not dreams. To be human, deprived of humanity.

I slowly drift back into consciousness until I feel steady enough to prepare another shot. I note with despair that this is the last load. After this wears off, I will have to return to the land of the living.

I ram the horse needle into my chest and shoot heroin straight into my heart, moaning in bliss as I settle back into the chair, which farts softly as it takes my 230 pounds. I really should get a catheter and do the full IV thing. I could stay knocked out for days . . . but who would feed the dog? He might eat me—it could be worth a shot, as I've never been eaten. But I knew that killing myself wasn't an alternative.

If I killed myself I could not fulfill my task—a task which was an attempt to wrest my destiny into my own blood-soaked hands. I had set before myself a mission, a holy quest, and an act of grand redemption that might erase the ugly blot that had been my life.

Something had created me. Some sick thing had formed me from what I did not know, and had set me out upon the earth to rape and slay and maim, somehow feeding off my feeding to sustain its own hideous existence. But perhaps it did not realize that in my years amongst the humans that I might develop empathy or even sympathy for them.

I had to find my creator, and destroy it, so I might save my eternal soul.

To begin, I would have to unravel the clues of my past, things that I had forgotten in the space of my 50 years upon this planet. How had I gotten here? Who was I? *What* was I? This was the point of my drug-soaked, dream-drenched reveries—a search for the truth in the black pages of my mind. The more time I could spend in this manner, the better chance there was of my remembering the things I had made myself forget. Then it would be payback time.

I sink back into delirium, disappearing into myself, and notice a tangled mass of protoplasmic material. I move towards it, bumping into its gelatinous fringe. It is like discovering a cancer in yourself and the hateful energy repulses me, sending me to other regions, other times.

After WWII, I had slipped away. I was lucky, and not overly Aryan looking. Plus I spoke several languages perfectly, and had money and papers. I had seen the end coming and had made preparations accordingly. This was my second incarnation—what I had become after Stalingrad, and in that time I had done some things—terrible, awful things. And I had felt great about doing them. It had brought me tremendous power, and earned me formidable enemies. But I needed a vacation.

So I went to France, the south of France, near the Spanish border in the foothills of the Pyrenees. It was only ten miles from the Mediterranean, and the climate was delightful. The people were simple, and it was an easy matter to procure a sun-washed villa atop a mountain with an excellent view of the only approach route. I fixed the place up and settled in, taking great satisfaction in my first real house. And I began to out-wait my fate. I began to grow old. And the older I got, the more I believed that at some point in the recent past, I had gone mad, and totally lost track of all my family and friends. It seemed reasonable and certainly preferable to an image of me behind a machine-gun, massacring prisoners. Me slobbering about in a feeding-hive. I began to fantasize about my old relatives coming to visit, and the joyous reunion, and the food they brought. It was good to have a vivid imagination because, of course, they never came. So I planted grapes, and began a modest vineyard so that when they arrived we could drink a great toast. In the meantime, I drank alone. I became quite the drunk, and cultivated specific wines to knock my ass out. That and the considerable supply of morphine ampoules I had managed to hoard. Ahh . . . the south of France.

My features settled at 30 to 50 years old, depending on how drunk I got. I made a lot of wine, good wine. At one point I even had a local boy helping me bottle the stuff. But he became too bright, too curious, and I had to get rid of him. I even forged a relationship with a local prostitute. A fledgling romance, sustained by occasional bouts of mad sex. Yes, I enjoyed sex, but not as much as Gabby did. She started coming over all the time!

I was convinced, as were the locals, that I was an eccentric, rich, reclusive drunk, with an old face but a young body. The hardest time to believe this was when I would run naked through the hills in the middle of the night. I would find myself atop a local precipice, howling, stripped to the primal, the shield of alcohol burned from my blood. The locals heard my screams and warned me the hills were haunted. Only I knew the truth—they were haunted by me.

In Stalingrad, it had been easy. I had fit in, becoming a legend in the city, a mercenary from nowhere with an unwavering lust for mayhem. It was all I knew and it was how I lived and besides, everyone else was doing it—how could it be wrong?

They let me go, knew better than to give me orders. I would just appear out of the rubble, ammo draped around my broad shoulders, clutching an evil gun, grinning . . .

"Where's the war?" I'd say.

Night fighting was my specialty. It helped being able to see in the dark. I'd take the men on the darkest ways, through the sewers. Then we'd come at them, from below, spilling into their midst in an orgy of hand-to-hand combat. We would beat, stomp and stab them to death, trying to conserve ammo. We'd quickly pillage the place for valuables—I'd go for weapons, watches, drugs and liquor, and then return to the underworld, to my vault, where I would make obscene love to mangled corpses until I was whole. Usually, most of my men would also die. I never led them to a deliberate death, but that didn't stop me from feeding on them if I had to. In this place it was not unheard for a thousand to die in a single day in one building. But I was one of the few who knew where the corpses went. Figuring out the food chain, I had realized my days as a link were numbered. I had to move up or be consumed by it.

I think that's why they killed me. That's why I switched sides. That's when I joined the SS.

2
SERVANTS OF DEATH'S HEAD

The "Shutzschtaffel," or as they are more simply known, the "SS," are best remembered as the henchmen of the Holocaust, killing upwards of 12 million in the death camps. The organization, with a lot of help, ran the camps for which the Third Reich was so famous.

But the SS also produced numerous combat divisions, which saw extensive action in Russia and the West. So while their colleagues were busy slaughtering millions behind the lines, these formations were busy killing millions in the field—resulting in an incalculable number of plundered souls.

The fighting divisions (and a full-strength division is anywhere from 8,000-20,000 men) bore colorful names such as "Viking" and "Prince Eugen," but were referred to collectively as the Waffen SS. It was one of the best-equipped, trained, and motivated fighting forces ever assembled. The mailed fist of Grofaz, the Führer, Adolf Hitler. To many, they were the devil and his demonic legion, set loose upon the world to slay. To my masters, they were servants of the harvest, tools to herd humans into the maw. Fire-belching titans tore up the landscape, reducing men to a fine pulp. Hitler, giving orders he could not understand, a biological construct with the will of a wind-up doll. Something touching his spine. The SS, obeying with grim fanaticism, believing themselves mystical warriors, receiving their brand-new Tiger tanks at crowded marshalling yards, a new toy in return for their oft-eternal commitment.

Training and morale were outstanding in 1943, despite Germany's colossal defeat at Stalingrad, from which the SS had emerged unscathed. Hitler would not have wasted his pet monster in that wretched kettle. There were other plans for them, plans coming from below. Plans that made them build the camps.

SS men often bragged of their honored and elite status. They drank and talked loudly to forget the things they'd seen. They were hated and feared by all, but few Germans would shun their company on the battlefield. Most Germans, and indeed the rest of the world, sometimes even those who fought against them, tolerated, ignored, admired or even encouraged their actions. Like the fucking Pope.

They wore a grinning skull as their badge, proudly signifying themselves as servants in death's army. They didn't wear a star or a cross. They wanted to wear a skull. They reveled in their evil aspects, and the beast they secretly served empowered them with the unholy strength needed to commit their crimes, and later smile proudly in the face of their executioners.

And for a time, I was one of them.

After Stalingrad had ceased its corpse grinding, I made my way west, following the retreat of the Wehrmacht to Rostov. It was easy to play the wounded straggler, considering my appearance. You see, I had been subjected to a concentrated and sustained blast from a flame-thrower, as well as a considerable amount of additional abuse. This had been my first of many deaths. My flesh was growing back gray and lumpy, stretched tightly across my bones. My face was a mask of scar tissue. The ears were gone, the nose was gone, and my hair was a patch of burnt tar. Over-large teeth glared whitely through the mess. To say I was hideous was a considerable understatement.

When I first came up, after an indeterminable period of blindly questing through the flesh-sewers, I passed through a steppe village that was relatively undamaged. The only people left were old women. When they saw me they began screaming and ran away. I stumbled behind, pleading for directions. Soon after I was picked up by a German patrol who were truly appalled at my appearance, so much so that they were tempted to shoot me. All I could do was sob and collapse into their arms. My charred and bloodied uniform made me a German soldier but that was it. Wrapped in a Wehrmacht blanket I grinned all the way to the hospital, apparently near-death but filled with glee.

The hospital was in an old school on the western edge of Rostov. It was a quiet area except for the screams and pleadings of the wounded. I gazed languidly at them as I was carried in, delighting in their misery. I was taken to a burn ward, and here I stayed, in a bed, twitching and clawing at my sheets. Officers came to question me but I would just stare back with my ruined face until they grew nervous and left. I was a horribly wounded man who had lost his mind trying to walk home from Stalingrad, and that was good cover.

I was very impressed by the Germans and their nurses, especially this buxom blonde from Heidelburg who ran our wing. She was nice to me, especially when she changed my bedpan, which I filled with a pungent green discharge, confounding the doctors. The Germans were more organized than the Russians were and I couldn't just slip into the ranks. My best bet was to continue to grow flesh and pretend to be brain-damaged until opportunity beckoned. I never spoke, just moaned until I got drugs. I lay and drooled, and healed. In fact my rate of tissue regeneration was quite rapid, and the doctors were astounded. I began to eat their food, though I didn't need it. All the while, men were dying around me, and I was becoming stronger. But I wanted to make a real turd for Nurse Faber, whose name I could now whisper. She put up a curtain to give me more privacy. I think I knew what it was really for. She had the hots for me.

My ears had healed enough for me to eavesdrop again. It was good to know my ultra-senses still worked. In this way I discovered the SS Obersturmbannführer was coming to visit. My heart leapt!

Nervously, I began to count down the days until the Nazi party.

Nurse Faber could tell I was excited, as I had ceased soiling myself. There would be no more of that . . .

Through a crack in the curtain I could see a great swastika banner hung on the wall. Preparations went on for a full day before the event. Many pastries were baked, and a special sausage was unpacked.

I bellow in the middle of the night. When the nurse arrives I am staring straight at her, covers thrown back, my relatively unburned penis draped across my leg, oozing juice.

"Ach du lieber!" she says into her tiny fists, scuttling out to spread the rumors of my size, rumors that would reach the ears of Nurse Faber, and perhaps even the SS man. I wanted both of them to know I was of good stock.

Finally came the night before his arrival. I lay there, assimilating flesh from the soul-fume, stroking my tool until Nurse Faber slipped through my curtain, bearing a hypodermic needle between her fragrant breasts.

My worm-like lips writhe into a ghastly smile as she administers the dose. Its a huge one, much too big . . . my vision melts into a blissful, roaring vacuum and I spin into a warm and furry oblivion. It's experiences like that one that have left me deeply addicted to all manner of drugs.

After a time, I start to drift back in to hear a confused babble of voices.

"This is the man from Stalingrad?" says a sharp, accusatory voice. "The man who walked over 500 kilometers?"

"Yes, Mein Herr. We thought it best to keep him separate." This is Nurse Faber, and this is not my room.

"Well perhaps you think too much, Nurse!" he suddenly bellows, then just as quickly grows suave. "Or perhaps you think of . . . inappropriate things. Jewish things. Perhaps you should think more of preparing your body for the rigors of Aryan pregnancy. The Fuhrer has willed it!"

"I merely meant that he was sometimes violent—"

"He is a soldier! He is supposed to be violent! He is a hero! And he is to be treated with glorious consideration, not hidden away like some freak!"

There are other men in the room, and I can smell their guns. He walks to them, slowly putting on a pair of leather gloves with his back to the rest. Then he snaps about, clapping his hands with a thunderous report.

"I want him and all the rest I have chosen ready to move tomorrow at dawn. We must get these poor wretches out of your hospital and back into combat where they can be men again. You destroy their spirit!"

His boots, followed by a swarm of others, thunder away.

I had done it! I was headed back to combat. He had called me "the man who had walked from Stalingrad." He knew about me. Feeling flushed with delight, I decide to celebrate. Celebrate by heaping abuse upon a helpless unfortunate. The woman who had almost prevented me from meeting my hero. The woman I longed to rape. Nurse Faber.

That night I take a little life from a man in the opposite bed, a little too much . . . and he dies.

I am very strong now. My sinewy arms, not yet fully formed, could still snap necks. I can smell Nurse Faber in the hall, preparing to leave after a 20-hour stint. When she does, I rise quickly and place the corpse from dinner in my bed. Then I'm out the window, scuttling down the wall and dashing across the yard to a copse of trees beside the road. I hear her bicycle coming, the urgent squeak it makes powered by the svelte calves of Nurse Alexandra Faber. In her self-assured way she has, as usual, left without her guard. Her hair, a shimmering blonde wake behind her lovely face, which is alert and poised and suddenly terrified as I rush out of the darkness, clamping one hand over her mouth and grabbing the bike with the other. Then I run, holding her beneath my arm and her bike in the air. Despite her struggles, I run until I am at the river, in the bushes that border its depth. Here the bike finds its grave.

She is on the ground recovering from the chokehold and I wait until she is aware of what's happening. Her hair is tousled, her shirt ripped open. The mouth is wet, with a piece of straw stuck to the saliva on her cheek.

I slowly wrap a length of gauze about my peeling head.

"Don't scream," I hiss, hiking up my pajamas.

She would have if she'd had the breath. She does succeed in making a noise, a sound full of many different emotions but most palatably pure fear. Then my hand is on her mouth, her teeth sinking into my palm. My blood squirts into her as I snatch away her clothing. She fights fiercely, writhing her naked body against me as I force myself into her, bulling her into the dirt. It usually takes me a long time to come so I immediately lay into her at a frenzied clip, hitting her hard with my whole torso and grinding my balls into the mud. I keep my eyes closed, much preferring the image of her bustling about in her nurse outfit, and fuck her with incredible speed and impact. I feel our asses sliding across the bank of the stream and into the bushes as frightened animals thrash away. By now I have pistoned my full length into her, the slamming action creating vacuum. Chunks of soil and small rocks are humped into her, and my shaft begans to swell with molten cum. An exploding sun slowly passes the length of my obese penis. It feels like sperm is falling out of me for several minutes as my body twists against her unseen form, filling places deep within her with my excessive load. Then I collapse upon her.

In my defense I must say that I was not really aware that rape was wrong. I had learned about sex from the whores in Stalingrad. They liked getting raped.

Alexandra Faber was the first unwilling sexual victim I had ever encountered, and it was when I heard her crying beneath me that I realized I had done what some would call a "bad thing." I equated crying with soldiers weeping over their dead friends. I didn't do it or understand it. But now it filled me with panic and remorse.

So I break her neck with a twist that kills her in a split-second. Dragging her corpse under the surface of the water, I weigh it down with rocks. Still her arms rise, wraith-like, from the deep, as if she were still seeking my murderous embrace. So I pile her bicycle on top of the corpse and sneak back into the hospital, getting some new pajamas and putting the dead man back in his bed. As usual, I don't sleep.

The truck arrived at dawn. It was cold, March 1943. I was still fumbling with my feelings about the whole Alex thing. I had never felt bad about killing someone before.

The truck trundled up, piloted by a couple of soldiers. The inmates picked by the Obersturmbannführer stood there by the side of the road. I noted with relief the driver and his companion were members of the SS Totenkopf Division, the Death's Head Division. Even through the dust they had a superior air, as they climbed down from their vehicle and approached the wretched mass of wounded men. Their guns were leveled towards us, and for a moment I thought they were going to open fire.

"Get in!" one screams.

I fairly leap in, followed by the shuffling others. A Wehrmacht man with a crutch starts asking questions.

"What's this, Corporal? You notice I outrank you," he says to the young SS man. "Several of these men are under my command. And we will not mount until we report to our Division."

"Yes Sergeant, I see . . ." replies the driver, expertly driving his boot into the Sergeant's balls, who doubles over and receives a kick to the temple. As he collapses in the road, the other SS man quickly walks up, produces a pistol and holds it to the man's bleeding head. He turns back to us.

"Get in!" he screams.

We bounce along, my usual cheery demeanor restored. The

other men don't talk to me, but they can't help but look. They can't help but notice how quickly my flesh is restoring itself, like worms weaving into each other to form a living tapestry of meat. Rude masses of scabby tissue form into the beginnings of a face, and my hands begin to thicken. But I need a good feed.

I peered through a flap at the passing land. It was a place I'd only just been exposed to, rolling, wooded country, not like the steppe lands I wandered, and nothing like Stalingrad. I wasn't sure if I liked it. It smelt clean—and I'd never known clean. But then the blackened buildings and empty towns appear, and the far-off and skeletal remains of Rostov jutting out of the horizon denote a return to the war-zone.

Suddenly we pull up in the middle of a German army supply dump. There is a lot of activity around us but we don't have time to observe as we are chased into a large tent. Here, we are given new boots! We also get a greatcoat, helmet, a belt and some rations.

"Listen!" yells the driver, whose name was Kranz. "You will be returned to your units. But in the meantime, you are indentured to the SS Totenkopf Division, owing us the sum of 58 marks for your new coat and boots. You will follow my orders, and the orders of any member of the Division, to the point of death. Fail to do so and you will be shot. Say nothing of what your duties are to anyone. Fail to do so and you and your family will be shot."

"We will make you," says the other one, Wotten, in an almost singsong whisper. ." . . shoot . . . your own family."

We load the truck with rifle and machine-gun ammo. I can see tanks at a welding shop and great piles of supplies covered with vast camouflage nets. The soldiers watch and smoke. I work and listen.

"We must get up there quickly." says Kranz. "We'll miss all the fun . . ."

"To have them in your sights, at your mercy, cowering and crying, yet you are unable to carry out the task . . . the Obersturmbannführer will be very upset," says Wotten in that same cooing tone.

Kranz shoots him an ashen look. "That won't happen," he says stiffly, fingering his throat. "Work faster, you sons of whores!"

The men tie all the flaps of the truck down and tell us not to look out, as we crowd in behind the crates. Soon we are flying down the road, bouncing down a degrading scale of rutted passages until I can hear the unmistakable ripping sounds of German MG's. My companions begin to exchange nervous glances. The fire is constant, heavy, and unanswered. There are occasional pauses and during one of these we pull up very close to where the guns are.

Suddenly, a wave of pleasure washes over me, jerking my back straight and causing my head to begin burning. My flesh crawls with ravenous delight.

The guns spit again, a long vicious lashing, and I feel a great death near. I grab several cases of ammo and push through the back flap, depositing them and leaping back for more. I stay up in the gate, shoveling out crates and staring wildly into the woods that surround us. The air is thick with cordite smoke, but there is no burning, no shellholes, no dead cows lying wasted in the field. Then the guns crash silent again, and I feel men sink to earth, feel souls spent. There, through that belt of trees, that is where it is happening.

Kranz walks up.

"No need to worry. Just killing Jews," he says.

Other soldiers begin to move the ammo off through the woods, towards the killing zone. I make a move to follow but Kranz interdicts. It takes all my self-control not to tear his throat out as I reel back towards the truck, staring madly at the dark spaces between the trees. Machine-guns bark again and the guards snap their heads towards the sound, startled. I see this and leap straight up into a tree, not stopping until my head pierces the canopy, and for one moment I behold the clearing beyond the thicket. One moment to hold forever, one titanic feeding I am denied as others glut. I drop back to the ground in full view of one the men of my squad, jumping back into the truck before his stupefied face can ask a question.

A Kubelwagen occupied by a Hauptsturmführer and two soldiers pulls alongside and orders our truck to follow him to the dump. They joke a little about all the Jews they have killed, and then we drive off. The men stare morosely at the floorboards, contemplating what they had been party to.

In the field there had been a great ditch, filled with corpses. Close to the ditch, which was easily 100 meters long, was a stockade filled with victims. Parties of what they had called "Jews" were driven, nude, from the stockade into the ditch, where they made to stand atop the freshly slain. Then they were shot. Other ditches were being dug and still others were being sealed over. All this I took in with a glance.

We had brought over 30,000 rounds to the scene, where they were running out of bullets. It was vast, a new form of killing, different than combat in that there was no energy wasted in conflict, just power gained by unhampered feeding.

The beast I served apparently was not sated by mere war—it craved genocide.

The mere brushings of the power fringe had refreshed and charged me—now I yearned for the embrace of lustful violence—an embrace I would now receive.

As we roar across a wooden bridge a sudden explosion kicks the truck into the air. A huge mine ignites the span beneath us as the truck dances atop the fireball, poised yet failing, slipping through space made cruel by flame and splintered wood, which enters our abode, rending and burning. Men fly out the back or sprawl into the burning canvas. All scream.

I burst through the tarp, kicking away from the flying juggernaut as it plummets to the bottom of a bleak ravine, crumpling with impact as it is showered by falling timbers. The men are tossed about like toys—some burn in the wreck while others thud into the ground with audible splinterings. All of them die—Kranz, Wotten, and the man who saw me jump. I relax and mostly absorb my fall, though ribs crack and my breath is knocked out of me.

I'm still aware enough to keep moving, avoiding the landslide of rubble even as I look for dying men on which to feed. I stand, and my broken thighbone rudely juts out of leg. I dully regard its snapped end as a great cloud of smoke rushes upon me, as does my pain. I slump, gasping, feeling the burnt souls sluice past me but lacking the focus to absorb them.

I lie there, watching the bridge burn. I can't see the Kubelwagen but as it was ahead of us there was a good chance they made it. Then to confirm my suspicions I hear the cough of a Russian MG from above the far lip of the ravine, answered by the submachine guns of the officer's guard.

Even far behind the front, Russian partisan groups conducted operations. It seems obvious we had just been operated on. I begin to drag myself to the far wall but freeze in a patch of smoldering grass as I see figures attempting to stealthily make their way towards me and the wreck. Four figures clad in scraps of camouflage and civilian clothing, holding obsolete weapons as they came to loot or capture or kill. Partisans. I lie motionless, close to a pair of other bodies as they approach, gaining courage as they scan the scene and see only death.

From above, the firing continues. They move quickly, these three men, one old, and one woman, just a girl. A family operation. Maybe that's Mom on the machine-gun.

"Quick, check those bodies—we must get back to Gregor," spits the old man. "The evil ones will come soon!"

With a blood-curdling howl I leap to my feet, paralyzing the group with shock, jumping at and grabbing one man by the coat, hoisting him aloft and tearing into his face. Hot blood jets forth as I ram my tongue into his eye socket, holding him close like a shield. His companions scream as I madly hop with his struggling body, clawing out until I scoop the girl into my death-dance. I grasp both of them by the skulls, my nails digging into their scalps. I bring them together with a brain-dashing wallop, shedding the "ism" of their beings, which gurgles down my arms and into my hide. I hold my victims aloft, cackling insanely.

The old man runs forward, crying, raising an ancient Wembly pistol, which misfires and explodes in his face, sending lead into his brain and him to a deserved rest.

The remaining son, who has now seen his entire family die at one time or another, throws his gun down and runs for the opposite wall. I release the bodies, which drop in bloody heaps at my feet, still emitting the fume, which begins to mutate my form, cracking my mouth at the corners as pus spews down my molten face. Bones are becoming spines, spines are becoming talons, which pursue the sobbing lad, slicing his coat and the flesh beneath into flapping chasms of scarlet ichor, releasing energy which I devour and in doing so become whole. Then I'm up the wall in a series of bounds, my leg holding in place through sheer strength of muscle as my bone re-knits. Atop the slope a grassy plain stretches away, a road bisecting its expanse. In the ditch beside this road sits the Kubelwagen, a squat gray bug behind which two men cower from the partisan MG, which is projecting death from the low-rise 300 meters away. It fires again, tracers lashing, tearing the hood off the buggy and kicking up dirt around a corpse in the road. There is a muffled thud and the vehicle begins to burn, as I begin my patented "crab-scuttle," moving towards the enemy through the waist-high grass that renders me invisible. My joints become elastic, adapting to the movement as I move towards the rise. I don't have to look, I can hear and smell them. They are packing up the MG, satisfied with their work and desiring safety—two of them.

About 20 meters away I rapidly accelerate and start to rise up. I hit full speed and leap into the air, flying over a patch of brush and sighting my prey right in front of me—two brown clad men crouched over a half-disassembled Maxim gun. They look up and perfectly expose their throats as I flash between them, trailing two fingernails and landing ten feet away, turning to compare the identical qualities of the two wounds I have delivered, running to them to admire the fact they both die at once. I slobber at the wounds, now glutting myself.

"Gregor . . ." I croak, sucking and questing for the magic juice.

Finally, I am satiated, no longer hungering and fused with power. The bodies I search and I take a flask of liquor, powerful peasant stuff. I smash their heavy weapon and jog to the Kubelwagen. The vehicle has been charred and still emits lazy sweeps of flame. The man in the road is dead, shot through the chest. I see the grinning skull on his tunic and know he is a member of the Totenkopf SS. A large amount of blood has come out of him and he has assumed a deflated look. Behind the vehicles there are two more bodies, another soldier and the SS Haupsturmfuhrer. The soldier's jaw has been knocked off and his legs set afire. The officer seems to be sleeping, with his cap knocked off, and only a small wound to his forehead. He has the look of a staff officer, with a brown leather attaché case clutched in a gloved hand. I look more closely at him, into him, and detect life still within his frame, life lurking at the edges of his being, unsure of where to go.

Quickly I bandage his head wound, which is small but producing lots of blood. I sense metal in his head, but manage to stop the bleeding. I grab some clips and a SMG, then gently swing the Haupsturmfuhrer onto my shoulder, tucking his case into my coat and making my way back towards the depot, loping along like an ape, moving beside the road through the brush. I cover a lot of ground until I see the approaching dust cloud of a panzer recon column—two armored cars and a half-track sent undoubtedly to investigate that explosion that was heard as far away as Lyosk. But the first thing they find is me, covered in blood, in the middle of the road. I'm holding the Haupsturmfuhrer, and I wave them down.

A head appears above the armor plate and removes its goggles. It talks.

"What happened? Is that Haupsturmfuhrer Frederick?"

"Back at the bridge . . . ambush." I slowly wave back where I had come from, and then turn back to them.

"All dead . . ." I say.

I return the attaché case (filled with stuff about me) as they load up the officer and take off. He'll live. An armored car takes me to the ambush site. I show them the bodies and tell them the story in as few words as possible. The leader, a short, dark man with a puzzled and suspicious face, listens in silence. I show them the wounds I made with my hands. They seem impressed, even fearful. We retrieve the SS dead, strapping them to the hull.

"Well, it all makes sense except for you," says the leader as he draws himself up before me, lighting a cigarette. He seems brave.

I slowly turn to him and then find his eyes. My own are dead smudges, lumps of coal that smolder with an interior heat, all pupil. He tries to hold my gaze, but looks away. I look at the driver and bore into his head with them. I speak slowly, towering over all, dominating.

"I was wounded." I say louder. " They said I'd lost my memory. I don't know my name or my unit, but they said that I had walked out of Stalingrad."

The crew stares at each other and me incredulously. I tilt my head back and rasp out a long breath to the sky. Far-off thunder rumbles, artillery.

"I know I am German. I know I want to kill . . ." I search for the word, "Jews. I know I want to join the SS."

My eyes turn to the nervous commander, as I spread my stained hand towards him in a pained yet eloquent gesture.

"What else must I know?" I say.

I became a servant of Death's Head. My condition was judged fit, if unusual. The accepted report was that I was a German soldier still suffering from the effects of acute amnesia, caused by wounds inflicted during the retreat from Stalingrad. I had been burned badly, to the point of deformity, but I was otherwise totally recovered. Indeed, my appearance enhanced my performance. All that remained in me was an unswerving desire to kill. Knowing what I did, I displayed considerable aptitude. They needed me, and I ended up in "Das Reich" SS Panzer Division.

I was sullen and resolute, wearing the "speckled egg" camouflage of the SS trooper. Too big for tanks, it was my job to give them support, and I rode atop them from place to place, destroying all. Using cover, I would engage enemy infantry with flame-throwers and demo charges, moving beyond the Panzers who would sit in a dominant position and deal with the enemy armor at long range. Our success would signal the next advance of the tanks behind us, and we would shelter in the debris of our making, gasping our thanks. At such times we would smoke, and find great comfort sprawled out in the mud, observing the approach of our friends, the tanks, becoming ever larger, sounding as if they were about to shake themselves apart at any moment. Dragons. They roared by and we followed.

Of course, the Russians continually strove to upset our plans. The space of earth had been altered in that towns, rivers, and woods had been suffused with new, sinister purposes. This fine road that had taken much produce to market now became the perfect enfilade to send blazing shot into advancing ranks.

Ahh . . . to burn to death inside a tank. A tank is basically a rolling bomb, heavily protected but a bomb nonetheless. A bomb which four or five men might live within, packed alongside ammo and gas. You get a tank and train in it for months within the closely monitored confines of the armored proving ground, working with your crew well in advance of their deaths and forging a rude yet elaborate empathy with them. It seemed that perhaps it was not totally meaningless. You went to war on a train, your tank lashed to a flatcar. You and your men, drunk, gambling. Camp life in a strange country. Blubberingly asinine revelations, twisted by drink. A local girl who gave not one shit about nations. Rumors. Then orders. Movement, always at night. Thousands of people moving around you at all times, yet unseen, from the homey confines of your tank. Doodles would sprout across the walls; stashed food and dirty socks would transform the metal edges. You could cook potatoes next to the exhaust duct.

I stand beneath an unyielding expanse, a canopy of sky. I could turn 360 degrees and still see the same thing, endless blue sky broken by flat brown plains. Springtime in Russia, and only a few clouds dot the infinite vista. The steppe land rolls away in all directions, alive with scrub and the occasional copse of trees. There is warmth upon my clammy face, a pleasant feeling which would sometimes bring back unwanted emotions like pity, or fear. But the breath becomes a diesel fart as my Panzer section rolls by. We are fielding PZ-IV's, and I hoist my demo charge, trotting behind. Other elements in the Battalion are fielding the new "Panther" tank, which looks like a heavier version of the Russian T-34, a beast we all fear. But they say the Panther's gun is better. We do not know because these machines are untested in combat. Rushing these tanks to the front may have been a mistake. These "wonder weapons" seem to belch flame out of their exhaust every time you start them. Several have broken down already, and one's engine has caught afire.

Many idiotic details are discussed as our section takes lunch. Water trucks come up and a field kitchen is organized. We can see elements of our division and others fanning out on our flanks, and the men cheer as a formation of Stukas thunder over, their wings sprouting "tank-buster" 37mm cannons. It's quite a show. The shattered legions, which had reeled back from the winter's debacle, had been quickly replenished by new formations. Mine was one of them. By spring, 1943, OKW was ready to resume offensive operations in central Russia. And now, on the plains surrounding the city of Kursk, our armored fist stood poised to smash.

"How quickly can all this go to shit?" I say to Kepler, who is scribbling in his book.

He looks up and smiles.

"Scary, sit . . ." he says, re-arranging objects on his ground roll.

They call me "Scary," for lack of a better name, "they" being the few men in the battalion who would dare talk to me. I sprawl out next to Kepler, staring outwards into oblivion.

"Murder, murder, murder," I muse. "Why can't we have some rape?"

"High Command has decided that we fight better if our balls are full." Kepler says.

"Seems like a waste of good sperm. We should organize a company circle-jerk."

I liked Kepler. He was perceptive, humorous, and not intimidated by my grotesque appearance. They called him "the poet" because he was constantly scribbling in a black sketchbook, which he would suffer no one to look at. Because of this, many in our outfit considered him odd and anti-social. He was actually quite talkative; he just didn't like talking to stupid people. One time Big Carl, an ex-circus strongman from Essen, stole his book. Two days later Carl was dead, apparently murdered by partisans. Three days later Kepler was scribbling away again. I don't know who had killed Big Carl, but Kepler was my friend.

We sit in silence and gaze at the parade of steel, which surrounds us. It is a huge operation; the biggest since Stalingrad, and we're really amazed at how fast the Wehrmacht has bounced back. But what really is amazing is that as morale soars, and as this awesome juggernaut crawls forward, everybody seems to have forgotten that the Russians are out there.

We are ordered into platoons and then addressed by our squad leader, Sgt. Pitz. He is a bear of a man, fearless in combat, inexplicably violent away from it, qualities that doom him to die. A decomposing Russian head adorns the front of his half-track, and someone has put a cigarette between the moldering lips. Pitz grabs it, and the guy's lower lip falls off. Lighting the stub, he turns to the men.

"Today we will strike a death blow to the Red Army! Due to our recent successes in this area, the Russian line has bulged out in a great salient around the city of Kursk. We stand upon the southern edge of this salient." He turns and takes the severed head in his hands, holding it at waist level. Flies follow.

"Today we attack!" he says, delivering a drop kick to the head, sending rotting chunks of flesh and dislodged maggots into our ranks. The head flies into a nearby gully, where a dog pees on it. The ranks roar with laughter.

There follows more inane chatter as the men take heart in foul jokes and meaningless maps. The general point is to drive north, destroying all in our path, until we link up with the units driving south. This will cut off thousands of Russians and restore stability to the front. The prisoners will be herded to the rear and processed into a more manageable form. This is the plan anyway. Regardless of our success or failure, death will triumph.

Finally, we mount up on half-tracks and crowd onto the metal benches. We smoke, and I pass around a flask of vodka. As we drink the fiery stuff, we hear the first rumblings of far-off artillery fire. The armored plates are folded down, effectively blinding us. We bounce along in our darkened box, and the noise of the barrage grows steadily louder. Each report rouses us all the more until they sound very close, and the sharp crack of our tank cannons can be discerned. Pitz is at the door, trying to anticipate the moment that they will unload us. Dirt clods and spattering steel rain upon our rolling coffin, which suddenly drops down a steep grade and slews to a halt, as we bounce off each other in a clatter of weapons and equipment.

The doors screech open—a gush of cordite pours in as we pour out, Pitz screaming at us. We are at the bottom of a gully; smoke all around but covered from enemy fire, which lashes across the sky above. We advance down the defile as the MG section sets up near the lip and the tanks take position in the shallower areas of the ditch, with only the great turrets exposed.

How do I feel? Like I'm on my way to score drugs. I've been

cooped-up for weeks and haven't been able to feed. I need to do so in a manner that will leave me with enough strength to be comfortable until my next action. I need to kill as many men as possible, just in case the next battle was not for some time, though on the Russian Front that usually was not the case. I grind my teeth and move faster, sensing a great slaughter coming. I have lived in shadows since my last transformation, and now I feel it falling away from me like vapor. I sense the enormity of this happening and howl, sending my sense out, feeling the shape of the battlefield and the positions of the enemy.

We have reached the first of Ivan's defensive belts. It stretches directly across our line of advance, first consisting of mines, then wire, then anti-tank ditches. Amongst and beyond are trenches and tunnels, dugouts and revenants, and worst of all pillboxes made of concrete reinforced with steel. The approaches to this area are well-coordinated with the gunsights of the Red Army artillery and the bombsights of the Red Air Force, and of course the entire place is infested with Red Army ants.

The lead element of our battalion is already engaged. I hear small arms fire and grenades exploding from around the bend in the defile. There is a strong point here and the first assaults have failed as is evidenced by the groaning men with their guts hanging out. I move to the assault position with several others, Kepler amongst them.

"Stick close," I say.

Our tanks plaster the fort with high explosive and smoke and we move out to destroy it. The man ahead of me suddenly explodes as he steps on a land mine, plastering me with scraps of flesh and cloth. I blink away the blood and take off, knowing exactly where not to step. Swirling smoke clouds, rent by orange bursts as they fire blindly through it, obscure the fort. Its good enough to kill the man next to me, and I suck in the fume of his death as I pause to prime my demo charge, bullets kicking up dirt around me. Hurling a 40-pound charge at my tormentors, I eat earth.

WHOOM! It is an appalling soundtrack.

In the seconds following the explosion, anyone within 50 meters is knocked senseless except for me. But I'm up at once; blood streaming out of my nostrils and ears, moving through the huge gap in the wire my charge has created. I run past the firing apertures and around the back of the pillbox, ripping the door off the hinges and leaping within. I use my shovel.

Kepler appears at the door, as I'm finishing up. What can you say? I grin, bursting with vigor, and slip past him. We've broken into the defensive belt, and the Russians are beginning to abandon their positions. Some are running across the fields and others are surrendering. I amuse myself by shooting people from a position of relative safety. They run faster, terrified by my accuracy. I shoot them one-by-one and then have a smoke. It hadn't been very difficult to crack this first belt. It was almost like they gave it to us, and I begin to smell a trap. Then Kepler is behind me.

"You killed eight men in there!" he exclaims.

"I most certainly did not!" I say, feigning concern. "Two of them were women" (Russian women often fought alongside their men).

He just stands there slowly shaking his head. He is a perceptive one and at that moment I think he knows what I am or at least what I am not.

"You better get down," I say, pulling his legs out from under him.

There is a sudden, savage shrieking. Stalin's organs, as we call them by the hideous music that they make. The pipes of hell blaze martial glory as our position is enveloped in 200 mm rocket projectiles.

The earth turns over in a shuddering tongue of soil, which buries me alive and just as quickly disinters me, slapped senseless by the concussions. My helmet is torn off, my body lacerated by flaming steel. When I come to I am being dragged by the heels towards a truck full of bodies, leaving crushed and bloody grass behind me.

"I'm not dead, you bastards!" I snarl, jumping up and weaving away.

Ivan's reason for giving up this position is now obvious—they wanted to trap us in a pre-registered barrage. As soon as we had taken the place, they pulverized it, caring not if they killed their own men in the process. The rocket attack is over but shells are bursting all around us. Men stagger about as if drunk, missing pieces of clothing and occasionally limbs. The landscape is covered in dead dogs and scraps of ragged flesh, burning equipment and scattered personal effects. We've been hurt, and I can't find Kepler or Pitz. Luckily our tanks have escaped damage and are now moving up. It takes about an hour to consolidate our position and during this time I grow almost frantic as I search for Kepler. I see Pitz squatting in a trench, only his head visible. When I get closer I see only his head is remaining, propped against a rock. The rest of his body is nowhere to be seen, though I can smell it. But I do finally find Kepler sitting next to a slew of dead Russian prisoners, scribbling madly in his book, which he snaps shut at my approach. I thud to the ground next to him, smiling stupidly.

At this point I am bubbling with glee, eyes glazing over as thousands draw closer to the point of their deaths. The battle is raging all around us for hundreds of square miles. Above, the Luftwaffe is striving to keep the air clear of Russian Sturmovik ground-attack craft. We sit in silence with each other, listening to the roaring maelstrom, which surrounds and threatens to engulf us. Finally orders come to move out. We load again into the half-tracks, and button up.

"I give up!" exclaims Kepler, his features assuming a bemused and livid look. "We have just lived through a scene most unprecedented in the annals of carnage. I can't figure out what the hell I am doing here, why I became a part of this madness, but you—you seem to enjoy it!"

BLAM! A shell, close, rattles our armor. Kepler begins to laugh hysterically, tears of blood rolling down his face from a small scalp wound, and he removes his book from his tunic, thumping its anonymous black cover. "I just can't do it justice—its really quite insane! A story about some sort of ghoul who feeds on war. The fucking Whargoul!"

We cringe as we hear Russian engines above. The vehicle twists violently, weaving to avoid attack, sending us sprawling into each other.

"You are the new squad leader!" Kepler screams.

For an answer I leap to the cupola and unbutton the steel hatch, wrenching the MG around in time to see a group of Sturmoviks being chased off by a flight of ME-109's. There is a burning half-track alongside of our own and men spill out, aflame. My tongue sprouts out of my mouth like an erection, a divining rod whose length crawls with delight. Around me, all rushing forward, are more armored vehicles than I have ever seen. It's truly magnificent, surpassing the legions of Pharaoh, or Caesar, or the mighty Khan. Everywhere are Tigers, Panthers, PZ-IV's, armored cars, half-tracks and hulking assault guns. Endless infantry, some mounted, some afoot. The sky, so clear earlier, is now black with smoke as we move towards what appears to be a sea of flame blocking the horizon. We are approaching the second defensive belt. The Russians have dug huge pits filled with logs, which they have set aflame, thus channeling our advance into their killing zones. We are already running afoul of mines and tank traps, as the air battle above us increases in ferocity. It is impossible to determine who is winning, so darkness takes the day, before we can begin to assault the second belt.

At that point we did not know that there were twenty more beyond it. The Russians had known our supposed "secret" plans for months, and they had been busily preparing for our arrival.

Worse still, we knew that they knew, and we didn't care. That was part of the plan.

3
THE MIND OF A CHILD

Walking through the city at night I search for a meal, and pizza just won't do. I have a special need and a new plan, and am confident in my ability to pull it off. Usually I don't kill this close to my fort but tonight I'm going to, for reasons I don't yet understand. After all, there are murders every night anyway, and nobody gives a damn.

Slinking down a trash-strewn alley I see a group of young toughs approaching me. I have taken the look of a vagrant tonight and they spot me as an easy victim upon which to vent their hate. I let them surround and beat me, and fall to the ground laughing.

"Stop—you're tickling me to death." But then one pulls out a knife and I have to hurt him, whirling him around by his legs and using him like a human club.

"Go on, get outta here," I say as I hurl him out of his sneakers and after his retreating companions, knocking them over like a set of bowling pins.

"Go beat up some white people!" They do.

Twenty minutes later I am slumped next to a rotting tenement from which the howls of a forgotten baby echo. Yet another broken life, sprawled out on the pavement, wrapped in puke-smeared clothing, drooling bile and stinking of excrement. Most people give me a wide berth and that is just how I want it. For it gives me time to settle into myself, drawing my life force deep into my chest, leaving my limbs cold and useless. Nothing moves except the trail of viscous barf running down my chin, but inside my guts churn as I begin to extend myself down the interior length of my right arm. Truly an uncanny experience to house your conscience in your elbow and sense your own head as a spectator would. But there was no time for reflection—my hunger beckoned and I continue the journey within myself until I had placed all that I needed in my right index finger, which no longer looked like an index finger.

I detach myself from myself with a crunching sound and begin crawling up the wall. I am a worm with six legs per side, ending in hooked claws with which I scurry quickly up to the third floor. Through a broken pane of glass I gain entrance to the baby chamber and then the urine-soaked cardboard box which serves as its crib. The baby's cries become shriller as my lamprey-like mouth begins to bore into its skull through the ear canal, seeking the sweetness that only an infant's brain can bestow. The sound of grinding cartilage fades into that of squishing pulp. The screams become silent as the child's life force passes into me.

My surrogate container cannot handle the energy for long—I must return to myself and deposit my load. Squirming out of the brainpan through the bloody pothole I'd chewed, I scuttle back, across the room and down the wall to reattach myself to my hand. I transfer what I need to lurch to my feet and stumble from the area. In about twenty minutes I feel and look like myself again, basic black Whargoul. My hunger has abated, for the time being.

My experiment had worked better than I'd hoped, though it had taken over an hour. Transmutation was a useful ability to have, though it was often unpredictable. I was always learning new things about myself. Like how when I kill babies, I stayed sated longer. And when I stayed full, I didn't have to go kill people. Generally speaking a baby, even a crack baby, is worth three or four adults. The younger the human, the sweeter the taste, the longer the high. So I was cutting the humans some slack. Besides, what kind of life did that kid have in store for it anyway?

Funny how you can rationalize just about anything . . .

***

"Did I dream it?" I wonder as I stare across the drifting desert plains, where I had been on station with my new unit for two weeks. Did I dream about my youth, like I dreamt about my death, and all the life in-between? Had I been a child, toiling on shining plains, working endlessly but not thinking it cruel? It was the way my village had existed for centuries, and I did not question the orders of my father.

I dreamt that I had a father, other than my Father.

If we wanted to eat and stay warm we had to work, and work hard, and I saw nothing in my future but becoming my father one day, with my own children, probably living in this same house. And if the party men took too much from us at the end of our harvest, well my mother (yes, I had a mother as well!) always hid something to take away the sting of their state-sponsored theft. But when commissars came to lecture us about the growing storm, which would become "The Great Patriotic War," my mother did not think to hide her child.

They had smart uniforms, and a wondrous machine called a motorcycle, and being a boy I was very impressed, running up to them as they addressed the collective. It was 1941, and the Germans had just invaded us. At this moment they were raging eastwards, a murdering mob, coming to burn our babies.

My joy became horror. I was 16 years old, large and muscular for my age, so I was amongst the first that they grabbed. They put a gun in my hand, a WWI relic, likely to explode, although they gave me no bullets for it. Words pumping from a well-oiled throat, we are ordered into formation.

"March!" the commissar barks, pointing across the fields to the West, beyond which the monsters known as "The Huns" are gathered.

We are not given the option of saying "no" as a small truck full of soldiers rolls up. I am not able to say goodbye to my parents, but my dog, Nevsky, catches up to me, bounding and frantic. He paws at me, imploring me with his eyes and mouth. I feel the grief of my parents as the dog jerks about, trying to reach me in the most basic of terms, annoyed at my human stupidity, not understanding the guns. Bundled figures clutching obsolete weapons stumble past, warning me of "the commissar." But my dog and myself have become a steaming tableau, and I follow his beckoning head to the far-off figures of my parents, who had realized the end had come but were still trying to deliver unto me a bag containing food and warm clothing.

I dreamt of love. Love, and the sudden loss of it. My brain was warm, my face flushed. I think I began to cry. A memory of tears I never had, wept for a family that never was. My father's huge beard bobbing towards me, helping my mother across a puddle. His mission fulfilled, Nevsky gives in to ecstasy, barking messily and rolling in the grass. And now my father and my mother, their voices calling to me, their only child . . .

But I didn't have a father or a mother. I didn't even have a name, except for Whargoul. This dream didn't even surprise me, because it was my fondest wish, to be human. Yes, that may surprise you, but I would trade my life for yours in an instant. My existence is a curse. With the perspective of hindsight, I saw that my life had become an atrocity.

I am grabbed roughly and do not resist. Smiling blankly, I ignore my parents. There is a gun sprouting from a black glove, and I am shoved forward. It feels good, but I don't know why. Watching from the truck, smoking a cheroot, the commissar—well, he smiles too. After all, he has come here to get me.

My parents are led away, along with wailing others, but not before everything they carry was confiscated. The village is looted. There is a lie that the goods will be "adequately distributed" even as brutish hands violate my mother's sack, pawing the treats into their greasy mouths. Nevsky follows still, barking from a distance as I walk away from everything I have ever known towards something no one ever should. I am lucky—most of the conscripted "soldiers" of my village have neither coats nor weapons, just an order given from the end of a gun.

We march towards the arena, feeling as a Nubian would, brought to Rome to fight and die, brought to Harlem to shoot dope into his heart. Ahead the Coliseum looms like a beckoning tomb, the crowd within raging with wine and lust. The New York skyline swirls with hell-dust. A lion trots about with a human spine in its mouth, glorious droplets of blood staining the thirsty ground.

That day they stole all the young men. They beat my father and took his coat. They shot my dog and raped my Mom.

Know what? I didn't feel a fucking thing.

My eyes open as I snap from a drug-induced coma to the lair of the living dead. The familiar angles of my space, the flickering TV, my gun rack, and another slobbering dog . . . licking my face. Another drug-drenched reverie is over, and I am back in Harlem.

How had I been made? Had I actually been human once? I knew the answers were in my mind, but how could I distinguish between fanciful dreams and actual memories? The fact was that I could not. But wasn't that as good as truth? After all, what really mattered except what I thought?

This story seemed as good as any. I'd been born a human, a strong and healthy one. Then something had happened that had turned me into Whargoul. I had been unleashed upon the world to rape and slay. My mission was both to create and destroy life.

The mere fact that I existed seemed to contradict rather radically a number of popular mindsets, most notably the idea of a benevolent God, which ruled the Kingdom of Heaven, and Earth, was all-powerful (created everything), and only suffered Hell to exist as a punishment camp for sinners. This seemed rather quaint after visiting Auschwitz. I could believe perhaps that this god was an evil one.

Hell's domain existed on the surface of the Earth as well as in its bowels—and its estates were spreading. If this white-bearded, male, cracker-assed God was supposed to protect the humans, and he does claim you as children, then dock that God a days pay for napping on the job. The innocent (weak) were usually the first ones lined up against the wall, and their murder supplied the evil ones with the energy to thrive. This is how I lived. Thriving on the harvesting of souls. The killing continued, unabated, all sides thinking they were just. Men did much of the killing, men who were devils, who followed devils that were not men. I was a devil. Where was the "all-mighty" while all of this was going on?

Man created God out of wishful thinking, granting him the powers that men could never wield, and transcribing his laws into words for the humans to govern their lives by. These "Ten Commandments" are supposedly the WORDS OF GOD, but even they are open to interpretation.

For instance, lets look at "*Thou shalt not kill.*" Sounds pretty straight-up, huh? Don't kill each other! But no son, God didn't really mean that. He meant not to kill the good people, the ones on our side. That's why you joined the military, to know who's who. But what about when good people got killed? Well, that was God's will, son, and we can't question his cosmic designs. There is a greater good he does, even as he allows children to be thrown into pits full of starving rats. Now get in your plane and drop an atomic bomb on Hiroshima.

I'd come to believe that their God was a lie, often used to seduce and suck choirboy cock, or lead millions to their deaths. You'd be better off without him clouding your senses.

And your Jesus was highly overrated. After all, I'd come back from the grave half a dozen times, forming whole bodies from the juice of dead ones, growing new skin, tissue, hair . . . and I'd played the martyr, with the best intentions a martyr can possibly have. I had thrown myself on grenades to save others, taken bullets that violated me in the most hideous of ways, stayed behind to cover my men's retreat as shells tore my guts apart—who was to say that his sacrifice was greater than mine?

Mine, the poor Whargoul who has cried to your heaven for

mercy countless times, and had never received anything but pain. You are not good and you are not all-powerful, for you simply do not exist. And I've come to the painful conclusion that you cannot help me.

God was a misdirection play from the other side.

But I was alive. And I enjoyed playing the martyr. I was recyclable. I had already outlived Jesus by at least 20 years, but had died five times. Maybe there was something of the savior in me. The only thing I truly believed in was that anything was possible. Why couldn't I transform myself into a redeemer, why couldn't I save the world? But there were reasons, reasons that had to be destroyed. And the biggest one was that I had been designed to do exactly the opposite.

They make me do bad things. They make it feel so good that I want to do them. So I shoot-up and sprawl around, ignoring the call. But I have to eat, and they make it hurt so badly when I don't.

I lie on my couch for days. The drugs are wearing off and I have none left to prolong my narcoleptic stupor. In about a day the inside of my bones will start to itch. I'll try to ignore the signs, fight back with beer or food indulgence, but sooner or later I will have to kill a human.

My gut will start to grumble, my head will begin burning, and obsessive thoughts of bloodlust will return with increasing frequency. A craving, a necessity, that I am ultimately powerless to control. Over the space of a few days the pains will grow from annoyance to agony. Ropy veins will bunch about my temples and heave with fluid, causing excruciating headaches that threaten to blind me. My muscles will start throbbing with their own life, sending me in circles, walking from place to place in my house, dizzy and twitching, forgetting what I'm doing and losing things I'll need. The sweet spew of the cortex kiss is all that can relieve my torment, but still I resist.

Now, even huge doses of alcohol and sedatives are powerless against the surging tide of hatred that encompasses me. Then the visions begin, the nightmares, the horror of myself. First come whirling patterns of rotting flesh, which drape my inner eye. I can't turn it off. The dead rise from within me, muttering their accusations, as they approach my paralyzed form, across which spiny maggots writhe.

I am re-wounded, and sometimes I replay episodes where I have been tortured. I relive the pain, all the pain, made even worse by my pre-knowledge of it. I bite the carpet so my howls won't be heard for blocks. And then my victims are upon me. I become them for their final seconds, feel them being throttled, or stomped, feel knives being rammed into their guts, feel improvised weapons, like cinder blocks, smashing their skulls, and then finally the guns, bombs, and shells which have been my greatest tool of harvest. I feel what it's liked to be raped to death. I feel what it is like to be destroyed by the Whargoul, and it is the cruelest of fates.

The worst part about it is that I do not recognize the vast majority of the people I have slain. So far, I had not repeated any of these episodes, so I really had no idea as to the scope of my crimes. Suffice to say that they were vast beyond comprehension, brought me unimaginable suffering, and could only be temporarily relieved by committing even more hideous acts.

So I roll around on the floor screaming, bellowing at the walls and smashing up my apartment. That is the extreme state of the deprivation, and I don't often go that far. I usually cave-in as soon as I run out of drugs, before I reach the final and most unbearable stage, the pure and raw physical torture of starvation, unfulfilled bloodlust, and heroin withdrawal. Usually I kill before it gets that bad, but sometimes I wait too long, and that's when I make mistakes, like the one I made the other day, another mistake . . .

The man in the expensive suit had come into the neighborhood to stump for votes. Any attention from the city was rare but what really surprised me was that he was white, with a mixed-color entourage of supporters, including a couple of security goons. The guy was running for city council, and his name was Moyer. All this I discern through binoculars from my upper observation post, as I examine the parked orange van, the politician and his cronies, and the small crowd of people that is beginning to clot around him.

A banner goes up—MOYER NOW! it proclaims. Moyer removes his jacket and rolls his sleeves up around his beefy arms, facing the locals who eye him with suspicion. I can't hear what he's saying, but he gestures with vigor, sweeping his arms across the wretched landscape as if he could magically transform the rotting structures into tenable dwellings.

Normally I would have applauded the man's courage—it took nuts to come into the projects, especially this one, and try to talk to people who generally despise you. But my thoughts were not my own, and my hunger burned like an atomic ulcer. Who was this white motherfucker to come in here and pretend he gave a damn about these people, just so he could get on the evening news? You have damned us, and your pathetic attempts to right these wrongs are as transparent as your skin is pale. His admirable qualities become highlights on the menu, and I decide to kill him and as many of his lackeys as possible.

Pulling on my black ski mask, I am instantly flushed with relief, as if I am being rewarded with a blessing from hell to affirm in myself the correctness of my decision. I pause to grab a couple of items I'll need, and then leap to the elevator door, moving through it into the open shaft. My pathetic attempts at morality have vanished, my burgeoning humanity again postponed by my irresistible lust, though I don't yet realize it. My mind is too full of the contemplation of my attack, the review of my positions and the anticipation of all possible variables. I fully realize the consequences of the situation. Racial tension was high and the mid-summer sun didn't help much. This would really aggravate the situation. But for reasons at this point unknown, it doesn't bother me. I have become my original self again, and the more violence that this spawned, the happier I would be.

I move into the underworld, knowing my passages are secure, as I don't allow the terrain to go too deep. I'd blocked holes, drained certain areas, and installed supplies. I even had a boat down here somewhere. Reasonably cocky near my Harlem H.Q., I barely encroached upon the underworld of New York City, 2001. I suspected that it was far vaster than its surface-oriented counterpart, and just as populated.

Scurrying up a concrete tube, I elongate my body. My hunger pains disappear as I rush like water, and it feels so good to shift my strength to where it propels me the quickest, lightening and lifting, and plunging my now snake-like form through a web of difficult passages, finally entering a main artery half-filled with rancid sludge. Moving along the edge, I shake myself back into form and enter a pentagonal intersection of several tunnels. Rudely, I realize they probably put more effort into the construction of this place than any of the inhabited buildings above. Graffiti is evident as is trash and other signs of subterranean activity, highlighted by the slashing sunlight, which shafts into the pillbox from two street-level gutters. To one of these I go, sighting Moyer and his liar's party engaged in a lively debate with a now 50-strong group of locals. I hear the word " bullshit" repeatedly as I remove the first of the two items I have brought, setting it up facing the street in some weeds, just inside the aperture. Now I hear shouts concerning "Baby Kiesha" and "rats," angry shouts. I connect the wires and arm the device as the shouts grow to that of a belligerent mob.

"Now I know you're upset," blares a bullhorn in the hands of the candidate, slowly backpedaling in front of the pressing throng. There is an unexpected shriek of feedback from his loudhailer and he stares at it confusedly for a split-second, a split-second that several men in the crowd use to good advantage by stepping aggressively forward. He raises his horn just in time for it to catch the sound of him being struck in the head with a sweeping fist-to-elbow blow. Horn meets head and both break, sending Moyer reeling onto the van. Blood rushes to his face as his attacker melds back into the mass, which instantly erupts into cheers.

I also hear a helicopter.

The mob surges forward, held back only by the two goons who become the new victims. Ironically, they are both black. A smartly-dressed female helps the bleeding politician into his van. Laughing hysterically I remove the manhole cover above me, and then scramble out of the sewer, trailing wire. I stand behind a pole and observe the vehicle, now fully loaded. People pound loudly on its side as it begins to pull away. A bottle strikes it, glittering shards expanding like the voluminous throb in my skull, and then a volley of rocks. Moyer is behind the wheel with blood streaming from the bridge of his nose, his face pale and terrified. Clearing the milling crowd, he guns it towards my position and the exit beyond, leaving the security guards behind. As he passes I detonate the Claymore anti-personnel mine at what I am certain is the perfect time.

The weapon blows, hurling 500 steel balls of buckshot in an expanding cone with a one-foot base. The van is only ten feet away and hopefully takes 100% of the balls. It's as if a giant shotgun were discharged into the vehicle. The swirl of flame, the report and impact all occur simultaneously, as I leap behind the blast as close as I dare to behold the ruined thing, shuddering to a halt in a gush of smoke. There is a great hole where the driver's door used to be, surrounded by a perforated expanse of smaller holes, each denoting potential death and covering a wide swath of the vehicle's hide. The tires, the windows, and mirrors are all blown-out, and flames begin to sprout from beneath the hood. The tank will blow soon so I have to work fast, bulling through the hole and over the mangled corpse of Moyer—a bloody potato with protruding ribs, devoid of clothing from the waist up, headless. The van's interior and all victims are pasted with most of his head and upper chest, and everywhere are jagged bits of bone and soggy brain, mingled with chunks of meat sprouting hairs or draped with smoking skin. The body of the woman next to him is jerking in her death-throes, charred face graced with 12 black holes, running red. I elbow her aside, jumping into the back where three of them are still alive. One is gagging from the fumes of the wreck, and I move to him with my second item, a polished metal tube a little bigger than a common drinking straw. Its sharpened end finds easy purchase in the flesh at the base of his skull. I grind it in, and then deliver a sharp blow to the other end of the tube. With a crunch it bites through the skull and lodges in the cerebral cortex. I suck.

"It's in the brainstem," would read the cover of my brochure as to why I coveted the consumption of brain juice, and recommended it for all. Why? I don't know for sure, but I had arrived at certain conclusions: your brain is the most complicated and mysterious organ in your body, and it thrives on the finest of nutrients and proteins. Think of it as the engine of a sophisticated racing machine. This machine is made up of wheels and cables, fiberglass and wire—a variety of parts that would be totally inert unless driven by the engine—an engine that could not start unless it was primed with high-octane racing gasoline. Before the gas even reached the engine it was strained and filtered in a variety of ways so that only the most volatile mixture was ignited, ensuring top performance. The brain is much the same. All the shit you humans cram into your festering pie-holes is broken down into essential elements for the continuation of life. The finest of these elements go to the brain—high-octane gas for your mental engine. This substance collects in the brainstem and is drawn, as needed, into the vaulted spaces of your mind, and for whatever reasons (which I did not yet understand) I required it for the sustenance of my own existence.

So think of me as the punk kid who siphons the gas out of your brain.

As the van begins to consume itself, and the helicopter hovers like some voyeuristic insect, I slump, overwhelmed by the relief which courses through my being. The hunger dissipates, replaced by a glowing, giggling glee, which is augmented by the fact that I have more food close at hand, which I bend to with alacrity, jamming my feeding device into yet another skull and sucking out his ism as the gas tank explodes.

"Yowch!" The cab fills with flame as I take my leave, bursting out the back doors and into the street, rolling once to extinguish my clothing and come to my feet right in full view of the stupefied crowd, the hovering TV news helicopter, and the previously unseen cop car rolling in my direction.

I hightail it for the sewer, flatten my form and pour into it like a gush of slime. Then I'm gone, ignoring the shouts and the sirens, racing through my maze and at one point blocking the tunnel with a plug three men couldn't move. I don't stop until I'm back in my fort, up to the lookout post on top and gazing upon the carnage in the street four blocks away.

Normally the cops didn't even come into my neighborhood unless there was a corpse to pick up, and that day they had several. The aftermath of my actions would be the first step on the way to the troubles I would experience over the next few months. You just can't go around exploding Claymores and brain-sucking potential council-members, no matter how strongly you might disagree with their policies. My methods were usually much more covert and most of my victims were never found, plus I preferred hunting those that society would never miss anyway.

On orders from those that I had sworn to destroy, I had violated my own code. I had committed a flagrantly violent public action, murdering a prominent figure. It drew unwanted attention to my realm. For the next few days the police presence was heavy, as the cops imposed a curfew and ransacked local dwellings for evidence, inflaming the bad feelings on both sides. Several humans were hauled away and beaten half to death; one had a mop-handle rammed up his ass. The area around the crime was cordoned off for days and meticulously searched. They even sent dogs into the sewer and I think Maug (my dog) killed one, as he came back slick with blood, panting and happy. It was dumb luck that my domicile was not discovered, but I was ready to defend it if it had been. And that would have been a real mess. Had I known the real reason that I'd committed the crime, I scarcely would have believed it myself. As it was, I wouldn't begin to realize the full implications until a week later when my growing hunger compelled me to venture once again out of my fort.

My first week in "Das Reich" was an eventful one.

My flesh had stopped regenerating for once, even though I didn't have any skin. I felt fairly certain that it would return with my next feeding, which could wait, if need be, for some time. This was due to my experiences in the hospital, sucking the soul-wafts of the mangled. My batteries were fully charged. It was a good thing because I had been under intense pressure and scrutiny since my enrollment in the division.

A black truck filled with soldiers takes me to a small and isolated camp, deep in the Romanian wilderness. I am under strict guard—ten soldiers with heavy weapons that follow me everywhere. They do not speak, and they have faces that look like turnips.

In a cool concrete chamber, I am interrogated about the Russians, their tactics, and weapons. The voices come through the wall. I tell them everything I can, and I knew a lot. The questions about my personal history never came. Where I'd been born, what my name was, what my family was doing—these were questions at that point unpondered by me, and already known to them. I was assigned a name: "Josef Mueller," which was just about as generic as you could imagine. Then they teach me about the German army, just the facts and the manner in which I must behave in order to "fit in." There are also visual aids. It takes a couple days.

Then it's off to the range. I am taught war skills. Usually I train alone, though I am always under guard. I am instructed and supervised by Sturmscharführer Trengret, a member of the "Werewolf" order. We are followed by a large armored car, an Sd. Kfz. 232 with eight wheels and numerous MG's, along with a 37 mm cannon in the turret. Trengret reports to the vehicle for orders. He talks to it, and it talks back. The German small arms I am already familiar with, so they teach me how to drive a tank, how to shoot a rocket launcher, and many other techniques of murder that will prove useful. I ask to fly planes but they will not let me. So I shoot guns and blow stuff up all day. Nice work, when I can get it.

I rest in one room, the guards in the other. I am instructed not to speak with them. They don't talk to each other either, and eat brown paste that comes out a hole in the wall. I am brought food, which I don't need but still enjoy. After a week I'm getting pretty hungry, and the guards are starting to look good. But I act with the iron will that is expected of me.

One day I realize that training is over. Alone in a field, I watch the soldiers pile in the truck and drive off towards camp without me. The Sd. Kfz. sits for a moment, regarding me, then also moves off in a different direction at high speed. Grabbing my weapons, I run towards camp, taking a short leap off a cliff and arriving before the truck. I take up a position outside the camp and wait. The SdKfz comes into view first, atop a small hill overlooking the whole scene. Then comes the truck, barreling down the road. I fire my Panzershrek (shoulder-mounted rocket launcher) in a flurry of angry sparks. The truck erupts in flame and slews to a halt, a chorus of high, piping screams escaping. Blazing men stumble out, their ammo exploding. I cut them down with my sub-machine gun and advance, looking for a feed. I barely see the grenade explode and take a heavy blow. Dropped to the earth, I scuttle away, leaving the dead and my filthy prize. There is metal in my face and chest, but I'm not badly hurt.

Trengret bursts into view through a wall of smoke, upon me with a dagger. I twist about and take the blade in the shoulder, hardening the flesh and snapping the blade as my hands grasp his throat and then his skull, forcing him down while driving my claws into his flesh. I break open his neck at the base of the skull and force my tongue into the hole, not missing a drop.

Finishing my meal, I hear the familiar rattling of tank treads. It is the PZ IV I had been training on, rushing down the road to the scene of carnage and loosing a shell at me. I duck under the explosion and run off in a great looping circle. The tank turns with me, rotating its turret and firing madly, bullets striking just behind me as I outrun its axis of fire and get behind it. The driver throws the transmission into reverse and tries to run me over, but I bound onto the rear of the tank, ripping open the engine cover and dropping a grenade inside, just as the rotating main gun knocks me off. The grenade explodes, doing unknown damage. The tank continues to grind about, searching for me as a sudden gush of black smoke rushes from the rear deck. I leap onto the front deck and ram my SMG into the vision slit, spraying a stream of lead into the aperture from point blank range. Metal explodes into the drivers face, and I jam the muzzle of my weapon further into the small opening, pumping a full clip of fire into the tank's interior, filling it with shredding lead which is dense enough to—*BLAM!*—set off a shell just as my gun explodes—I pitch into space boots first as the shattered weapon melds with my arm and face in a glorious ripping of flesh and steel, arranged in a cone of fire. The beast immolates itself as I thud into the earth.

Rising painfully, I regard the burning tank. They are all aflame, so there is no food. Brain juice burned up quick.

"What a waste," I sniffle.

Suddenly I hear a voice, from a distance, calling to me. A metallic voice, rising from a speaker attached to the front of an armored car.

"Mueller! It is I, the Obersturmbannführer!"

I look towards the hollow sound.

"You have made me proud. I can see I was right about you. It is good that you are back with us."

I stand there, covered in blood, uniform aflame, a dopey look on my writhing face.

"There will be no more mistakes. There is a new offensive. This time you shall fight on the correct side. If you return, I shall tell you more. Walk down the road. A vehicle will meet you. Inside will be normal soldiers. Do not kill them. They will furnish you with papers and you shall assume the identity described within. There will no longer be a guard upon you. You shall be conveyed to a front-line unit, which you shall join as a replacement soldier of the "Das Reich" division. Your new life begins today."

I stare back, deeply satisfied. I had waded through rivers of gore for this moment, and I knew that I deserved it. Finally I was hanging around with people of quality.

"And one more thing. You'll be pleased to know your seed has found able purchase in the womb of Nurse Faber. She has been conveyed below and will be used to create new material. If the material is satisfactory you may be allowed to mate with her again."

But hadn't I had left her lifeless corpse at the bottom of a stream?

"Now go. Go and reap the whirlwind . . ."

I stride off, breathing heavily as I continue to regenerate. No, I wouldn't kill them. I could wait. They were to become a part of the greater killing. The Obersturmbannführer respected me, understood my special needs. And needed me. Needed me to kill, needed me to rape. All I had to do was play along. Play with my favorite things at my favorite playground.

I was off to a place they called Kursk.

Maug was my loyal and trusted dog, a 160-pound pit bull with something of the devil up his butt. He was usually good-tempered, but sometimes prone to random fits of mindless violence against my furniture and me. I still trusted him a lot more than most humans I had met, with the exception of Cheng.

Maug had just shown up one day, and would often disappear for extended periods of time, rummaging through the underworld and doing dog knew what. I'd occasionally drive him out to the country for extended romps, but his main purpose was guarding my abode during my periods of absence, or potentially fighting with me in its defense. It was also nice when he would lick my face.

I had several vehicles tucked about the New York area, my favorite being a black panel van, a Ford, with a steel mesh cargo cage, fat tires and a ball-shrinking growl. It was my battlewagon. There were other machines, like the Riviera and a couple of motorcycles. I would take these vehicles on my "beer runs," always changing my positions and avenues of approach. I never drove up to or out of my fort, and that night I decided to walk all the way.

I needed to score dope, good dope, and maybe fuck a whore. It was that or kill somebody. Still bloated from my last feed, I felt confident about my chances of controlling my lustful urges. That night I just wanted to have fun.

So I got dressed—boots, sweat pants, and hooded sweatshirt, all black. I had my money belt and a thousand bucks in my pocket. My watch read 9:38 pm, E.S.T. Saturday night in sin city. I finished off my ensemble with a nasty stiletto tucked into my boot and a double shot of Bushmills. Patting Maug goodbye, I slipped into the shaft and made my way to the outside, his plaintive whine fading behind me.

In a few minutes I appear beside the railroad tracks, which I begin to creep along, listening for movement, feeling a colony of rats scurrying along beneath me. Moving down the track through the greasy blackness I come to a rusty metal ladder that I leap up, avoiding the security screen with ease. I plop down in an alley and begin to make my way through the glowing and raucous streets of New York City.

Foremost on my agenda is Fat Lenny's, a notorious open-air drug market that I don't get within a block of due to the copious amount of swirling blue lights that denote a large police action in progress. There are shouts and blows as skulls are cracked. I give them a wide berth, silently cursing. I've always hated cops, and since becoming black I have felt their heat even more so. As I furtively move along, the police presence is noticeably greater than usual and does not slacken until I begin to enter the more affluent areas of mid-town. Apparently my latest attack has rattled city hall.

Away from the black neighborhoods, the streets are packed with the insane variety of humanity that only New York City can bring forth. Punks, pimps, professionals—a panoply of persons cross my path, all looking wary and confused. There is a tense feeling in the city tonight and I get more than a few suspicious looks. I slip into a deli, buy some malt liquor and suck it from a brown paper bag. You might not think that a creature that feasts on brainstems semi-regularly would enjoy a cold 40 of Olde English, but I appreciate the numbing effect it has on me.

Me. What the fuck was me? I stare at my reflection in a store window, packed with gadgetry. So many devices. Tiny screens and fighting figures. Personal computers and pocket pussies. And my black face staring back at me.

Then I'm on TV.

The hot blonde newscaster reports the story from behind the wall of glass, as I tune in my hearing. The footage shot from the news 'copter is played for the millionth time that week. People want to see the blow to Moyer's face, the retreat and then the unexpected explosion, and finally me, leaping from the flames and rolling, then rushing into the sewer.

This is what I get for only ever watching the History Channel—I'd become a celebrity and didn't even know it.

They zoom in as close as they can until the fuzzy outlines of my frame fill the screen, my body blurring, the ski mask anonymously terrifying. They show it again, in slow-mo. Next, a horribly burned survivor is interviewed. Then the officer in charge of the investigation, a great, meat-faced man whose harsh voice is somehow familiar . . . I'm fascinated by the level of attention my story has received. I mean, bombs went off all the time.

Then I realize I'm still wearing the same clothes, except for the mask, which is hanging out of my back pocket.

"Fuckin' piece o' shit . . ." says a white guy to his drunk friends. "They ought put a wall around Harlem."

"Then cart us off to the death-camps, right?" I turn on him with a roar, blowing them backwards with the sheer volume of my voice. They scuttle off into the crowd.

But he is right. They need a wall, if only to keep me in. Me, the monster, the rat that ate Baby Kiesha's brain.

I remember the shouts from that day—shouts of "Baby Kiesha," and "rats." A baby girl had been found dead in her crib, apparently killed and partially devoured by a rat. The rally I had attacked had been part of a last-ditch effort by city hall to head off a rising condition in the black community, a condition widely known as "black rage," a condition which had led to a citywide crisis and manhunt.

I stumble down Broadway, panic suddenly assailing me like a cloud of wasps. Once again, I was the pawn. I thought they had forgotten me, I had prayed they'd never find me . . . but they were using me, using me to start another filthy war. And this time I didn't want to play.

I throw my sweatshirt away and purchase a *Simpsons* color print T-shirt. In the store the radio blares "the suspect is described as a 6'5" black male, powerfully built, wearing a black sweatshirt, gym pants and combat boots." I throw a fifty at the black shopkeeper, mumbling sheepishly about us being "brothers" as I grab another 40 oz. from the fridge and run into the street.

Feeling vulnerable, I lose myself in the mob. Soon, the streets are packed to the point where I can barely move. I wriggle madly, assailed by a thousand vapors, an infinite set of possibilities, all pointing towards my doom. Three-card Monte is jamming the curb, limos are arrogantly parked three-deep, and boxes of jewelry are shoved in my face.

Then from across the street something catches my attention, a commotion, a sound I am somehow drawn to. A crowd has gathered about a junkyard percussion unit-trashcans, 5-gallon drums and the like. It's a good beat, and I strain to get closer.

The crowd has focused on the antics of one maniacal individual, a middle aged, rattily dressed Asian. As soon as I see him I forget my panic and stand, dumbfounded. He's prancing about to the beat, doing some sort of a bizarre mantis dance, like a kind of drunken Tai Chi. Occasionally and without warning, he whirls up to an onlooker and exhorts them to join him in this mad waltz. He only goes after those most likely to say "no," like a group of burly bikers, who invariably turn beet-red and insultingly refuse. Undaunted, he capers about into an amazingly adroit kick-jump, landing directly in front of me.

"I'm Chinese!" he says. "Time to dance!"

Something about his face made him suddenly appear younger than his visible years, yet ageless. My hand touches his and a discernible energy passes up my arm, as I effortlessly slip into the ring. We begin twirling about, staring without embarrassment into each other's eyes as the crowd erupts with delighted squeals. I lift him high and toss him, and he flips, dirty clothing flapping in slow-motion, and then he does the same with me—all 240 of my pounds. The panic and confusion of the evening slips away in this suspended interlude. I feel unfettered, free, unstained by my bloody deeds, and sensing the proximity of my energy, the band redoubles their efforts, garbage drums pounding a relentless staccato. The dance reaches its furious climax and I tear myself away, shaking with uncontrollable laughter, moving as quickly as the crowd will let me, the Chinese man capering behind me, calling to me to return . . .

Hailing a cab, I ride almost all the way home, staring at the back of the cabby's neck but not thinking about sucking his brainstem dry. Instead all I can feel is the touch of the Chinese Man, a warm and lingering sensation that now permeates my being. I feel relaxed and composed as I enter the fort, feed my dog, and put on a movie (*Old Yeller*). Stretching out on the couch, my eyelids begin to grow heavy.

I forgot to score drugs, and have also returned without beer. Oh well. It's warm here, and I am weary. The TV sings sweetly. It's comforting as it sifts visions into my mind, whispering of redemption, soothing my soul. Baby killing and brain-sucking seem far away as I slide gently towards a velvet abyss, a part of me that had been hidden but which had now expanded to swallow me. Did he drug me? The feeling is overpoweringly disarming.

For the first time in my life, I fall asleep.

4
THE GRINDER

I must tell you the story of Stalingrad, city on the Volga, "Papa Joe's" showpiece, the communist dream realized in block and being. Hitler believed that to take the city bearing Stalin's name would mean the end of Russia; just as the death of Berlin three years later would herald his own personal götterdämmerung. Of course Hitler would believe just about anything they fed him.

Germany invaded Russia in June of 1941 (for about the hundredth time) and a year-and-a-half later they reached the limit of their advance at the industrial city of Stalingrad. Here the "greatest" battle ever was waged. This was the place of my birth, and my first death.

Over 2,000,000 people were killed there in less than 8 months. What a momentous figure that was! For instance, once I heard of an elementary school where the students set out to amass 1,000,000 bottle caps. Hundreds of students collected every cap they could find for an entire year, and still could not reach their goal. They guzzled soda until their fat faces were glazed with fructose. They filled the gym with trash bags full of caps and finally gave up. But other humans at another time, my time, did succeed in amassing 2,000,000 corpses, all of whom met agonizing and terrifying deaths. A corpse was so much bigger than a cap. Now *that* was a pile.

I must tell you what happened there, how I helped them reach their goal, tell you specifically how men will behave in the face and wake of death as devils drive them forward. The true story of war—not the lie you have been taught.

But maybe you don't want to know about it. The story of a pregnant woman with her belly flapping open, fetus glistening, is rather unappealing; how I ate it even worse. Trying to describe the sound of bodies being offloaded from a cattle car can conjure a vision unpleasant before dinner. Fine and good, but try to not be too torn up when your loved ones are reduced to gristle.

The war would go like this: the Germans would come with their blitzkrieg and the Russians would defend to the last man, only retreating when they were dragged, boots first, to the mass grave dug by the victors. The survivors blew up or burned anything that remained, leaving the Germans nothing but scorched earth from which to plan their next attack. And so it would go—from line to line and town to town, assault, defend, retreat, falling back almost 700 miles until they came to Stalingrad. And then even the lowliest foot soldier could tell that there was nowhere left to fall back to except the trackless wasteland which stretched to the Ural Mountains and beyond. It was do or die, and most often both.

We had been fighting for weeks around the gun factory. A perfectly ghastly place to have a war. The biggest factory in town (in a city of factories), it was over a mile long, and was made up of hundreds of rooms, both tiny and vast. There were great manufacturing halls, workshops and storerooms, metal lathes which could bore out guns built for battleships. Showers, vaults, great smelters and furnaces, dynamos and slag heaps, catwalks and subterranean tunnels, interior railways, all were joined together to create a behemoth of our modern world, a gigantic toad belching evil vapor, squatting over the city like a ravenous god, pumped with life supplied by the thousands of workers who dutifully appeared every day, summoned from the squalid wooden structures which surrounded the factory for blocks.

Of course now it was blown to shit. The Luftwaffe had bombed it for weeks and then the artillery had begun to fall. The factory had gone from workshop to fortress to ruin. Three of the four gigantic chimneys had fallen, with horrific results. The workers, their houses knocked flat, had still come to work, and were given weapons to replace their tools. It was, after all, a gun factory.

In front of the factory was the devastated city. It had taken years to build and weeks to annihilate. Behind it was the river, the Volga, depthless and beginning to freeze. Existing in the city were the Germans, wondering why the hell they were there but knowing only further carnage could deliver them. They had paid in blood for their real estate, and now sought to complete their investment by driving us into the river from whence I had arisen. Standing against them were the Russian army and I, bled white by months of savagery, and pushed into a tiny section of the city dominated by the factory. We'd been beaten and abused, shelled, shot and mangled, resigned and confirmed to death or glory. This was my place, my life, and my stomping ground. At that point in my existence, these events seemed a perfectly normal way to behave.

I rise from my vault before the dawn, greeting the corpses I have dragged here to suck dry. They are strewn about like broken dolls, heads smashed, limbs charred, lives ruined. I really have to clean up in here.

I arm myself with a submachine gun, grenades and finally a foot-long trench knife with a spiked lead ball for a pommel. My boots leave sticky imprints in the coagulated blood which carpets the rough floor as I take my leave of the feasting chamber, gorged on death and ready for another day of killing.

I had only been alive a couple of weeks and had yet to meet Batz, or Eurich, had yet to experience the first of my many deaths. I knew I was different, knew I could survive fatal wounds, but still respected the power of war, because I did not know at that point that I could return from the dead. Plus it hurt to have your arm ripped out of the socket, even if it did grow back.

Appearing through the mist like a lonesome wraith, I felt the bitter cold of another winter's day in Stalingrad. Of course, surface cold couldn't hurt me, but it played hell on my men. I'd make the rounds and find people I'd just talked to frozen stiff. Between that, the lack of food and of course the Germans, this was the most dangerous place in the world if you were a human being. Still, civilians clung to life amongst the rubble. That had been Stalin's idea. He wouldn't evacuate the city because he knew the civilians would help fight for it.

I scuttle up Chimney #2, our highest observation point, surprising the guard who lurks on duty there. Stupidly, he is smoking, his brazen cherry blazing through the night. It doesn't take much for the German snipers to draw a bead on you, and I thrash him quickly, covering his face with my clammy hand and forcing back a desire to snap his neck, quickly gorge, and then throw his body down the chimney shaft. But no . . . we need the men and besides, I have just fed.

"Idiot!" I hiss. "You want to get your head blown off?" I take the field phone and move a little way back down the circular metal stairway, half expecting a fullisade of German lead to tear it up behind me. The guard, regaining his composure, follows me at a cautious distance. I slowly peer over the railing and feel the vastness of the city around me. I send my senses out, through the swirling pre-dawn mist, out towards the Germans and the dull brown embankment, which marks the beginnings of their lines.

I was anxious. It had been too long since we had faced an attack, and the Germans wanted our factory so very badly. They had already lost thousands of men trying. It was not like them to leave a bill half-paid. Plus there were other evil signs. At night low-flying German planes would deafen us with their screaming engines. The Stukas had whistles in their wings which terrified the men, often sending them streaming out of the best of cover, only to be mown down by a pre-sighted MG. The Germans did this to mask the sound of their heavy armor moving around so we would not know where the next assault would come from. But they didn't know how good my ears were. I think I knew where their armor was.

A bitter wind suddenly whirls over us like a specter of the terror to come. It sends my companion into a shivering fit, his equipment rattling. But I am unmoved, sending my being out to the wind, and the mangled chunk of crust that was this place. Out to the brown mound of the railway embankment, tunneled and burrowed by the gray-clad soldiers that live and lurk there, waiting to come across that shattered expanse, waiting to strike. Our factory had become a symbol of all they hated, and they believe if they wrest it from us, if they can achieve victory, that somehow they can reach salvation from the white and icy death that threaten to consume them. Every morning I come up here to see if they are coming.

Through the pallor of yesterday's destruction and the doom of today's dawn I seek them with my eyes. In this moment, right before the sun, they would be at their starting points, waiting for the barrage to begin. Atop the railway embankment I see dark smudges, squat and grotesque forms that emanate unyielding solidity. Behind them I see small dots moving, men swarming to their assault positions.

I grab the phone and crank it up, calling Batyuk's Tower. The structure stands at the furthest part of our lines, a battered stone building of impressive height in a generally flattened city. It is defended by a memorable collection of psychopaths under the command of Lieutenant Batyuk, a dark and swarthy Mongolian whom I enjoy drinking with. He lies all the time about casualties so he can receive the dead mens' booze. It is rumored he once shelled his own supply lines when he had not received his vodka. They were going to court-martial him but he got a Red Star the next day for valor in combat. Now they send him double rations, and I do my part to help him consume them. I like getting drunk.

"What?" comes a muffled voice from the phone.

"Good morning fatty. Quit humping that dead nurse and listen to me."

After a short but noisy pause, his voice returns.

"Ahh, pale one. Kill anyone lately?"

"Only Germans, but who's counting. Listen, did you get your AP last night?"

"Ten shells only. Why?"

"Now look out a window—see where the railway should be?"

"I can't see a damn thing," he growls, not liking the sound of this.

"Just keep watching . . ." I quickly stand and launch a flare in the direction of the tower.

The effect is immediate and chaotic. As soon as the rocket launches across the battlefield, people begin shooting wildly. Tracers lash the sky. The flare goes off with a dull "pop" about 30 feet above the tower, suddenly bathing the whole area in harsh phosphorescent light while making a spitting and angry sound, globs of fire dropping to the ground. There is the edifice—once a stone office building, now a pockmarked ruin. And there are the tanks, hulking German monster tanks a mere 200 feet away, poised with muzzles agape to blow murder into Batyuk's Tower. Tiny flashes erupt from the tower as the Russians fire at the suddenly scattering figures, which had been assembling behind the steel behemoths.

"You have guests," I say into the phone. I hear a series of muffled curses and then the first sounds of the German barrage, the far off cough of cannons, and then, much closer, volleys of flaming projectiles leap aloft with a rending roar—Nebelwerfers. They are rockets, and carry a huge charge. The blasts can make whole companies of men simply disappear. I hurl myself over the railing, leaping 20 feet down to the street, striving to hit the ground before the first shells do.

I don't quite make it as a charge airbursts close by, interrupting my flight with a concussive wave. It's really quite nice for a moment—it feels like I'm flying—then I'm flying mouth first into a pile of rubble. Spitting teeth, I barely attain the dubious safety of a crater as the Germans lay a blanket of ruin on our beloved fort. Today the Germans were coming.

I usually reserve my hate for things, not people. I hated artillery. There was nothing you could do but take it so I tried to be good at that, smashing my form into the dirt and broken rock, digging in as best I could, trying to differentiate between the various types of reports while keeping my mouth and nostrils plugged. An exploding shell could create a vacuum that would rip your lungs out through your mouth.

Beyond hell there is the extended barrage. All my endeavors became useless as the individual explosions merge into a solid roar. Stones pound me and the ground begins to heave. A sudden and sharp pain lashes my ass, as my pants are torn open by a burning splinter. Ahead of me, next to the building, is a trench that leads to a bombproof tunnel, and I leap for it, hopping and scrabbling, dog paddling in mid air. I crash into the trench, bowling over a group of terrified men making for the shelter, crawling through their midst with judicious use of elbows and boots, and finally breaking free into a section of tunnel. Behind me the men are screaming, so entangled they cannot move, then the floor rushes up into the ceiling, then back down into them, hurling me down the tunnel which rotates 180 degrees as I fly into a metal door. Bracing my back to it I am plastered by the God of War. The only thing that saves me from being torn apart by shrapnel is the gigantic wave of dirt scooped up and rammed down on me with excessive force. For a moment, as I sit there in the cool darkness, I think the barrage must be over, then I realize I'm just deaf. The ground is still heaving like a fat whore. Then someone wrenches open the door behind me and I feel arms dragging me into a room. I can't see a damn thing due to the dirt packed into my eyes, which I madly rub at as the explosions continue.

The bombproof is not all that. It is packed with men and filled with smoke, and shakes constantly. Occasionally it takes a blow as if from a giant sledgehammer and the men look quickly up, caught in the truly horrible state of potentially being reduced to bloody rags at any moment. Part of the ceiling curls up at the corner, and a cascade of sparks showers us. The noise becomes greater as men shrink away from the rent, knowing death was searching for such holes. One man grabs a log and tries to shove it into the gap. There is a sharp report and he flies back violently. He impacts with the opposite wall and his skull is smashed between it and the flying log. Despite all the noise, everyone feels his brain die, especially me. The hole is bigger now, and flames are right outside. The men are howling and jumping all over each other, fighting to get away. But I am the strongest, the most sinuous. I writhe into the bottom of the heap before the next shell explodes. And when it does, the curtain of flesh protects me. The men are sprayed with burning steel. Many are killed outright, others are crying in agony and bleeding profusely. The roof has fallen in and the broken block channels the red rivulets into a curving descent towards my gaping soul. I lurk beneath, grinning, shifting the corpse above me into a more convenient position. Shells burst all about but I feel secure, cloaked in bodies as I feast.

It's good to be able to hear so well. It's made me really love music, and to be able to distinguish the individual reports of varying guns, the character of the different shell bursts, so as to know when to keep my head down. But that doesn't matter now as the barrage continues without let-up—a martial symphony of impressive scale. They must have been saving shells for weeks, shells born in German factories, lovingly transported to the front by the million. They pumped in shells, we pumped out death. Supply and demand. I lay there with my face up and let the blood run over it, wondering what's happening at Batyuk's Tower. They are probably getting assaulted with flame-throwers and point-blank tank fire.

I hoped Batyuk was still alive—I liked that fat fuck.

I am buried at the bottom of a mass grave, between me and heaven is a layer of fire. Teeth are stretching into needles, drawing forth the life force I need to heal my ass. Soon I am singing sweetly, my soul alight. My butt glows from within and I grow impatient with the sustained abuse we are receiving. The instant I sense the barrage begin to slacken I leap upwards with all the force I can muster, through the corpses, tearing aside a large hunk of corrugated metal while firing my gun into the air.

"C'mon you bastards!" I yell as I stumble through the dust, colliding with a wall that yields an opening past a heap of burning bricks. I scramble over them and enter Manufacturing Hall # 2.

Men are milling around in confusion, others are down, and some are burrowing into the ground like dogs. I kick several asses, urging the men towards the firing wall where the line of resistance is forming. There is a great red glare coming from the terrain outside, a great burning which bathes us all in bloody light. I peer through a hole and gaze out over the killing field. It's hard to see much as smoke is everywhere, but in the direction of Batyuk's Tower I see stabs of flame rend the fog. I hear guns stuttering and blocks collapsing. This is where the fight begins.

I move to the tunnel that will take me there, rushing down its length straight into a group of retreating men.

"The tower is down," gasps one. "The Germans are in the shops!" Then he falls down dead.

I snarl in disgust and duck up a shaft, which ends with an iron disc. I push against it and it yields slowly as a rush of thick red liquid dumps through the expanding crack. I squirm through and into the bottom of a slit trench stuffed with mangled flesh. I'm about thirty yards from the Great Hall and halfway to the tower. Tracers whip the air and I keep my head down as I duck around the corner straight into two Germans.

"Hands up!" I bark. They do so, dropping their weapons. I open fire from a foot away, blowing their heads apart.

"Oh sorry, I'm still fairly new at this." I say as I stomp over the bodies.

I keep moving, leaping out of the trench and running for the tower that I immediately see is now only a heap of blasted rubble. Germans now see me, as they are swarming over the embankment and tower ruins, voicing a many-throated yell of pure war-lust, assaulting towards the shops that are my goal as well. Bullets begin to strike around me and I run at full speed until a tank shell explodes directly behind me, lifting me with ease and hurling me into an iron-grilled window which rips out of its foundation with the impact of my 6'5," 220-pound body, landing me directly at the feet of Batyuk who stands, half-naked in his underwear, firing a pistol at the squad of Germans attempting to enter the room through the shattered north wall. I lurch to a halt in a cloud of dust just as his bare and hairy chest erupts in a series of crimson divots.

"You're late…" he gurgles, collapsing.

No more vodka rations for him!

Bullets cleave the air above and I pull a sheet of corrugated metal over me. Batyuk sputters and dies, fingers clawing at my leg. A shudder of pleasure runs through me as Germans toss smoke grenades into the room. They burst around me, cloaking me in chemical mist. The first soldier who enters the room sets off a booby trap, filling his face with nails. Then a squad of Russians charges from behind me, stomping across my position and mashing me into the bloody floor. A large shell detonates amongst them, right in front of me, wiping their lives out in an eye blink and hurling tattered chunks of their bodies and possessions in all directions. From the other side of the wall I hear the clanking sounds of the monster tank, nosing about in the rubble and looking for new targets. No barricade can stop this beast—it must be killed.

I look about through the rubble, knowing at any moment that the Germans could come spilling through the door and fill me full of lead. But before that happens I find a demo charge in the death grip of an amputated Russian arm. I pick it up on the run and charge towards the door, the amputated arm still dangling from it, at that moment not knowing that I am the only soldier holding up an entire German battalion.

Their vanguard reaches the doorway just as I do, bursting from the smoke and through their ranks, leaping for the tank which is lurking just a few meters beyond them. It is a gigantic thing, a model that I do not recognize, and I become a blur of motion, so quick they cannot fire. I clamber up the front of the machine before they even know what is happening. I prime the demo and wedge it beneath the gaping maw of the main gun—it emits an angry hiss and a column of smoke as I turn back towards the safety of the shops, hurling myself into space, surrounded by beckoning death on all sides while never having felt so alive even as gunners get their range and send a whizzing swarm of bullets after me. One strikes my left shoulder, spinning me around in mid-air and passing out the front of my chest. As I rotate, I see a German trooper atop the tank where I had just been standing, bending to the demo, trying to scoop it up and throw it away from the friendly monster but without luck as the charge detonates in his grasp.

WHOOM! The charge, the man, the tank and all the ammunition aboard explode at more or less the same time. Shrieking splinters and lashing flames pulverize the area and for a moment people stop shooting at each other to behold the unleashed chaos of my making. I am grabbed and hurled by the force which slams me back through the northern brick wall, shattering numerous bones and propelling me into a whirling vortex of scalding dust and down a collapsing stairwell. Clothing aflame, I pass out.

When I come to, I sense a large black shape next to me. It's a tank! No, it's not trying to kill me. There are black metal pipes protruding from it at all angles and it is surrounded by shadowy figures that in turn surround me. I'm flat on my back, lying next to a boiler. I feel my head lifted from behind, as a cool and slick object is placed between my lips. Fiery liquid spills from it, reviving me somewhat. I cough and sputter, raising myself to a sitting position. I'm in a darkened cellar, Russian soldiers around me, staring down at my nude and blackened body. My wounds itching, I lie still until I have summoned the strength to speak.

"I need a weapon," I mumble through smashed lips.

I pass on several until I find my favorite, a submachine gun. Somebody gives me a greatcoat with a moist hole in the back denoting its former owner. We are huddled in a boiler room underneath the shower level. The men found my charring body half buried in a heap of bloody rubble and dragged me here. Since then, more explosions have sealed the entrance and we are now trapped. From above I can hear the dull rumble of continuing combat and I search about for a way to return to it. My wounded shoulder is throbbing with the pulse of it's healing and I stretch out my arm, cracking the joints into place and relishing my body's necrotic power. I am healing fast, the proximity of death giving me new life. The dying wounded in the corner do their part. They die. They die and I take their strength.

Apparently, many observed my defense of the room and they babble excitedly about my exploits. I ignore their praise and glug the rest of their vodka. They seem quite happy to stay here, as it seems rather safe and that is a rare quality for any place in Stalingrad. There are about 20 men in here, a mixed gaggle of survivors from a variety of units forced together into this space by the tides of war. They sit about and do their best to ignore it as they trade stories and rations. How strange that we should all end up here, in this miserable hole, facing death together. How strange that I should look upon these men as a living deli-tray.

Sudden knocking sounds come from above. Twenty necks snap upwards as one. Germans are searching for us in the hollow spaces beneath the floor. They know these unseen chasms could be full of Russians just waiting for the right moment to make their presence known in a murderous manner. They begin to pour gasoline down the broken pipes into our sanctuary causing immediate panic amongst the men. They throw themselves onto the mound of debris blocking the exit, hurling bricks aside as they try to escape the death trap. I leap to their aid, caring only about myself. Above us, and unseen, a German assault pioneer hoses the area with a flame-thrower, and the gushing gas becomes pillars of flame, igniting several men who blunder into the other men, setting them on fire as well. The smell of burning flesh fills the air as I clear a gap big enough for me to squeeze through. I fall down a pile and into a corridor, then jump back to the opening. A soldier is trying to squeeze through the gap that only a Whargoul could manage, behind him the men are screaming in terror and agony and he reaches to me for help. I grab him by the face and twist his head around, snapping the bone and ripping the cartilage with a sloppy sound. I do it without thinking, forgetting they are on my side. He dies quickly with his head on the wrong way and I bite him in the back of the neck. His body plugs up the hole and the rest die behind him in the inferno. He becomes the conduit for the soul-suck and I take them all, glutting myself on the energy of the harvest, finally falling back to the opposite wall, intoxicated and swooning with the unholy power of death's making.

It has already been a busy day but I'm just getting started. My shoulder wound has totally healed and more—I am at the height of my ability. Barely a month old, today I will kill a thousand years of life.

The corridor I'm in runs the length of the building and I rush down it, sensing an opening ahead. It sounds like a tank roars above me but then all is wiped by a shattering explosion somewhere close ahead. The corridor collapses in a shower of burning block that I run through at top speed, bricks bouncing off my head. I almost make it to the end before my legs are trapped behind me. Squirming like an eel, I writhe to daylight. When my head pokes free of the rubble I see I am entering a gigantic shell hole about halfway up one of the crater's walls. The area is blanketed with thick smoke and small fires burn what they can find. In the center of the crater is a German tank, a Mark III with a 50mm gun. The tank is on its side thrashing like a crippled dinosaur, one length of steel track unwound from the sprockets, hanging limp and useless. It has crashed into what used to be the building above, setting off a huge charge left by the Russians who have abandoned this area. Still falling chunks of rubble are testimony to the force of the explosion that has left this fine piece of German machinery helpless, treads churning. I watch, mesmerized by the spectacle, as the front and turret hatches clank open. From one crawls the tank commander in his black panzer uniform. Swearing, he moves to the front hatch. A bloody arm flops out. By now he has been joined by another crewman who has exited the tank from its belly hatch. Together they inspect the vehicle and remove the mangled driver as the battle rages unseen around them. Apparently, a stray shell has struck the vision slit, killing the driver and sending the tank careening into a building which has set off a hidden charge. The survivors are lucky to be alive. The vehicle is not too badly damaged and will fight again once it is righted and repaired.

Several other Germans clamber into the hole, which offers protection from stray bullets and shrapnel. They smoke and pass around a flask after they drag their dead comrade aside. The crewman seems shaken, the commander unmoved. I start to fire from cover, gun erupting in a geyser of flame, bullets, and spent cartridges. The commander's face is torn off by the heavy lead, which rips into the crewman's chest, blowing out his back in a geyser of angry red droplets. The soldiers scatter as I chase them with my bullets, mowing down two more as one escapes over the lip. I leap out of my hole and rush to the tank, stomping a head into pulp as I pass. A soldier appears, firing. I accelerate and leap for the closest cover, the open turret hatch of the crippled tank, squirming through the cramped interior until I sit in the blood-smeared driver's seat. I am momentarily comfortable, though I feel somewhat claustrophobic. Fire ricochets off the armor as I enjoy the feeling of invulnerability. The main gun is pointed straight at the sky, and I wonder if I could use it to kill their god. Surely he must be watching the antics at Stalingrad, delighting in the torment, feasting on the death as did I, but harvesting on a much grander scale. I would enjoy putting a shell into his baleful eye. Maybe he would think twice before he again indulged in his murderous voyeurism. To feed on the soul of a god—now that would be glorious.

But was it possible? Or would the missile harmlessly pass through the fabric of the being, and, trailing vapor, pirouette perfectly, and fall back to terra firma, re-entering the barrel of its birth to obliterate the sender, Whargoul.

My reverie is rudely interrupted as the inside of the tank abruptly boils with flame. I am enveloped in agony and leap out of the hatch, screaming, a burning bolt of flesh. The Germans had expected me to die under the burst but I don't oblige them—instead I shrug off my blazing coat and charge at them nude, my hair aflame. They are above me and I bound into their midst, grasping, clawing and rolling in a wretched and joyous fusing of death and redemption. I ram my gun's barrel into a chest and pull the trigger, spraying bone and lead, finding and pulling the pin on a grenade, which explodes with flesh-shredding force amidst the fray, and now there are four more dead men to add to my hellish tally-sheet. I barely feel the wound I receive as the blast rushes over me, though I am pocked with shrapnel. There is a trench here, and more men charge from it. I block a blow from a spade, pivot and cleave the edge of my hand into a man's dirty face. A bullet strikes me in the leg, passing through muscle and fatty chasm. It hurts but the leg holds as I hoist a man aloft and disembowel him with a sweeping stroke. His guts trail loosely, freed from their holy place, where they had controlled the release of shit for over 23 years. I am spattered with fluid. Two men grab my legs, and another crashes into my chest, knocking me off balance. We fall in a tangle of limbs as there is a brief writhing, generating a huge cloud of dust. Then I'm on my feet, killing with my hands as I smother another one between my legs, his teeth gnawing at my cock. It feels as if raw adrenaline is being pumped directly into my heart. Three men die in as many seconds and I notice the gunfire slacken for reasons unknown. I'm right in the middle of the German advance wedge and I'm ruining everything, exposing their assault positions. Our rolling ball of men flails madly about in the wreckage of our making. Torn belts trailing equipment are tossed about, and a mist of blood and spent souls surround us. And still they come, curiously drawn to the whirling maelstrom of havoc, though they see man after man slain and lain in the ghastly harvest of gore and guts which drapes the shattered landscape and flecks the spinning sky above.

Boots, severed limbs, smashed weapons and teeth arc skyward and fall back to earth as I smash skulls, snap necks, tear throats and burst testicles. The shooting stops. The Germans won't fire into the hand-to-hand struggle for fear of killing their own men, and the Russians just can't believe what they are seeing. A muted roar fills my ears. Wielding a large iron pipe, I club madly. It slams into a man's skull with a crack half the city hears, hurling his brain 20 meters where it lands with a wet plop. The upper half of his head is gone but he takes a step towards me, imploring me to bend to the pulped socket and have my fill, which I do. Somehow a SMG has found its way into my scabby hands and I fire until the clip is empty, hopping into a trench filled with deflating bodies. I move deeper into it, looking for more Germans to kill when suddenly I realize the sound I'm hearing is the Russians *cheering for me*.

Cheering the blatant display of my murderous hell born abilities, like they would a star player at a football game. I pause in my grisly work, assailed with feelings I do not understand. I feel a lump in my throat as I stare back at the blackened fort, smoking and defiant on the horizon. I almost feel bad about killing men from my own side, but don't know why.

Around me I feel the Germans preparing to renew their attack upon the factory and I swear that they shall fail. They will lose this day and they shall lose the struggle for this city of the damned. So I swear, the Whargoul, standing on a moistened heap of the dead. As much as I admired the Germans, at this point I enjoyed killing them more.

One comes around the corner, gun leveled. I stare back, drenched in blood from head to toe, slathered in gore and emanating steam, my skin hanging from me in tatters. My face splits, displaying my set of dog-like teeth from which pieces of shredded flesh dangle. I reach out for him while making strange sucking noises. His face blanches in fear and he runs for it. I pursue him around the corner just in time to see him disappear into a tunnel into which I also duck. Then unseen hands push the plunger, which leads to the wire, which leads to the demo charge which sets off the blast I run directly into. I'm at the peak of my power and this is probably what saves me, for the blast is huge and close at hand. Timbers fly, the floor drops and the void below is exposed. An underground expanse of corpse-choked water rushes towards me, and in colliding with its surface I imbed myself into it, momentarily losing myself in the ecstasy of death.

The mass of dead flesh rolls past the circle of light, debris draping its edges, rats scurrying over its gelatinous skin. I am stuck in it up to my knees, awake yet senseless, eyes spinning in my boiling skull. Many of the dead found their way into the sewers, and then to the river, and their skin crawls over my bones as we chug slowly along through the maze. Devious creatures note our passage and report below. The city has extensive sewers and all sides make use of them. Softly quivering, I return to myself, suffused with feeding-filth as the tunnel passes into the light, back to the Volga, the great river the city stood against, the river from which I had come. Here a large drainage pipe spews the rotting water into the river, right next to a ferry landing where many are gathered. They begin to look as my island of plundered flesh slugs into view. Imbedded to my ankles, I am nude, lit by the flaming sky. I wave, staring at them blankly.

"The battle goes well," I say without meaning. "Look at how many have died."

The large group of people pause in their various works and gaze at me in horror until a shell explodes in their midst. Agonized wails fill the air as I snap and dart at escaping souls.

Some do escape, but where to? Why wasn't I a part of that, or more accurately, who ate the souls that I could not?

Birthing from out of my flesh raft I splash to the shore, calves yearning, pouncing at a dead man's boots and uniform, and hurriedly dressing myself. I had learned to like clothes, and was sick of running around naked. My swinging dick tended to get caught on things and through comparison I had learned it was a rather large one. As I check the dead soldier's weapon, a couple of officers come running up to me. I turn, taking a great breath, and bark at them. They fly backwards, knocked off their feet, hats flying. A beet-faced commissar is sent sprawling in the mud. Amused at the force of my verbal blow, I veer off towards the cliff which faces the river, releasing the bolt of my weapon which slides home with a satisfying click, gleaming with the fire. I run straight up the cliff wall and leap into a giant sewer entrance. Rats scatter as I land and wheel about, gazing back at the Volga and the many ships passing to and fro upon it. The Germans are attacking them with planes. I am attracted to the designs the German pilots or their talented ground crews have painted on the cowlings. The shrieking birds drop like stones and release their bombs, then reverse themselves and claw their way back into the ether. At this point of the battle the Russians are still short of planes and can do little to stop the mauling. The bombs explode amongst the confused jumbles of ships. Men and women are thrown screaming into the river where they find their way to the bottom. There, a maw awaited them, sucking in water like a drain. Sometimes the maw would spit things out. The boats get wrecked, sunk and forgotten. A pity, that. Boats were pretty, and it took skill to make them.

Behind me, the continuous roar reminds me of the battle that I must rejoin. I run up the pipe. It is a drainage vessel from beneath the smelter vats. I squirm through the wet stone and come out at the bottom of a coral-encrusted slag pit. There is a sharp report and a man sails through my sight, trailing entrails. Shells rain again, then tank cannons fire at a flat trajectory, bolts of thunder which crash through three walls and then explode. The Germans are shelling the fort anew and preparing their final assault.

Emerging on the plateau behind the great factory complex I break into a full sprint, rushing across the broken ground towards the mighty fortress. If the Germans take the complex then they will use the factory as a staging point to drive us into the river, back where I had come from, back to the bitter night that had been before my day. It means the closest thing I know to death, and I don't want to go back there.

The Germans have renewed the attack through an office complex that were the last large buildings before the first great hall. As I enter its cavernous interior I see the Russians busily preparing its defense. The workshop floor is honeycombed with trenches connecting to various strongpoints reinforced with unfinished gun barrels. Men crouch in these pits and sight weapons. Many more troops are being siphoned into this maze of forts in a great brown wave of men and bobbing weapons. Screaming officers point the way. Instantly I see Necrosov.

He is at the head of them, blaring orders, surveying the scene from atop the pillbox at the base of a huge chimney. Necrosov is the senior officer in the Barricade, and I had heard many stories of him and his squad, the "Voiden" or "devils" of local myth. Necrosov and his men were respected, feared, and shunned . . . they were based in an oppressive black building situated at the center of the factory complex, an old church called "The Black Temple." From here he directed the defense of the factory. Rumors of devil worship and human sacrifice ran rife. Captured Germans were also brought here and you could often here their screams from outside, as they were tortured to death, indeed these cries were broadcast on loudspeakers. Stories of his exploits in combat, like the time he took a tank shell, always preceded his arrival on the battlefield. He made me uneasy and I usually took pains to avoid him. Today that had proven impossible. As soon as I enter the arena he snaps towards me and points at a position beneath his.

"Get on that weapon," he screams at me with a voice that sounds like shredding metal. He is tall, and bald, with a huge black scar roughly the shape of Brazil dominating his head. Clad in a black long coat bristling with grenades and ammo, his steel eye patch glares redly at me. I obey.

The weapon is a Browning .50 caliber heavy machine gun. A beautiful piece of death, sent to us from our good (and convenient) friends in the U.S.A. The ammo belt coils out of its gleaming breach, and my loader scrambles into position at my side.

"Hello human. What's your name?" I say with a bristling grin.

"Uh . . . Peter . . ." he says sheepishly.

I grasp the handles and peer down the barrel, sighting the various lanes of fire from which I am sure the Germans will be coming. My position is excellent, above the factory floor and nestled at the base of the great chimney that rises above the complex. I breathe in deeply and await the joy of the killing.

A sound at the edge of my senses alerts me to the coming death. A whistling, the piercing cries of the fell war birds that dip their wings and drop like liberated gargoyles, towards the hall we have sworn to defend to the death. Now the men in the trenches hear the same thing and look at the roof in panic.

Stukas!

The gray rectangle grows in the bombsights of the approaching machines. This building, filled to bursting with men, cannot defend itself from this attack. The sound of the shrieking wings grows louder, and as it does it becomes more terrifying to the men here. Wide-eyed and foam-flecked, many leap up from their positions and run wildly about, screaming and spreading panic as they seek an escape route in vain. Officers seek to beat them back into position, causing even more confusion. The sound grows to a deafening level and even I cringe beneath the edge of my position as the salvo of bombs burst through the roof, detonating with vengeance ahead of me. The explosion is tremendous in its force and rips a huge hole in the roof, which collapses in a swath of flaming debris amongst the building's interior. Men are mangled en masse as our forward positions are wiped out. If only the pilots could see the carnage they had caused. Then perhaps they would choose another vocation for the application of their energies. The simultaneous blasts of several

500 kg bombs create a great inferno that engulfs the front two thirds of our building. Men are sucked into the whirling maelstrom of fire. Water pours through the gaping hole in the roof as the snow melts. Men begin staggering out of the devastated area, their clothing burned off, great oozing wounds dripping red, flesh blackened and charred, eyes staring wildly at their entrails, bulging and purple. They fall into our trench—some lay still, others pick up weapons. Truly appalling to most, I am delighted by the hideous spectacle as I prepare for the German assault that is sure to follow.

I doesn't take too long until I hear the grinding of metal treads soon followed by the hulking black silhouette of the monster tank. Its cannon erupts in flame and it sends a 150 mm projectile into the center of our line, sending sandbags and bodies flying. Smoke grenades burst before us and now I fire, pumping lead into the areas where I know the German assault parties must be. Red tracers strike metal and bounce crazily as bullets tear into their ranks. 50 cal. slugs rip into flesh, tearing off arms, shattering bone and spattering brain. The rest of the line follows suit as the Germans move into a hornet's nest of Soviet fire. But they have more support as I behold another tank nosing up alongside the first. It fires and the shell explodes directly beneath my position, tearing off my gun's barrel and my loader's face. I fall to him and jam my tongue into the bloody hole, feeding quickly as bullets rip the air above me. The inside of the factory has become a wonderland for me, a parade ground of Death's pale steed as the advancing German assault squads and the Russian line engage each other at close range with a deafening cacophony of small arms and grenades. I hazard a peek over the lip of the trench and behold the gaping maw of the assault gun a mere 20 meters away. It grinds through a perfect mess of smashed tile, twisted metal and flattened men, looking straight back at me and belching a shell in my direction. There is a roar that blots out all as the shell rips into the metal covering of my position, tearing it from its welded foundation and into me, swatting me backwards. Me, the shell, and the wreckage collide with the casing of the chimney, smashing through the three-brick-deep wall with bone-shattering force.

I wake up moments later flat on my back at the bottom of the tube, tendrils of smoke drifting across my field of vision. High above me I see a dull disc of sky. Nestled at my side is the smoking shell, dented by my head.

It was a dud.

As I rise, I feel bones shift and crack in my back and shoulders. Painfully, I crawl back out the hole of my making, back into position. There are shouts of surprise and shrill shrieks of agony. Russians are swarming over the tank with crowbars, tearing at the hatches and tracks. And there is Necrosov, hurling a grenade and firing wildly after it, hoisting a man aloft by the neck and blowing out his guts in a greasy smear of fire. Germans rush into the fray and a savage hand-to-hand fight quickly develops. I throw myself into it. Hands find a throat and squeeze, the vessel bursts open with a gush and the pain leaves me. I suck out his adrenaline and continue with my murder motion, fighting alongside Necrosov, spinning and pumping and surging and killing. I hear his mechanical parts whining and I know he is different but the same, manufactured by the master, the Father. Where I am purely organic, he sports implants.

There is a savage hissing as a flame-thrower vomits liquid death upon the knot of struggling men. Several are set alight and my new coat is showered with the searing stuff. The tank is also sprouting flame as the men inside it cease to be anything but dead. The flames break up the melee and I stumble back into the trench. Necrosov disappears into a hole in the wall, firing. Broken and mangled bodies are heaped about, wounded and helpless men bemoan their misery, I revel in it while above the roof begins to burn, dropping flaming pieces of debris into our ranks. The German assault wave has ceased for the moment as they regroup just beyond our vision. A crew appears, dragging a cannon. In a singularly blatant display of my power, I hoist the entire gun out of their grasp and place it in position where the 50 cal. once stood. The Germans surge forward again in a last-ditch effort to storm into the trench. Their battle cry merges with that of the Russians and the screams of the dying to form a hideous chorus of unrelenting misery and terror. The shred of shell, the rip of metal, the feeling of tearing meat, we kill, burying shovels into each other's faces. All along the line the soldiers leap and clutch and form into a timeless ballet, with this, their greatest performance. The combatants merge into one great flailing organism bent on self-flagellation. Blurs of motion explode in spurts of red. I slam a shell into the breech of the gun. The second metal monster tank nudges around the flaming outlines of the first seeking a clear shot. I pull the lanyard of the cannon just as the tank gunner pulls his and simultaneously the two shells leap towards each other. My smaller shell strikes the casing of the larger one in mid-air, knocking it off course just enough to send it over my head, plunging into the hole at the bottom of the chimney, where it meets its wayward brother, the dud dented by my head. The two now combine their power and merge into a new truth, a blossoming of force that the chimney cannot swallow. The burst takes out the base of the chimney and sprays us with swarms of burning stone. It kills stone, it kills flesh. People, killing people, are ripped apart. But this is all secondary to the dull rumbling which adds a sinister undercurrent to the cacophony of carnage. The floor begins to heave and buckle, sending men sprawling into the mud and blood, still tearing at each other's throats even though their limbs have been amputated and are afire. As if they can somehow gain new life through the death of another. As if they aspire to be me.

The chimney is coming down. First the bricks and then the beams. I know well before the others, but also know that I cannot escape. Through the hole in the roof I see the huge cylinder shudder, then shed a skin of bricks, and then begin a horrid crumpling towards us, like some crippled colossus. It blots out the sun and I gather all my strength, crouching and then leaping into its 100-ton falling mass. The air is the last thing to escape.

Someone kicks me in the head. My eyes bulge open and a

stream of obscenities pours forth from my foaming mouth. I have been kicked, but because I am not decapitated, my head cannot roll. So it just hurts.

I am buried up to my neck in a vast pile of rubble. I had almost made it to the top. They dig me out and fill me in.

Night is coming. The attack has ended. The Germans have gained ground today though to what end we know not. Of Necrosov there is no sign, though none will say that he has died. I can guess where he is—back in his fortress, laying naked, attended by his gibbering slaves. We are already digging in for the next day's fight, and the Germans have fallen back to lick their wounds. The rubble of Manufacturing Hall # 2, "The Grinder," has become the tomb for the 2,000 men who have died there this morning. But it is not a silent one. We can hear the moans and whimperings, the desperately phrased pleas for help in two languages, as the entombed wounded expire. We can't dig them out as snipers kill any who approach the mound. They die as the night comes and soon it is silent.

I sit in my vault and rest, scratching lead and stone fragments out of my hide, champing and yawning, still feeling the lingering pleasure of the soulsuck. You could ask me why this had happened and I would have been hard pressed to supply you with an answer. You may as well have asked me where I had come from, and at that point it certainly was not something that I put much thought into.

But I was beginning to. Something vast was occurring, something I was an important part of, yet knew next to nothing about. They called it "World War II," but it was so much more. As I pondered the day's events, for the first time I wondered where it all was leading. Where had it come from, where had I come from? And for what purpose? Who was calling the shots, and could I get an appointment? I resented being left in the dark. I thought I knew where to start looking for answers.

The Black Temple of Necrosov.

5
SUPER BOWL SLAUGHTER

The war that destroyed America began during the Super Bowl. A supposedly harmless sporting event became the powder keg which would erupt to ultimately claim billions of lives.

Sports events often represent the best and worst qualities of the countries that host them. And they often are used as gaudy sideshows to mask other more significant events. Like the forbidden love men often feel for each other. Human males were not supposed to be touchy-feely, at least not with each other, unless of course they were gay. Some men were, and that generally alarmed other men. In elevators people keep their space, especially males. They don't want to rub up against other men—the feeling repels them. Yet these same men will jump all over each other, they will hug, slap each other's buttocks and even kiss, if one of them scores a touchdown.

Football masked other, more sinister practices. Like the organized drug use, graft and gambling which was rife throughout the game since its inception. It was a sad fact that many of the games were fixed, and that players, coaches, and especially the referees conspired to keep it that way. Those phone calls on the sideline often were from Mafia bosses telling anxious quarterbacks that their families were safe.

The less obvious evil was by far more dangerous—the one that set off the bomb. Football promoted the idea that whites were superior to blacks. The white slave masters of the U.S. government needed to keep the blacks under control. That meant, at first, outright slavery and then a campaign of social strangulation. But as time went by they realized that the money that was to be made off the blacks' many talents was too lucrative to ignore. One way to hold them back but still cash in was to channel their efforts into the realms of sports and entertainment. But even then they needed to be reminded that they were considered inferior, even as they basked in the adulation of millions. The symbolism of 22 powerful black men being bossed around by five old white guys was unmistakable. That was the power of the referees, the power of the man.

There were many problems with the game and an attempt was made to address them with a strike. The shit dragged on and on as people increasingly turned to the other leagues. Arena football and newer, more violent sports flourished. But people missed their football, and the players missed their paychecks too much. And those giant stadiums simply had to be filled.

People were sick of just about everything, sick of the Mid East War, and the Apache Terrorists, and White Jihad (fanatic white Muslims led by Cat Stevens). They were terrified by a campaign against drugs that had become a real war. The growing German and Japanese colonies in South America had transformed that continent from a U.S. coke farm into a disputed territory. They wanted a bigger cut. As the flow of coke began to dwindle, the Ghetto Wars became more violent. In some cities, Houston being the largest, cushy suburbanites could hear the fighting rage nightly.

Finally the football strike was resolved and the schedule was announced. The country heaved a collective sigh of relief. Maybe the very fabric of society wasn't unraveling after all. Then, as if to affirm this, Saddam Hussein was assassinated. Drunken Americans danced in the streets, delighted by the death of their old foe. His killer, Cat Stevens, who had taken the name Mohammed Ali Khomeni, usurped him. Cat had been, in western eyes, radical in his sudden conversion to fundamental Muslim beliefs and scary when he had moved to Iran to support the Ayatollah Khomeni. The lungs behind

"*Peace Train*" burst forth with a new rhetoric that amongst other, more spiritual things, had called for the death of Salmon Rushdie for his novel, "The Satanic Verses."

He forges a military pact with Iran, and begins to build up forces on the border of Kuwait. The U.S. predictably responds by sending carriers towards the region. One of these carriers is the brand-new U.S.S. Ronald Reagan, a gleaming multi-billion dollar death machine with an onboard shopping mall. As it passes through the Straits of Gibraltar it is destroyed by a nuclear mine.

The carrier is vaporized. Ali denies any involvement and backs off on Kuwait. We bomb the shit out of him (well his people anyway) but the damage is done. The deadliest terrorist attack in history has left over 8,000 American sailors dead. Ali, safe in his bunker, begins to forge a Pan-Arabic alliance with himself as the leader and the final destruction of Israel as the goal.

As a country, the U.S. felt truly threatened for the first time since the Cuban Missile Crisis. Panic gripped urban centers as people fled to the country. But the "One-Shot-War" was over. The act was never traced to any group nor did any take credit. So nobody knew when they might do it again. This had the result of creating an even more oppressive atmosphere in the U.S. No one was to be trusted.

Finally the football season, dedicated to the dead sailors of the U.S.S. Reagan, opened to record-high crowds. People wanted to forget about their dying child empire (it was only a couple of hundred years old) and go to the big game, even though in many areas it was unsafe to travel.

The TV ratings are still huge. The whole country is coming down around us but we still having our mother-fucking Super Bowl. The rest of the world can fuck off and play soccer—that's right, soccer, and I'll call it anything I fucking want you back-stabbing piece of Euro-shit—we are having a FOOTBALL season here, and after we are done kicking each others asses for a few months you better pray we don't come for yours.

***

Desert Storm. On the receiving end.

"They are coming. See them?"

I can tell he's terrified. He's been underground for most of the last few weeks, hiding from machines that were trying to kill him.

I put down my binoculars.

"There are many of them. Close to 300, and more behind. Mostly tanks, M-1's, but also Bradley's drawn up behind the tank wedge. Infantry in those."

There is a giant cloud of dust on the horizon from which comes a solid and unrelenting roar. The sound grows slowly but steadily in scope and terror. But I'm not scared. I pause and turn to him.

"All coming this way to kill us. That's why they have come, to kill everyone of us and grind our bones into dust. What do you think of that, hmm?"

I glare at him. I know I am both wondrous and painful for him to behold. He doesn't turn to me, he just keeps staring out into the desert—into his onrushing death. He is, for the moment, truly beautiful.

"I really don't know why you won't talk to me. I could order you to speak but that would be no fun. But if you're in the mood come with me to my dugout. I'll make some tea and we will smoke some hashish. And we'll fuck awhile. Then we will go and deal with the American assault."

After a short delay I hear him following me up the trench. I duck into my dugout and turn just as he enters, my ass riding up on my small table. Now his face is flushed and angry. He throws his helmet to the floor.

"When I saw you fucking that man, I went crazy!"

Then we are on each other like wild dogs. His tongue pushes into my mouth as he goes after my tits, sucking off my fake mustache. I slide my uniform off my shoulders and drop it with a clank of medals.

Then I undo the elastic bandage that restrains my tits. His hot hands are all over me and my box begins to throb. We are soon without pants and I suck his cock until he's begging to fuck me.

"When the end of my life came, I always hoped I would be able to fuck a woman quickly, get off one last time before I died . . ." he manages to get out. "The Koran says that it is wrong . . . aah . . ."

He begins to erupt inside of me but I start bucking, forcing him out of me. He shudders violently and shoots a thick cable of hot cum right in my face. I squeeze and lick his balls. Several blobs drop onto my uniform

"There is nothing in the Koran about this, my pet," I say as I eat his hot and salty man-seed.

We both look up with concern as we hear artillery begin to detonate. Assad because he doesn't want to die, me because I do. We are in the fifth line of trenches from the first, which sounds like it is getting plastered. We hurriedly replace our clothing and grab our AKs.

Assad looks at me with concern. " Your breasts are just hanging out. At least button your uniform."

"No, today I shall meet my death with my tits hanging out. And if this repressive society cannot deal with that, then let it be trampled by the beasts of the infidel. Now to the battle, and that's an order!"

After the south of France, my mangled body lay on a hillside for many months. I had no arms or legs, or even a head. But still I was attractive. Attractive to bugs, and small animals, and even a bear. They kept eating off my constantly regenerating corpse, slowing the process that would lead to my return. To this day, I wonder what happened to those animals.

That is not to say that my consumers were my only company. I had the corpse of Gabrielle wired to me. We had died together, her first. That had been the worst part of my torture, watching her die. Worse even than having a propane torch held up to my instep. Still,

I had ingested her soul-fume which gave me the strength to survive. After they thought we were both dead they had bound our bodies together in a gruesome parody of a lovers embrace. Then they set an overly large charge of nitroglycerin under us and blew my charming sun-washed villa into smithereens. Clutching at each other, my whore girlfriend and myself had made one last trip together, as we where blown through the roof and over the cliff, where my rear porch and balcony had been. It had been a great locale, and from it I had been painting the surrounding countryside. In all my years spent there I had probably only killed a couple dozen people. Maybe I had fallen in love, maybe I had been happy here. Now my Shangri-La was a flaming wreck, my lover and I fused together in a sputtering ball of burning flesh lying in a silent vale at the bottom of Whargoul Mountain.

Yes, fused together. They had tortured us with battery acid as well. They didn't have to do that to her. But the bloody potholes the acid had made helped our bodies merge. We now resembled nothing quite as much as a meatball, devoid of features, just a red, wet, bubbling chunk of struggling flesh, struggling to find a new life with only the mangled remains of the Whargoul and his human whore lover to work with.

But somehow we had made it happen, even though animals kept eating our progress. It was the closest I had ever come to being obliterated, worse than my murder at the hands of Necrosov or the crash of the Warthog (which hadn't happened yet). And in the end Gabrielle would help me even in her death by supplying me with parts that were needed that I had lost. They fused our bodies to make me live again, to fulfill the ghastly purpose which I had been created for. They did a good job with what they had but the genetic material available imposed certain restrictions. Or maybe they just thought it was funny.

I had come back as a woman. I had tits and a pussy. And something that looked like a dick but did not work like one. But I was endowed with my normal omni sexual tendencies. I had fucked and been fucked by a large selection of fleshy configurations. Form could mean nothing. But sex was a way of opening the gateway between my spirit and my flesh.

I try to physically intimidate people because I am not clever enough to do it mentally. I always end up resorting to violence; indeed I rely on it, to solve my problems. It seemed like I had myself under control for a while there, before Iraq and the Gulf War. But my propensity for violence has increased steadily ever since. I was capable of great things but the source of my power had always been an evil one. It seemed as if I had almost been human, and I had been enjoying sex a lot more. But the transformation in the desert, which had made me the O.J. killer of Harlem, had also remade me back into a monster. Sure I looked human enough, but I knew what I was. I guess it made sense. In WW II the human race had glutted itself on war. They needed time to recover and assess the results. So did I. But soon the dogs had begun to howl anew, and we, the brethren of the damned, flocked to their call.

A battle, somewhere. I stumble into the field hospital. My arm is hanging by a strand of gristle. I approach the orderly behind the table. He looks forlorn as behind gauze walls men are drained.

"I need a doctor," I say, gesturing at my torn arm and accompanying stump.

"You need a doctor?" he says.

"Yes, a doctor please.'

"You need a doctor?" he repeats.

"Yes, a doctor you idiot! My arm's off!"

"A doctor?"

Suddenly several staff members rush in.

"There he is!" shouts one, pointing at my tormentor, who leaps up and runs off. Another orderly quickly sits behind the desk.

"Now, how may I help you—SHIT!" as he looks up and sees my horrible wound and the bright torrent of blood pouring from it.

I grin broadly, displaying my cracked and pointed teeth.

"Thanks but I have no problem shitting. It's this arm. I wonder if they could sew it on so I don't have to grow a whole new one."

He doesn't reply, so I rummage around through the contents of the room until I find a medical bag. I remove a needle and thread and set to work. Wounded men are brought in. That's good—the battle is still going strong. In 5 minutes the arm is back in the socket, held in place with ugly but strong stitches. I cough up a handful of phlegm and rub it in the crack, then run out to find someone to kill.

My Father had infected the world. Off-world species mated with the animals at hand, and controlling the mutating genes was always the primary concern. The goal—production of new life. The exploitation of that life was the reward. I was that new life. But I was just a tool. A powerful tool but a tool all the same. But I could never be truly controlled; only guided. To accomplish this I had been programmed with a series of subconscious brakes like memory loss, dementia, and hallucinations, all accompanied by physiological effects. This, compounded with an intense and unnatural craving for drugs, booze, and fast women, put me in the perpetually dangerous position which had killed me several times over.

My body exhibited other weird effects, like inexplicable diseases. Once my nose grew larger and increasingly more painful over a series of weeks, until it was three times its normal size and covered in pustules and warts. This occurred while I was in the south of France. I hid from Gabrielle, pretended I had gone on a trip, and waited for the condition to go away. However it just got worse as did my hunger. I went out to kill with a giant, throbbing nose. Then one day Gabby caught me rooting around in my garden, which I could not stand to let die. She tried to take me to a doctor but I refused. Then she brought one to the villa and surprised me. I could not let him examine me and my refusals made him even more curious. I attempted to disrupt the situation by bellowing at Gabby, and drove her from the room as the doctor chased me about with a stethoscope. At this point she stumbled into my "forbidden" room, which was filled with SS regalia and weapons, pictures of me riding tanks, standing next to piles of burning bodies, smiling and waving at the camera. She screamed in horror and the doctor came running. I suppose I wanted to be caught or I never would have been so sloppy, but after all I was quite the drunk. However the room's contents seemed to have had quite the opposite effect upon the doctor, who immediately snapped to attention and saluted me, standing rigidly until I returned it. He then muttered something about "understanding," and quickly left. Gabby, crying and horrified, was right behind him. I didn't see her for a while.

For months I have been working on my fortress. I purloin some construction materials, buy others, and convey them back to my fort in the dead of night. Sometimes my need for materials becomes greater than my need for secrecy, and I'll go shopping in daylight. It doesn't matter. I know one day they will find me. And when they do I'll be ready.

I've blocked up the windows with brick, and strengthened the wall with braces of concrete. Basically, I am building several skins around the central blockhouse. There are parapets and walkways leading to several firing positions, all of which I can fall back from to the central area. Here I also have my van, poised to burst through whatever is left of the wall and spew death into their midst. The whole place is mined and I've got plenty of ammo.

I had quite inadvertently become a symbol of defiance, terror, and twisted inspiration to many with my attack upon Moyer and now the many other murders the media claimed that my ilk and I had committed.

New York had remained relatively peaceful, as other cities had fallen into street violence and open warfare. It was the last bastion of reason, New York, the only town tough enough to take it. Take me and my reign-of-terror town, where I left victims charred and then promptly forgot about them. Where had I gutted schools. For years I had been oblivious to the pain I had caused until I was reminded. Until I was tortured. And all with design, all with purpose. I was being controlled, so he could control them. That was one of my reasons for going rogue—I resented any restrictions on my freedom. I had been set-up all my life, and my attempt at love had ended in fire as I had been dragged back to the crucible of war. Now they called again, they tortured me, and now they came to kill me.

Now we were surrounded but the enemy could not enter our territory unless he came in force. He watched from below, and from this subterranean vantage point he slowly saw the entire world burnt up to New York's doorstep. Barricades had sprung up, bombs and firefights were becoming more common after my attack, and of course my minions, the B.A., and I were credited with every one of them. When in reality they had done most of the killing, and I had nothing to do with them. I was locked in my fort, on heavy sedation, occasionally blowing off my head to relieve the tension. I wanted no part of their army or their movement.

But I could not help but be curious. The B.A. had no political agenda that could be discerned, and that was unusual for any terrorist group. That was always the top priority, after all wasn't war just an extension of policy, "by other means..." But the B.A. just wanted to kill.

The date for the first mass assault was scheduled for 10:00 p.m. EST, Jan. 24th, 2002. The best time to start a war against the whites—during the fourth quarter of the Super Bowl. Everybody would be drunk and occupied and the absolute absurdity of a Toyota pick-up full of screaming Negroes emptying a 50 cal. into your house was the last thing anybody would have expected. And it's just what they got.

All day the game had been plagued with questionable calls. Penalties had dismantled a couple of touchdowns and nullified other examples of excellent play. There was no doubt as to who was controlling the game despite the best efforts of the players. It was the zebras and their unseen masters. Even the whirling chaos of pro football had to be controlled, indeed it was essential that it was, otherwise what kind of message were you trying to promote to these people? That they could control their own destinies? That they, through the force of their own actions, could rise above the lot that society had set for them? Certainly not.

So when the only white player on the field got that critical, and totally bogus, pass interference call with only three seconds to go there was stupefied disbelief. When it led to the winning field goal there was absolute fucking bedlam. In the crowd, on the sidelines, and on the field. And in a million bars and homes where millions of people were getting drunk. People were pissed. The losers couldn't accept it, and the winners couldn't believe it. Everybody knew they had been cheated.

It was a defining moment in American history. Wasn't the strike supposed to have fixed all this? Never had so many people at once been confronted by the fact that something was very wrong with the system, the entire system and not just the fucking N.F.L. The whole gaudy charade held back a potential tidal wave of brimming bullshit. Of course, a lot of other people already knew that, or had a strong enough suspicion that they were ready that very night to die in pursuit of the destruction of that wall. So at just about the same time that #86 came running across the field (he had already been ejected), took his helmet, and smashed the head referee right in the face, the rest of America got smashed as well.

That night, war came to the U.S.A.

There were a lot of things that terrified people about the Black Army, or "B.A.." They got to see it all on TV that night in the year 2002, Super Bowl Sunday, and it scared the shit out of just about everybody. Even me.

First of all, they were very well funded. The first round of attacks in the U.S. must have cost millions of dollars to prep and execute. Bombs went off in front of hundreds of police stations across the nation almost simultaneously. Individual strike teams carried out over 2,000 murders. Mayors, judges, Klan members, ordinary folks. But all white. Across the nation, bands of well-armed death squads laid waste to life and property on a level undreamed of on U.S. soil. Some of it seemed random, some seemed deliberate. Whole families were wiped out save one child.

Another aspect of the attacks was the level of hatred they inspired. Within two hours of the initial series of attacks most cities had riot alerts in the ghetto areas. Whitey had been given a bloody nose and it was time to follow it up with a kick in the nuts.

They claimed no responsibility, left no names. The name, "Black Army" came from the media. They had no visible leader, no discernible dogma other than the bloody disruption of the status quo. No bases were found, no vehicles tracked. And the few corpses they left behind were utterly unidentifiable, unrecorded as any human being on the face of the planet. They were a faceless, formless terrorist army living in our midst, ready to attack with horrific intensity at any moment. And no one knew where they would strike next.

On the field the players fight. In the stands the people fight. On the sidelines the coaches fight. Some fight to stop others who fight, others fight in self-defense; others run to escape and cause even more harm, trampling many. Others fight because they are drunk on bloodlust. In fact, that's why most of them fight—because they like it. Referee "Bud" Tarlatan lies in the grass, bleeding profusely. People begin to scream, "Kill the white (or black) motherfuckers!"

Others just scream "Kill!"

I watch from my belfry as the crowd surges across Crown Avenue, towards the liquor store.

They save the best for last. A Black Army Suicide Squad attacks the White House, crashing through the security blocks with a series of expert demo-attacks, and then crushing into the gates with an 18-wheeler, which disgorges 40 men armed with AKs, Uzi's, and rocket launchers. Other assault squads come from below. Despite heroic resistance from Secret Service agents and Marine guards, the

White House is stormed and the first family taken hostage. The end result is the release of over 18,000 inmates from mostly American, but also Israeli, French, and British prisons. In America, most of these people go straight from jail to the war zones, swelling the ranks of the uprising. It looks more like the PLO pulling out of Beirut than something that could happen in the good ole' USA. Key figures from Native American, militia, and Islamic groups also go free. The B.A. has finally disclosed their political agenda.

Necrosov led the attack and performed the negotiations. I know because I saw him on TV. His face was masked but his voice was unmistakable. His demands were of the most inflammatory manner, and the televised butt-fucking of the President was certainly uncalled for. And after Necrosov had completed his mission he disappeared back into the ground to prepare for his next assault.

My Father was slowed by the fact that he could not manipulate machinery as well as he could flesh. But that could hardly be construed as a weakness when you considered just how powerful he was. A being that could create life from death. He could build a vast army, or create a race. As long as he had the basic energy to work with, the livestock, he could populate a planet. But he needed lots of flesh. He used the tunnels, the sewers, and the mindless maggot mazes to suck the bits towards him from places far away. The world was a circular toilet—he was the drain. And everybody went straight into his maw.

But he could not do things with metal and mineral that he could with flesh. He could not give birth to a gun. So he would create the creatures that would create the hate, inspiring the legions of already living victims. So they would begin with primitive weapons, the weapons at hand, their brains slowly warping into the condition required for the insemination of the new death technology. My Father taught you war, your most monumental and useless skill. Before his arrival on Earth roughly 6,000 years ago, the humans had lived in a paradise. You had been animals; or rather you knew you were animals. My Father made you want to become gods. War gods.

The production of weapons of mass lethality was an alien idea my Father had implanted into you by defiling your corpse pool and then sending those soulless creatures out into the world to destroy your lives. I was one of them, and there were many others like me. Your resistance to these attacks from within had helped prevent my Father from achieving his goals. But within the course of this century he had known his greatest success. Three millennia worth of his corrupt influence had worn you down. Now you possessed the means not only to destroy yourselves but also to obliterate all life on the planet. Except for him. I didn't even know if you could kill Father. After all, he was several miles across.

I should stop calling him Father; after all he was a giant baby-making machine. But I suppose his war-like nature obliterated any feminine qualities he may have possessed. Perhaps I should just call him "it," but he had always addressed me in a masculine tone and called himself my Father. He was proud of his son. And I must admit, I had enjoyed the affection. He had created me, and up until the point of our first meeting I had thought I was an orphan. And the one thing I was desperate for was any sort of a family.

I can no longer make even the most basic decisions in life. The merest of complications reduces me to tears. I've been in the house, apertures cloaked from the sun, staring at my guns and weeping. I can't go outside, because the war has started and they are screaming for a leader. My father is calling me to lead the army of the damned. But I don't want to go.

Even Maug has deserted me, though I sense his presence nearby. I must have scared him as the visions are in full swing. I have chained myself to a huge boiler, which I am tearing out of the floor. Knowing full well the consequences of the action before it is committed, I raise the pistol to my head and pull the trigger in one motion, blowing off the side of my skull. My body drops, sitting down hard in a spray of thick droplets, and then slumping to the side as blood empties from my shattered braincase. This ends my pain for the moment, but I'll be back.

Days later I awake to a dull, continuous pain in my face that is still sharper than the groaning throb that encompasses my skull. My head is re-knit, my brain re-constituted. Maybe it took two days for me to fall again into the mode of life, and during that time I had dreamt—dreamt the malformed dreams of an annihilated mind. My senses converge on my center and I hear screams, and shots, as the cops go block-to-block with the National Guard and kill anyone that won't submit. And their underworld minions provide help from below as they finally find me.

I see a black shape rushing towards me, engulfing me in a suffocating embrace. Drugged, shot and confused, they almost take me. But I fight, I fight hard, tearing and straining at what feels like a wall of inflatable skin which attempts to surround and subdue me. My claws rip into its flesh, tearing out holes that I work my body through. I'm covered by the creature's fluid and numbness assails me. It's poisoned me. I stop trying to escape and just try to kill it, splitting the muscle blanket with a gristly pop, writhing through its mass. It retreats with a squeal, flopping towards the hole, spewing droplets. Pursuing it proves impossible as paralysis grips me.

Then a swirling, gaseous form comes into view, holding a rod with a glowing crystalline orb affixed to the end. Like a wraith it floats towards me as its servant flops into the floor behind it, wretchedly gibbering its agony. Desperately I strain against the drug as the pulsing globe draws closer, its gaseous tendrils oozing across my convulsing form. They're gonna get me.

But then an explosion of black motion leaps into the midst. A snarling mass of rending claws and jaws, just back from a two-week jaunt through doggy heaven. The specter reforms briefly as a mass of writhing gristle as Maug rips through its vapor into the throbbing flesh core, which is just big enough to sustain its power and support the artifact. It cannot defend itself and the attack is too sudden to retreat from. The thing has no mouth so it makes no noise as it is destroyed, save squishy ones. Maug tears the thing apart as I fight against the drug, finally gaining enough strength to stumble to a spider hole and observe the street outside, as I attempt to gain control of myself.

There are tanks outside. And riot police, and soldiers. Helicopters swirl overhead, fires burn out of control, and shots go off like popcorn. It looks like they are getting ready to storm my block. I duck to the upstairs cupola, the fort's highest point, with Maug at my heels. From here I can see the whole surrounding area as I rotate the turret in a quick 360. The drug is wearing off quickly as it is replaced by a surge of adrenaline, caused by my observance of the full vista of carnage.

There are armored vehicles moving down several streets at once in my neighborhood, and these advances are being opposed. I watch as a Molotov cocktail explodes on the front of an armored car, turning into a rolling torch that drives into a building. Shots are coming from everywhere, and people are hiding from them. I can see some National Guard men gathered behind a garage, waiting for an M-60 tank to suppress the block before they continue their attack. The tank opens up with a 50 cal., tearing up the fronts of buildings and knocking down porches. The N.G. advances and is met with a hail of lead that sends them scrambling back for cover, leaving a man in the street. He gestures for help that he cannot receive, as a helicopter appears overhead, framing him in their spotlight.

Holy shit! It's a fucking Apache! And it opens up with its Gattling cannon, punching great holes in brick, destroying unseen flesh, and just ripping up the joint. Things must have been bad for them to have brought in air support so soon. The creature goes about its deadly work, darting in and out of shadows in its quest for victims. They clear the block and begin to converge on mine, approaching my structure from all sides, save the track. The copter hangs back, observing.

I run to the basement, turning on CNN as I rush by. Then I'm in a tunnel that puts me in a dugout about 20 meters outside my garage door. I'd stolen this weapon from an armory in Buffalo on one of my many road trips. Its where I got most of my hardware, from the drunken and drug-addled soldiers who were more than willing to trade things of death for the things I offered (usually drugs). I would have stolen a tank if I could have gotten away quietly. But I did get this Stinger.

It's a complicated weapon that can blow up in your face, but I understand it instinctively. It's a ground-to-air missile, perfect for dealing with the helicopter. I pop up like toast, acquire my target and loose the missile from my shoulder in a flaming rush that annihilates the hovering death machine in a beauteous eruption of reds and purples. The mangled mess crashes into the earth scarcely 20 meters in front of me. I run back down the tunnel as bullets tear up the dugout. Then it's back upstairs to the cupola, where I man the 50 cal. and wait for the next attack.

For a while nothing happens as they realize that one of their 30-million dollar helicopters just got toasted, and that in general this operation was going considerably over budget. All over the city people were fighting back with skill and cohesion. The tactic of "the bum rush," 20 or so guys armed with Uzi's and RPG's, appearing from nowhere, attacking rear areas and then disappearing seemingly into the street is most disconcerting. My Father has prepared well. Of course, it helps when you sponsor both sides.

When they come back they come back strong. Apparently, my house has been targeted as a small plane flies over and drops a bomb on it. Luckily the device, an incendiary one, has missed and detonated out back, setting my "bum-maze" aflame. Unluckily this will probably set fire to my house. But this seems to be a common tactic employed by the enemy—burn them out. Just ask the Waco survivors. Not like in Stalingrad where the Germans at first tried to save certain buildings they wanted, for use as shelter later on. Soon they realized there would be no "later-on," unless they could destroy the entire city. Unless they could erase it from the map by grinding the very stones to dust and boiling its blood into the air. In the ghettos they used this tactic from the get-go, much like the SS had done in Warsaw under the command of Stroop. I had been there, too, and again I had found the underworld.

Warsaw was one of the oldest European cities and had suffered severe damage in the first months of the war. The Luftwaffe had bombed it repeatedly, killing tens of thousands. Many old and beautiful buildings which had stood for centuries had been destroyed. When I came there the city bore its scars under the harsh boot of military occupation. The Germans, with their customary disdain for the achievements of other cultures, had stripped the city of itself in its transformation into the major staging point for Germany's upcoming invasion of Russia. They also used the city as a round-up point for Jews from all over Poland, who were walled up in the ghetto. When the Death Camps began to run, they took their victims from these urban pens. They began training the Jews out in '43, and by '44 the operation was going full swing. Apparently the record was 40,000 gassed and burned in one day. Stories like that had brought me here, to ancient Poland.

After the failure of Operation Citadel, the Russians began their inexorable advance that would not climax until the fall of Berlin. I fought innumerable battles in a vain attempt at stopping it. And the closer the Russians got the more frantically Germans tried to murder everybody, as if they could save their own lives through the deaths of others. It was a misguided concept for the millions of common soldiers who died believing. They received nothing but death for their sacrifices. But others did gain—the harvesters, like myself.

How could I be German when I wasn't even human? And apparently many of the Germans believed the same thing, displaying little in the way of humanity.

So the order was given to liquidate all the ghettos of central Europe. Liquidation through extermination. No "revision" needed here—it happened. But that's not to say that the Jews were the only ones to die there—quite far from it. Everybody died there, even the guards. And most of the victims clung to pathetic shreds of hope right into the death rooms, making their deaths all the sweeter to the taste.

But the Jews of Warsaw fought back, fought back with guns and bombs, battery acid and rocks. They knew the truth about the trains and they resisted their eviction with deadly force.

It was almost laughable that they brought in an SS panzer division to suppress their rag-tag uprising. The accepted explanation for us was that it was "practice." As if they needed it. We were members of one of the most experienced combat units of the SS, under the command of Oberstgruppenführer Johann Stroop, a famous and awful man. But the truth was that members of OKW (high command) had no confidence in the Wehrmacht's ability to rout out the bastards. So the SS was sent in to crush this rebellion in the most violent and destructive way possible, to send a clear message to any that might be considering similar action. Disobedience meant a quicker death. But the real truth was that the master received a higher return rate on corpses when the SS killed them. They were just a lot more efficient than the regular units, and more of their members were ghouls.

I stare at the smoldering horizon and listen to the men snicker nervously. They are glad the Whargoul has joined them but they are still scared of me. I have befriended no one since the death of Kepler, and I miss my friend.

The fact that I had killed him didn't help.

It was wise not to make too many friends during a war like this. They died too quickly. And it had hurt me to watch Kepler die. I hadn't meant to kill him. Besides, most of these men were boorish louts, idiots at best. It was true—armies attracted vast pools of scum, lost and violent men who had come to the end of their collective rope. The army promised redemption, or death.

I had no time for their banter. They asked stupid questions, like where I was from or what I planned to do after the war. That in itself was a revelation of sorts. I had not known the war would "end." I just assumed it had been going on forever and would continue to do so. Inquiries as to my family were likewise in vain. I told everyone I thought that they were dead, but that perhaps my Father was living in the caverns beneath Auschwitz, and that I planned to visit him soon. Their orders I ignored, their officers I despised and avoided. I rode from place to place in my armored car, attaching myself to battles. I was never challenged and all were fearful of my presence. My only guidance was the strange and sometimes annoying creatures that whispered to me.

We wade into bloody block fighting as brutal as anything Stalingrad had offered me. The Jews have turned every street into a death maze, every sewer opening a potential pillbox. They fight with desperation and fanaticism and as the battle progresses they gain a measure of our respect. They catch us in clever crossfire's, using expert fire control. They don't shoot unless they know they are going to hit something German. They hate us so much, and they fight so hard, going hand-to-hand and refusing to surrender, knowing that they would have been shot anyway. But they can do little as 30-ton tanks belch shells into their houses. We blow up block after block, entombing the residents beneath tons of rubble and then dousing them with flame-throwers. Days of fighting merge into a bloody smear that finally reaches a climax at ZOG headquarters, where the leaders of the insurrection have holed up to make a last stand. It's an old police station and makes a great fort. Orders have come down to try and take some of them alive so they can be publicly flayed. I am there for the attack.

First comes smoke and plenty of it. It blinds them and us but is to our advantage as we set up our assault squads. Then comes the Goliath, a fiendish new machine—a remote controlled bomb that tears off the front of the building in a blast that scatters debris for blocks. Then we are up and out, pouring into the gaping fissure, guns spitting, searching for prey. They fire back from close range, toppling several of our men and wounding me through the chest in a manner that makes it difficult to breathe for several minutes. I spend this painful time clubbing and stomping madly, making short work of them, all the while blood spurting out of my chest. By the time the rest of the squad is up I've slain everyone, and I'm already making my way up the corridor. I fire through the walls with my Kar 15 rifle. Most people wouldn't fire a rifle right at a wall, as fragments fly in every direction with skin-splitting force, but then again no one would innately sense the people directly beyond the wall, much less enjoy the pain. I pump three rounds through it, filling the air with smoke and deafening sound. A good kick busts a hole through it (solid stone), and I follow it with a grenade. To escape its power I simply turn around and walk three steps away, shrugging off the blast with little effect save the ruining of my uniform. Then I stride back into the wall and burst though its charring mass in a surge of muscle. To those on the other side I now give my pity.

Everyone is on the far side of the room, away from my attack. They don't want to look at me as my hideous shrieking challenges the dying echoes of the blast. They begin to writhe about in the remnants of the command bunker as I stare at them, not understanding their action. Then I realize they are trying to kill themselves without the benefits of having any bullets left for their guns. So they gouge their throats with scraps of jagged metal, and the lucky ones throw themselves onto knifes. Two try to strangle each other. One of them stands on his head and lowers it into a bucket of water. I laugh at their suicidal little dance.

"Let me help," I say, tossing a grenade.

They're all dead.

I watch the man, a German, half a mile away. Is he sad? I bet he is. His family is thousands of miles behind him, his future a tomb. Being a human must suck, knowing you had but one shot at life. One shot.

I watch him smoke. I watch him take a piss. I watch him eat a cracker. I watch him through the sights of my sniper rifle.

"I bet you think nobody can see you," I think as I shoot him in the chest and then watch him die.

It was another ghastly night in Stalingrad. The sky glowed a lurid yellow against the clouds, heavy with snow, and lit by the pallid corpse-light of the leprous moon. Mangled facades leaned drunkenly in their death-throes, towering over heaps of rubble and soot. Black ice clung everywhere—and the snow was black too. It was cold, cold in a way that would freeze your lungs to crystal. No one moved, no one dared to. It was too cold and too light out. Everything was still but it was not a silent night.

Terrible screams were coming from the Black Temple. Horrific shrieks of men in agony, sobbing for their lives in German. And not just human cries—there were the wailing tones of some beast, a mournful hound perhaps, tones that would suddenly rise into a chorus of maniacal cackling, as the screams began anew. And this was played on loudspeakers so the whole city could hear its hellish din.

It terrified my men so I could guess what it did to the Germans. They cried out to their friends, their families. Their pleas were often cut short by brutish laughter and rattling iron. It must have been very loud as I could hear it clearly, even here, underground, in the tunnels beneath the battleground.

I was often here, searching the labyrinthine ways for secrets yet unguessed. I was drawn to the Black Temple from the throbbing guts beneath it—seemingly the whole area thrummed with a pulsing ebb, and my senses told me things are moving behind the walls. Through these passages would be my means of egress to the grim edifice, and hopefully its eldritch treasures.

I stand in the rough earthen tunnel and climb upwards through a vertical shaft that empties into the void, which until recently had housed a coffin. Now only broken shards and scraps of cloth remained as I raise my head above the lip of the grave. I was in the workers plot, a gaggle of rude tombs, torn by shell and bomb, which was nestled in a courtyard behind the house of Necrosov, master of Stalingrad. And the screams poured down upon me, like a horrid radio play.

A volley of Russian shells tear across the sky, briefly lighting the church. It was simply built, and any decoration had long since been scraped away by the fires of war. But the building had not taken many direct hits due to its location in the midst of several huge factory buildings. It was well protected, and this is why Necrosov had chosen it as his home. The building itself was very solidly built and didn't even resemble a church—the commissars frowned on religion but the factory managers found it essential. It was one of their graves I peered out of now, gazing upwards at the bloated building that all but blotted out the sky. I would know your secrets, Necrosov. I wanted in.

This was how it went. The cities were becoming depopulated according to plan. In a sense it was very close to what had happened to the Jews. The "undesirables" were herded into the ghettos. When they were all in one place, they were destroyed. The same thing was happening to the blacks. Except instead of Zyklon B they used crack and cheap guns. They used crumbling schools and low-grade health care, lies and deceit, false hope and fake money. It was undetectable genocide, cities built with bone.

Young black men killing young black men wasn't a cultural phenomenon. It was population control. And men killing men wasn't the only payoff. It was also the countless retroactive abortions their premature deaths caused. That was why black men seemingly had no concern for birth control. It was because they could instinctively feel what was happening to them as a race, and they were determined to fuck themselves into continuance.

"I am the death of America!"

The screaming man stands on the edge of the ledge, teetering in the wind. He is a young black man wrapped in an American flag, with a gun in one hand and a megaphone in the other.

"I am the death of America!" he screams at the backs of the retreating crowd. "I am going to die today, and you can't stop me, and when I die, America will die with me!"

I watch on TV as the spectacle unfolds. Somehow this guy has gotten into the Empire State Building with his hardware and taken up a position on the ledge of huge lights above the main observation deck. Holding a gun to his head, he screams and rails against the injustices of the world as the crowd of observers grows. First they try to talk him down, then they consider shooting him. Then they try some reverse psychology.

"Go ahead and jump asshole, you'll just be another splat on the pavement."

The man drops the megaphone and dumps a jar of gasoline on himself. He lights himself on fire.

" I am the death of AmericaaaaAAAAH!" He screams one last time as the police shoot at him. He leaps off the building, trailing flames, and plummets earthward. At the last second he shoots himself in the head and impacts, exploding like a watermelon.

A woman has survived my attack upon the prison and she flees into the sewers, me pursuing, popping off shots at the fleeing Jewess. My howls shake the stone. She stumbles along in terror, her arm bloody and mangled, hanging loosely at her side. I chase her droplets and watch her ass shake. She falls heavily and I come up behind her in a rush, cradling her from the filth and clutching at myself, rubbing my crotch the length of her leg, as I tear at her clothes in slobbery fashion.

Gods, she was a beauty. Wide and dark like a gentle rift to the world of comfort, the plane of pleasure, the completion of the ideal. And she wasn't afraid of me anymore. When she saw me she saw a devil, and when she saw a devil her belief in angels was confirmed. When she saw Whargoul she knew she would go to heaven. She stared through the piss-soaked gloom and I saw pity in her eyes, and tenderness, and understanding that I was powerless to do anything to avoid my existence. She accepted me and what I was. As a woman she understood me better than anyone in the world, even my dead friend Kepler. She was a creator, I was a destroyer. We needed each other.

My submachine tears off the top half of her head in an iron roar.

"Who are you, bitch?" I said. "Who are you bitch that is dead? Who are you, women, which I can't understand, who are you women, and who is your man?" I scoop the remaining brains out of her head and jab my tongue into the hole (it's warm).

Then I heard the whirling flesh mixture calling me all from behind. The slobbery slip of a thousand tongues all clutching each other from the river of filth which ran through these bowels, these foul holes where men poured the contents of their asses, which helped to plug up the works with their war-mangled carcasses, which went to feed the flesh-vats. My journey craft was built in the midst of the shit brown blood from the sub-tunnel, leading down but moving up. Leading far past the boundaries prescribed by the city planners, into the areas where no human could survive, but where their presence was required.

Her soul is sucked into the making, and there I cannot give chase. Her energy is used right in front of me. I can only behold as the river thing spews forth a pulsing cocoon, a glistening, hive-like, quivering array of molten flesh, which I move to become a part of, which moves in anticipation of my clutch. It wraps me in those same dreams of comfort, the feeling of belonging, the touch of a woman. The meat whirl swallows me, and I pass below the surface of the shit-choked water drawing me through these new canyons of undead pulp.

I have passed the surface world and surge to a new dawn. East Front no longer exists, and I go to greet the birth machine. I see now that my whole life has been building to this, from the first moment I was spewn forth from the icy Volga. I have been drawn back to the west the whole time, bearing buckets of blood that were the lessons I had absorbed to make me worthy of such an effort. I sensed that there were others who had failed similar tests. I had killed some of them. I was the victor here, the generals were my pawns, their leaders made of uncomprehending clay. I knew now that they were all to be killed, all to be sent below, sent to the center of the Earth where it lurked and lived and spat out its murder machines.

The creator of the destroyer. Warsaw is being destroyed. I ride a wave of fresh corpses back to the anti-womb. I'll be rewarded—I'll eat 'til I burst—I'll find a new form. I'll suck it in and spit it back out at you and the world, reveling in my love of spite.

And then—could it be done? Could I then achieve the goal I had barely let myself even dream about, yet knew in my blackened heart I had been created to accomplish?

I would murder everyone in the entire world.

6
ARMORED WHORE

Bear with me. I cannot tell my story in chronological order. I must write it down as I remember it, and it is good for my sanity to not remember everything at once.

I'm hiding by the side of a road. Not a nice paved American road, either, a rutted and gnarled goat track winding through inhospitable terrain. No lush forest here, only stunted growths clawing life from the land. Night enshrouds this world but does not prevent me from seeing the things that I see. Like a bug on a tree thirty meters away. Like the column of trucks and armored vehicles slowly snaking their way up the side of the valley whose side I perch upon.

They are Iraqi soldiers, and they have come for me.

They call me the Wolf-Woman. For years I have been working in this area. I'm naked, as usual. I haven't washed for over a decade and it really shows. Hair grows out of me in matted clumps, from my armpits, enshrouding me in a set of surrogate clothing, framing a face that would later be seen as a lovely one. I haven't cut my hair for years and it stinks. It's matted with shit and blood; bugs live in it. My breath is a fetid vapor that will wilt green leaves. My breasts jut with vigor from the filthy forest, baked by the sun, pendulous and bloated with undelivered milk. I revel in my wretchedness and use it as a shield against encroaching humanity. Especially my own.

This region was rent with misery and thus it was perfect for my hateful activity. The native people, the Kurds, were desperately trying to carve out an independent nation inbetween Turkey to the north and Iraq to the south. The Iraqis had lost much at my hands, and apparently they felt I was some kind of demon the Kurds had summoned to fight them with. The truth was I couldn't give a damn about either parties and did my best to inflict suffering on both.

I squatted on a rock and ground my clit across its rough surface as I watched the humans approach my mountain with mixed feelings regarding their arrival. Their lives were in my hands but for the first time in years I was filled with doubt.

Should I release my ambush of piled boulders and logs? It would certainly close the road down. Then I could hunt them at will through the vales and dark passages, cultivating their terror, as you would season a steak. I would kill them one by one until there were none left to report back as to why their mission had been a failure. There was just another mystery, another missing patrol, and another series of letters to write back to concerned and then grieving parents. And another glutted Whargoul, one slaked on souls and blood, fat and happy and filled with an unquenchable desire to inflict suffering on others in order to alleviate her own pain.

But if that was my plan then why had I let one escape the last time they had come for me? Why had I let that man with the torn and bloody uniform stumble eight miles through the snow with my howls driving his frozen feet?

It was easy to hate the humans and I'd been determined to never return to their midst. I had been living outdoors for ten years, ever since the Mossad had blown my lover and myself up. Since they had tortured us to the point of death with a blowtorch and liberal applications of battery acid. I could still feel the kiss of the naked flame upon my instep.

They had arrived unannounced in the middle of the night. They had Gabby at gunpoint and promised to release her if I acquiesced to their demands. So I had allowed myself to be wrapped in heavy chain.

Then they tore out her tongue. It took considerable effort as she had quite a strong mouth. I will never forget the sound it made as the last strand of muscle popped free.

It flopped to the ground and glistened wetly as one of them pulled up a chair and sat on it backwards, regarding me coolly through thick glasses perched on the front of his bland and egg-shaped face.

"Your name is Joachim Pieper. You were a member of the Waffen SS. In 1944 you commanded a Kampfgruppe in the Ardennes offensive. Your unit massacred both civilians and prisoners in the area of Malmedy, Belgium, on December 28th of that same year. We have come to exact some small measure of vengeance."

His voice was as bland as his face, as he paused to remove his glasses and wipe flecks of Gabby's blood from them. She mercifully had passed out, a torrent of crimson spilling down her chin as she was bound across from me by the other one in the immaculate dark suit. After this he unpacked a black leather bag, arranging the contents on the table in front of me. A pair of pliers, a hacksaw, a variety of drugs, and a propane torch. And let's not forget the hot glue gun. After he is done he turns to me and fixes his piggy-little eyes on me. His slash-mouth barely moves as he speaks.

"We are here to kill you. We will do this by hurting you for as long as possible. And there is nothing you can tell us to make us stop. We don't want to know anything about you—we know all that we need to. We have been sent here for no other reason than to torture you in the most agonizing way possible for as long as we can. When you begin to pass out we will give you stimulants. When we need to sleep we will give you sedatives. We are here to flay every molecule of your body."

I try, but could not telescope my tongue into his eye and suck out his brain. My powers, ignored for so long, had totally abandoned me.

"Let us now be to work. I want to see you cry before breakfast."

They had thought of everything. They had brought food. They

had brought reading material. They worked in shifts, the skinny one who never talked, and the fat one that never stopped. They pulled out my teeth, one by one. They ripped out my fingernails, poured acid on my genitals, and squirted hot glue up my ass. They had worked on us for days, and to their credit they really seemed to enjoy their work. And every now and then they would show me a photograph of a man they said I had killed. And gradually the memories I had worked so hard to erase came back to me, and I realized that I deserved every ounce of pain that they gave me. I prayed to the abyss for a death that I knew I could never have.

But Gabby could die, and she did. She died in sobbing agony, her mouth spouting foam as they poured acid down her gullet. They were amazed that I did not die, though they would not show it. So finally they just blew us up.

But I never cried, never screamed, never gave those bastards an ounce of satisfaction other than the blood they drained out of me.

This experience had left me filled with fucking hate until there was no room for anything else. Yes, I had done the things they accused me of. But I had been powerless to control myself; I had done these things because I thought it was the right thing. I had only been trying to impress my Father. I had been programmed. Everyone else was doing it—these and a thousand other reasons.

But certainly Gabby had not deserved it. She had been the only person to ever show me love, and left undisturbed she might have healed me.

And my paintings. My other love. The days I had spent under the blazing sun, fancying myself some demonic Van Gogh, painting and drinking with Gabby at my side, gobbling at my rod. After a few years the work had begun to get quite good, and the shed in which I was storing them soon was full. The Whargoul's boundless energy applied to the fine arts. Perhaps they are in there to this day, shining in the dark with the conviction and expression of a beast that for a time sought to heal his sin through pigment. How useless to think that could have worked. How self-indulgent. There was no way to paint over my sin. But if you could find them, perhaps you could get me a show.

They took me from my love, they took me from my art, and they brought me back the past I had tricked myself into forgetting. If they thought they were doing the human race a favor they were horribly mistaken. Because the vengeance I swore would take years to achieve and the body count would be unimaginable. Now, with my tits, pussy and strangely dark skin, I take leave of my past and walk towards my cursed future, crunching through the fresh snow in my bare feet.

I wander the Alps, staying high in the hills, skirting mountains and glaciers, occasionally attacking an isolated outpost of humanity and making quick work of any I find within. I had tried to outrun my destiny by staying in one place, tried to drown myself in wine instead of blood. How foolish of me to believe they would have let me escape.

I move to the south, shunning all except when hungry. I move at night, slinking like a shadow through the brush. And the whole time I puzzle at myself and the new bits that I have. Like the hole I must fill with my fingers in order to know glee. Like the useless dick-nub that pee no longer comes out of. Outcast, unsure, I become as wild as dirt and vow to never return to their world again.

But vows, like necks, were made to be broken. I await the column that will take me back to the humans, to once again lead them into the death maze. Men were on the moon and nuclear bombs sure had potential. I had wasted enough time painting and playing animal-woman. New wars were forming and I was missing all the fun.

I'm standing in the ruins of the Polish diner. I guess the bomb finally went off. I can't eat heavy bread so I just walk into the midst of the ruin, ducking under the yellow police tape and crunching through the debris until I stand where my favorite table used to be.

"I'll have bread, and make it heavy. Make it banal and tasteless, and keep it coming until I'm dead."

I sit down amongst the rubble. The whole block is gutted from the resulting fire my bomb caused. When the fire trucks arrive the locals attack them. Thirty eight people die that day.

I'm looking for the Chinese man. I know he can help me. He made me fall asleep. He knows what I am and he knows how to help me. If I could only find him.

I get in the Riv and cruise. Finally it runs out of gas and I leave it in the middle of the street. I walk around for several days, occasionally snorting huge bumps of heroin from a ketchup dispenser. Finally, I grasp the obvious and decide to look for him in Chinatown.

The streets are filled with raucous celebration. Giant beasts prowl the streets and suck writhing maidens into their champing jaws. The people applaud with glee every time a virgin is ripped apart. Nearby skeletal ducks applaud from rotating corpse-roasters as firecrackers ignite constantly or go out in the sticky blood that clogs the gutters. Everywhere there are slick and stylish young men with dangerously angled faces, leering from doorways, comparing guns and stories of pussyfucking. I am surrounded by deals and air charged with sweat and cordite, cooking flesh and Asian snatch. Gods, I'm giddy. Jesus, I'm horny.

At Lo's Noodle World there is a denser crowd of young people gathered outside, climbing up on trashcans and clinging to the window grates to get a glimpse inside. I wedge myself through their midst so I can understand.

"What's happening?" I barely ask one as the words plop out of my drug-addled mouth.

The man gives me a strange look but decides it may be prudent to answer my question, lest I bite half his face off.

"Happens every year. Some crazy old man eats a whole bathtub full of noodles."

I can't get closer without getting physical so I do. I use my expanding fingers to pry flesh apart and one-by-one the mass begins to relent. It's hot inside, and bright with lacquer. Impossible scenes of Asian bliss throw themselves off the walls as bodies squirm against me. Several times I'm off the ground but I make way, ignoring curses, threats, and finally a switchblade rammed into my back. I'm too fixated on my dream of salvation to care what anyone thinks and the fact that I am the only black and huge man in the place means nothing to me. I'm finally in the inner chamber where the spectacle will unfold, as I pop my joints out and gain another six inches.

The room is a huge dining area packed with people, though none of them are eating. Instead they are gathered in a great sweaty circle around what appears to be a large bathtub full of noodles. They stand on tables and chairs. The mood is tense and expectant. Many are checking their watches; all are waiting for something to happen. Many puzzled and/or dirty looks are thrown in my direction as the crowd begins a chant, slowly at first but slowly growing in coordination and power-the chant of a name, over and over again, an evocation—

"CHENG-TZU! CHENG-TZU! CHENG-TZU!"

My own voice is added to their roar, adding a considerable amount of volume. Bottles are being passed around and I grab one, glugging the liquor and raising my fist with the others.

"CHENG-TZU! CHENG-TZU! CHENG-TZU!"

I don't know how to explain it. Simply that he was not there, and then he was. One moment the crowd was not erupting in glee . . . and then it was.

He was still wearing the same ratty, but spotless, clothing he wore upon my first encounter with him. Still wearing it with a regal quality that would shame a Pope. The same wizened and cheerful face, with the shining eyes. The awkward grace of a gibbon. The sight of him floods me with an emotion that I had not had in 30 years, since my last days with Gabby.

I was crowded with feelings from the other side. What did I feel for this man? Why did he taste different?

Was he a man at all?

He quiets the crowd with single gesture. There is nothing to be wasted with this man—every motion, every gesture is purposeful and deliberate, even when frivolous. Like the glance he shoots me. He can taste me too.

Silence reigns as Cheng lifts a single noodle, an incredibly long strand of pasta that I realize is one huge noodle. He places the end between his lips and holds it there, arms raised. There is a breathless moment—and then he begins to suck.

And suck. And suck. And as the endless noodle continues to disappear into his mouth the crowd is chanting in unison a word that I cannot understand but I know means—

" SUCK-SUCK-SUCK!"

And suck he does. There are easily 40 gallons of noodles and it becomes apparent that he intends to consume every ounce. I watch in amazement as his belly expands beneath the weight of his slobbery feast and know at that moment he is truly one of my kind. Why he would want to eat a half-ton of noodles at once was beyond me, but who would understand my peculiar appetite?

It turned out Cheng only ate one meal a year. He came here every New Years Day and ate enough to last him until the next one. He had been doing it for as many New Years as anyone could remember, and he never seemed to get older. And he only needed a light sauce, just enough to grease the noodle on the way down.

With a great POP, the last foot of noodle disappears into his face. His body, bloated to twice its normal size, falls back into the hands of several robed noodle-acolytes, who bear him out of the room accompanied by thunderous applause and cheering, of which I am a part. The crowd surges forward, madly licking at the empty tub. I squeeze myself into the street.

Later, I sit on a bench and contemplate the sweaty card that has somehow found its way into my hand.

"Tiki-BoBo's House of Pleasure. Massage, Acupuncture, Beautiful and Exotic Ladies. 188 Canal. 24 Hours." Then a phone number.

But that was not the inscription which had transfixed me, and turned my joy to dread. It was the words scribbled on the back in a spidery hand which I knew to be Cheng Tzu's.

"Your Father has returned and is searching for you. He sends powerful enemies to either recruit or destroy you. He prepares to unleash the final war with you as his general. But you still have one last chance to redeem and thus save your eternal soul. Come to me."

There it was. My chance, my dream. A shot at salvation. All I had to do was deny the nature which had been programmed into me since before my birth. But it was a chance.

My salvation awaited me—at the local whorehouse.

The first time I died was the night I met my brother for the second time. He explained much before he tried to kill me.

The city was the carcass, a great dead whale. We were journeying through its clotted cathedrals. The black church was its penis; I was the recurrent sperm, dying to get back in. The black church broadcast the howls of the dying as hounds worried at their genitals, within the building most shunned in Stalingrad—the place I most desired egress. I knew others of my kind were there, going about their bloody business in a manner most vocal.

The defense of Necrosov's building was surprisingly light. In fact, it was non-existent; the front door was wide open, guarded by the lifeless forms of two frozen men, still propped into position, drifts of black snow beginning to pile up about their legs. Though they were dead, I had no idea what creatures might be watching through their eyes, so I avoided that obvious passage. Instead I leapt from my hiding place in a great arcing bound which left me clinging to the pitted stone some thirty feet above the ransacked graveyard. I climbed quickly, digging my finger and toenails into invisible cracks, scrabbling at the stone. I didn't pause until I perched atop the highest steeple. The opposite tower's top has been shorn off by a rocket—a lucky hit. That will be my hole.

A hole beneath a sky around the world without a name. There was a whole world out there, a huge world, made up of billions of souls, all bending their wills to the pursuit of each other's murder. It was a World War—the whole world fighting! Nations striving and thriving, putting all else aside in their destructive quest. I knew the names of many of them-America, Japan, China. I wished to visit them all, astride my pale horse, whirling my gore-soaked scythe, spraying all with hellish pellets. For what else could be the quest of war save the end of it, only achieved when all have been destroyed.

And beyond that? An entire galaxy where unknown millions of worlds waited to be engulfed with the destructive mania that gripped this one. Millions of worlds containing billions of beings—this I felt instinctively. All waiting to be killed. If it went well enough here, then it would leap off this planet like chain lightning, smiting the cosmos with its curse. This was my destiny, to aid in this infection.

It made me smile, and I do, snow gathering on my teeth, as I sail through the nighted gulf between the two towers, my greatcoat spread like a pair of bat wings as I ride the frozen wind. I land on the broken belfry, slipping and clawing my way at the broken edge of the tower, pulling myself up and over the edge, dropping into the ruined room below and the sights of the frozen soldier who guard this chamber.

"Is your master in?" I hiss.

The screams erupt anew, several men, begging in rude Russian for their lives, this time accompanied by animal-like yelps and barks. I know the answer, and receive a grin from my companion in affirmation. Such an affable fellow, still possessing a sense of humor despite his long watch. Past him is a broken stairway, slickly adorned with black ice, leading below, and into this chasm I cautiously descend.

Even from here I smell roasting flesh, metal and unwashed bodies. The walls vibrate with screams, shouts, and various metallic and mechanical noises, always punctuated by brutish laughter. Chains rattle and animals snuffle about in their master's leavings. That's all below, and all that I can tell from here. The various chambers, which lead off of the circular staircase, are empty, save broken furniture and stone. The blown snow is devoid of boot prints, but marked by the passage of a large hound of some sort. Two bends down I leave the snow and ice behind In fact it begins to get hot quickly as a lurid glow begins to emanate up the stairs from the gloom below. As I descend deeper into the keep the sounds begin to change from the metallic blare of the loudspeakers to the infinitely richer and more expansive tones of the real thing. As I continue my passage I note the decor, much more ornate than your usual Stalingrad fare in that it was not totally shot-up and otherwise abused. The interior was utilitarian, more like a schoolhouse than a church. Gun leveled, I creep towards the glow of flame tossed upon the wall before me. Glued to the inner wall, I pause to remove my helmet and then slowly peer around the corner.

First a boot, then a leg, then a body upon a stool, laughing and pointing with a bottle at some unseen folly. The room is oppressively hot and the creature is stripped to the waist.

Yes, creature. Human in form, but much more muscular and tougher looking. The face was what stood out—it was under-developed, rougher in form, not unlike me but more lacking in character. I mean, at least I had lips. This creature had but a gash, twisted by its guttural tongue as it spat forth a venomous stream of what I assumed were obscenities. Its features were ugly and abbreviated, the eyes fish-like in their glinting malignance. It was hairless, except across its broad and scaly back, which seemed to bristle with a fairly prodigious collection of spines. Peering around a little further I saw more of these things, many half-clothed (some naked) and all gleaming with the fetid sweat which seemed to perpetually issue from their porous bodies. Several were pantless, and there was not a visible penis, just a small nub that may or may not have been a functioning organ. Obese beetles scuttled amongst the debris, and occasionally these would be scooped up. The creatures would bite into the head, tearing it off and sucking the juices out of the thing. All bore or had at hand a wide variety of weapons, and what clothing they did wear was of Russian issue.

These were the Voiden, Necrosov's followers. Here they were at rest, away from the battle, their inhuman faces no longer covered by wrappings against the cold. Good thing, too. If they had run around unmasked they would have caused panic in the ranks.

And they are partying. Empty bottles of German beer, Russian Vodka and American transmission fluid litter the floor. Bellowing, one raises a pistol and fires it in the air as the creatures begin a harsh chant, stomping in rhythm.

But I can only see the edge of the activity. The room is very large and to lean out anymore would be to risk exposing myself. So I retrace my steps back up the stairs, and along a passage I feel will lead to the upper galleries my ears tell me surround the room. I make my way through the shadow-filled alcoves until I peer into a room containing a railing overlooking the main chamber. Sulfurous vapor spills through the ornately carven railings and the air is full of sloppy sounds and soft rustlings, coming from the floor below, which is alive with the chittering resonance of a massive beetle swarm. They cloak like a carpet the tiled floor beneath, which I am sure must be made of dead flesh. These "feed-beetles" spread onto the walls and cling to the ceilings, sluggish and fat creatures which spill onto the railings and drop into the room below when they sense it is time to be devoured. They part from my passage, as I crawl slowly through them, cradling my weapon and propelling myself towards the edge of the balcony towards what I am sure is quite the little get together.

Peering through a gap in the railing I see Necrosov standing on a raised dais of black stone, streaked with rivulets of greasy gore. Like most of his "men" he is stripped to the waist, wearing only a loincloth. His coarse hide is criss-crossed with the mute testimony of a thousand murderous wounds. He is not of the same race as his followers, this much is obvious. He is much more humanoid. He is covered in thick, black hair though his head is shaven or perhaps burned clean. Yes, burned clean because his flesh is bright red. Mostly. There are parts of him that are black, and there are parts of him that are metal. And there are parts of him that are encrusted strings of sinew in various stages of curing. He creaks when he walks, and then the metal makes sounds. It hums when a part powers up, and sometimes he freezes up and pauses in his movement while rotors whirl.

He was a cyborg. Part-man, part-machine. And what the ratio was I could not determine, though visibly it was about sixty-forty, meaning forty percent of his body was a visible metal implant or connective device. A creature of flesh, woven through steel.

Borne aloft by the slobbering mass. You see, the room was vast. Vaster than my ears had known. It was built about a pool, a great stone bowl filled with foaming pink and purple liquid. This caused the prodigious mist, which fouled my sight. The heat rose into the upper chamber, clinging to the walls and causing bugs to thrive, and as they live, they move slowly towards the edge, dropping into the pool and then later rising from it, and then being devoured.

Even bugs have a soul. And by a soul I mean an eternal yet featureless quality. Just like yours. You just have more of it. It is the energy that makes the dead get up and walk. And it can be extracted in a physical manner in a wide variety of ways, only a few of which I can understand or take advantage of.

So the Voiden feed while Necrosov stands upon the black altar, a great and ancient block sloping into and lapped by the pool which seems to be water-based and chunky. Instead of pagan relics the area behind it and leading away into the opposite wall is filled with worktables strewn with tools and raw material; dead flesh and bits of metal. A cart stands, rusty and dripping with blood which leaks from a collection of cracked, dark pots, over the sides of which a variety of limbs or gutty pulp hung. Beyond that, lit by naked electric bulbs, are a large collection of stacked shelves. There seems to be a further area where the shrill cry of a power tool in use rise. It cuts off abruptly and is replaced by a snickering laugh, which comes through the rows towards the main chamber. All look in that direction.

First I see the tentacles and arms amongst them. I think several people are coming but the appendages all issue from a central mass with a face at the center. There are two arms sprouting from each shoulder and pairs of tentacle-like yet jointed limbs sprouting from the chest and back. They are all bearing objects, some long, slim and dangerous-looking, some loose and meaty. But these limbs are folded back, awaiting need. The two chestal appendages hold forth a metal object.

"Your new arm!" screams the creature.

Necrosov's squad howls with delight as it is brought to him.

"Quickly you fool," he rasps. "Attach the damn thing!"

Limbs press forward with needles as the thing works fast, ignoring the shouts of the three captive German soldiers who are chained to posts at the opposite end of the pool, staring with terror at its boiling surface and madly tearing at their shackles. I think they are praying as a horned snout emerges from the depths. A lamprey-like thing, all mouth, and the mouth was all teeth. It rips into the first German, not savaging him, just inserting its suckers into his chest. At the same time a fleshy tube has risen and is clinging to Necrosov's groin. His head leans back and emits a long and deeply satisfying groan as his body is fused with the new material. All the while bugs continue to plop into the steaming pool as Necrosov's body knits new flesh around the steel.

Appalled yet hardened by this blatant display of trans-mogrification, I don't hear the tread of the attacking hound until it bites me in the back of the neck and seizes me in a vise-like grip, shaking me in its normal killing fashion. I lock my neck and let the rest go limp as I slow down. Perception lurches into a sluggish meld of mass. I use this ability to avoid serious sudden injury, like falling off a cliff. It doesn't work so well against a live attacker but at least I can twist around enough to ram the snout of my gun into its side and pull the trigger. We crash into the railing as I try to rise to my feet. The hound stays on me, rising on its hind legs and trying to pull me the opposite way. So it is a matter of strength, and with this being an infernal creature the outcome is actually in doubt for a split-second.

I curl towards the rail lifting the beast from the ground, its body hanging from jaws still locked to my neck. Continuing to rise it is my feeling that the force of being flipped and dropped on its back will break its hold, before it breaks my neck.

From below, the Voiden open up with submachine guns.

"Ha!" barks Necrosov as he fires his new grenade launcher-arm. The railing erupts in a blossoming of force and flame just as the hound strikes the rail, only to be blown back up into the ceiling. The rail disintegrates but absorbs most of the blast. Still, I am sorely hurt and the death-lock jaws of the hound yet grip me. My form shudders under the application of damage, and it only takes a sickening instant for the floor to collapse into a vortex of flame. We slip into and through, to emerge below liquid frothing in the bug-pool that swallows us whole.

How long we stay below, locked in the bath, I cannot say. My skin is foamed away. I become anew, absorbing and melding with my foe, who becomes my fodder. My screams come bubbling up through the plasma, my great clawed hands pawing towards the altar that I wish to touch. But they are not done with me as I buck and jerk in a tremulous spasm, my being absorbing new energies.

My lolling head begins to emerge from the now-calmed pool, eyes rolling in their expanded and decidedly more canine skull as I seek the boundaries of my new being. My lengthened arm claws forth and finds the stone shore as I wash upon the altar. The bath has changed me; my senses are heightened but I am still unsure of what has happened to me.

I rise to my knees in the receding slime, stretching out my arms in a series of grisly pops and slowly bring my eyes around the room—the bugs, slowing their essential cascade; the Voiden, now as one, level their weapons on me; the maker-thing, with the crown of arms, who cowers behind his master; and Necrosov, Soviet super-soldier and legend of the state, who prepares to bid welcome to this latest, albeit unexpected, potential member of his malignant cadre.

He fires the flame-thrower at almost point-blank range, burning a hole into my chest and engulfing me in a searing blanket of agony. I'm stricken, melting, and never have I felt such intense pain in my necrotic life as I suffer now. I am roasted, bathed in the acid vat, burnt to a crisp under a sustained dosage of igniting gasoline. The liquid of the pool evaporates away from me as several other weapons join the hail. I am under the direct and close fire of two heavily armed Soviet engineer squads and their cybernetic commander, and it almost kills me.

But then comes the suction from below. They are slurping hard, drawing me into the meat drain. The sides of the pool heave with fresh filth as the gullet begins to force me down, taking me from the flames of the Voiden and the city that they ruled. Plucked away and senseless, guided by unknown feelers, I rush underearth in search of a bloody new dawn.

One of the biggest things that freaks me out about New York is the shit in the walls. Yes, it is a veritable city of shit. The whole city is made up of giant buildings, towering beyond life and filled with humans. Humans who have to shit at least once a day. And many shit much more than that, some actually prefer to take a series of smaller shits in order to escape their boss or simply because they enjoy shitting. And when they do shit, it goes into the walls, and travels through those walls that surround the humans who do the shitting in its unseen search for a final resting place. Standing at the water cooler, eating your lunch, sucking off the boss, or even adding to the turd pool—at any moment you may be surrounded by more turds than humans. I sometimes uncomfortably fantasize that the walls are made of glass and this parade of wiggling excrement is made painfully apparent to the people who would rather ignore this unseen reality. And where does it all go anyway? I mean, we are talking at least 12 million turds a day. It's enough to make you want to move.

"God, this is a terrible party," I think, as I swill a 150-dollar bottle of champagne. They really need to do something about the music. It's always the same band, the President's favorite, and all they ever play are songs about Saddam and how great he is. Everything from the thirty-foot-tall portrait, to the colossal ice sculpture, to the horrid, keening wail of the singer, Adel Akle, as he babbles "Oh great leader, Great Saddam, Great Saddam, we pledge our lives to you," everything's meant to invoke the presence of the mighty leader here, amongst his most privileged servants. This is essential, as he never comes to these parties.

My breasts are bound back hard with a heavy elastic bandage. My uniform is padded as to reduce my curves. A fake mustache is expertly attached to my upper lip. I have many qualities that make me valuable to the Iraqi military—but being a woman is not one of them.

Things had not yet degenerated into the drunken orgy which I knew would occur later. Mass quantities of alcohol would be consumed as the men and women drank themselves to the point of delirium. Clothes would start flying and copulation would occur between vomit-spackled deck chairs sent sprawling by the impaired thrashings of the idiot humans. There would be drugs, there would be guns, and there would be murder. I planned to make my exit well before then and return to the presidential palace where I would indulge in my own selfish pleasures. You see, I had done very well for myself since that night in the Kurdish highlands.

After all, this was Iraq, the America of the Mideast. Women were not required to wear veils, alcohol, gambling, and prostitution flourished, and indeed it was considered unmanly to offer prayers. Baghdad was the Babylon of old, and that worked well for me. I had returned to the civilized world with a vengeance and this was the perfect stage for my latest horrific performance.

This disdain for traditional Islamic law, or Sharia was one of the biggest reasons Iraq was at war with its neighbor, Iran. Iran was a strict Islamic state under the rule of Saddam's main rival in the region, the Ayatollah Khomeni. The Iranians were just emerging from decades of rule as a puppet state of the U.S., under the gluttonous leadership of the Shah. The Iranian people, miserable under the excesses of the ruling caste, had overthrown their ruler in a relatively bloodless coup and replaced him with the Ayatollah, a bearded troll with an iron will, the people's spiritual leader, who had been in exile overseas for decades. Saddam, always on the alert for a power grab, had misinterpreted the period of instability following the revolution as a period of weakness. Allowing himself to be influenced by American money, (the U.S. was thirsting for vengeance after the hostage crisis) Saddam's legions invaded Iran in 1980. Surprisingly, his opponent was perhaps a disorganized but certainly not a demoralized one. The Iranians were galvanized by this attack and responded with fanatical zeal. Millions of young men poured toward the front, ready to fight without weapons if necessary. Since then it had been a bloody war of attrition that had dragged on for six years and showed no signs of letting up. This party is in honor of this war, and the many phyrric victories of the last year.

Suddenly, a great roar goes up from the floor. Uday, the President's depraved son, has attacked an unfortunate guest with a battery-powered electric knife. He calls this device his "magic wand," and uses it to trim everything from roses to noses. Great gouts of blood splash across the buffet table as people clear out in a large semi-circle to watch the murder, careful to hide any reaction other than amusement. Most go blank and turn away, knowing the slightest sign of disapproval could mean not only their death but also the deaths of everyone they ever knew. Some, seeking to curry favor, openly applaud the Prince's behavior. The only one who truly expresses himself without self-conscience is the victim, whose howls of agony momentarily threaten to compete with the inane blather of the singer, who does not miss a beat, even when Uday produces a pistol and empties the entire magazine into the man's rapidly disintegrating head. As he reloads, I decide it is a good time to make my escape. I make for a back stairway that will take me to the underground railway which transports Baghdad's elite as Uday continues to pump bullets into the now inert corpe.

My bodyguards fall into step behind me as I move into the underground world that honeycombed the earth beneath the city. Saddam has been spending millions for years on an elaborate system of bunkers, tunnels and palaces that form an unseen city where he takes his refuge from the many peoples that are trying to kill him. Between the Kurds, the Iranians, the Israelis, and his own people, Saddam has many enemies. At this point the U.S. is not one of them.

I settle into the comfortable railcar which speeds off towards Mujamma al-Riasi, one of Saddam's many palaces. Germans had built this railway and Americans had built many of the bunkers and underground structures which sprouted away from it, like the heads of some transit-hydra. These were the same tunnels that will save Saddam and his family from assassination many times over in the coming years. It is ironic that the tunnels were built by the same people who will later try to kill him.

As the train gathers speed in the subterranean gloom my mind wanders to the events that brought me here—how I had come from my primitive existence as the Wolf-Woman of Kurdistan to one of Saddam's most trusted henchmen (I mean woman) in the space of only a few years.

I had lived for many years in the hills of the Kurds in the ruins of an ancient temple, built by a forgotten race that may or may not have come from this planet. There was a main temple area in ruins, and secret chambers beneath in which I had my quarters, in stark contrast to my present luxury apartment located within the presidential compound. I lived beneath the temple in absolute squalor, smeared with blood and hardened shit, determined to remake myself in an image so horrific that the humans would never be able to bear my presence again. But I was failing. I missed the company that some humans could give me, the conversation, the sex. I was curious about my new form and the pleasures it could give me. More and more I desired a return to the land of the living.

My den was littered with the scraps of civilization that I had taken from my victims. Wallets with photographs, scraps of paper scribbled with symbols, doodles, and personal notes, plastic containers, and old newspapers which I had no trouble reading even though they were in Arabic. One of my powers seemed to be language mastery, though I never quite got Chinese.

My curiosity regarding the outside world increased with every member of it I killed. I mostly preyed on the inhabitants of an Iraqi military base, located outside the only major city in the region. The Kurds actively tried to appease me by bringing baskets of goodies and leaving them on the slope below my lair. Once they even sent a holy man who yelled a whole bunch of shit up to me. I don't know if he was trying to convert or banish me. I sent him back down the hill, minus his head.

Finally the Iraqis mounted a major operation to rid the region of my presence. The first thing they did was attack my temple with Hind ground-assault helicopters, condensing times slow demolition of the structure into the space of an afternoon. Then a large group of soldiers sealed off the area and sent a powerful column up the side of the hill. It was their belief that their assault upon me would be hindered by the Pesh Mergas, the Kurdish freedom fighters they mistakenly believed I was allied with. I tended to kill more Iraqis, simply because they were more numerous and thus easier to find.

As I sit their upon my rock, deciding whether to attack now

or play possum. I am pissed. I really like my temple. It has a crude quality that appeals to me. Plus, there are the many carvings that I spend hours attempting to decipher. They have destroyed all that with their damn helicopters. But my decision is suddenly made for me. A rocket bursts from the brush aside the road and slams into the lead vehicle, a BMP armored transport which bursts into angry orange. The column is enveloped in a hail of small arms and machine gun fire that comes from all sides of the trail. Men spill from the trucks, clutching at themselves as metal rends their flesh. Enjoying the spectacle, I watch as rocket after rocket tears into the vehicles until the transport are reduced to flaming wrecks, belching their deaths into the once-calm summer sky.

All except one. One of the lead BMP's in the column is fighting back against his unseen foe. Another RPG slams into the vehicle but deflects off the hull, spinning into the underbrush before exploding. The 23mm. cannon atop the vehicle is spitting back, locating the position of the rocket launcher and momentarily silencing it with a well-placed burst. Bullets are hitting the BMP from all sides, kicking sparks off its hull, but armored and impervious, the machine begins to pick its way past the wreckage of the column, trying to maneuver through and escape the trap. I can see Pesh Mergas fighters moving closer to the road, preparing a volley of grenades. Their rocket launcher is momentarily out of action, and they are moving to finish their prey before air support, undoubtedly already called, arrives in the form of a Hind. The track is littered with dead and dying Iraqis and their equipment—AKs, RPGs, etc . . . they are good prizes for the poorly equipped guerrillas and they want them badly. The only thing stopping them is the BMP and its damn gun. They load their last RPG and fire it with a terrifying *whoosh!* This one strikes the BMP right in the front hull and it does considerable damage, tearing off a crew hatch and halting the things attempt to ram its way out of there. They wait a moment to approach, and then begin, satisfied the gun is dead as well.

It is not. It opens up just as the first fighter emerges from the brush and makes his way towards a dead soldier's ammo bag. The slugs tear the man in half and rip towards his fellows, who retreat again in a confused and babbling bundle.

The grim tableau, enacted with such terrifying swiftness at its onset, now assumes the character of a stalemate. The Pesh fighters change position, readying themselves for a last rush at the vehicle, which has settled in the middle of the road, unable to retreat or advance not due to the profusion of flaming wrecks, but to the dead driver within whose face has been pulpified. But the turret of the weapon continues to move, searching in a slow circle, occasionally letting loose with a belch of death. The defiant beast against the dark pine and its unseen occupants touches something within me—pity? Rooting for the underdog? After all, they have come here to kill me—but that have never meant much to something that can not die. Whatever the reason, I decide to wet my blade.

Yes, my blade. I had found it beneath my temple as I burrowed in the unseen ways which I littered with the bones of those I had brought here. I had found a tomb. A tomb with a low central dais upon which were the remains of an ancient king, a long-dead protector of some forgotten realm. The jewels that adorned his crown and scepter held little interest to me, though they betrayed no hint of time. But the sword, which the skeletal fingers held pried to its chest, well, that was an object I could utilize. A weapon that I instinctively knew how to apply in the most expert of ways. Looking at my eyes reflected in the gleaming blade, I trigger a rush of ancient memories. The times of the Variag, and the burning chaos-wheel, that filled the sky with the flame of change. The day the overlord had died. Other ages, other tales. Perhaps it was my corpse that sat upon this throne.

The gloom of centuries removed from light has not dulled its finish; the ticking of time unguessed has not blunted its edge. It leaps from its scabbard with a grateful cry, and flashing at the end of my arm in a gleaming trail it leads me crashing through the underbrush towards the carnage below, my war cry rising like a wave of doom.

They hear my wail and know that I have come. Two manage to pivot their position and lay down a pattern of fire which tears apart the bushes just ahead of me. A grenade explodes and I leap above the fire, trailing hair like a cloak as I emerge through the canopy of brush, nude, glittering blade raised on high, and I plummet earthwards in a deadly arc. Wild-eyed, a fighter raises his weapon, spitting death too late as my sword splits his body from neck to groin, spilling his vitals into the dirt. I continue with my movement, compressing and hacking to the right, extending my arm from its socket in an impossible blow that disembowels my victim, leaving him fumbling with his severed entrails.

I see the fighters like red blobs through the brush as I line up, coming in low and fast, striking with my weapon in one great slit, interrupted only by the blossoming of cloven flesh. I strike like lightening, bouncing off trees, the leaves whispering my passage as I heap the ground with writhing men.

As my scimitar projects in one direction, so my foot moves in another, clawed and knotted and lurking at the end of my leg, striking another man in the face, knocking his lower jaw clean out of the socket as his tongue flaps wetly. Arm raises, gun chatters, arm lowers, brains spurt. I spin a blood weaving, a manic expression which leaves my blade sheathed to the hilt in another man's chest. He feels the steel sliding into him and I fancy that he thinks—

"So this is what its like. This is what it feels like to die." All his worries are gone, and the biggest mystery in his life has been solved. And he realizes that it is really not as bad as he may have thought it would be, even considering the violent nature of his death, and the bad reputation that dying has. And I think that maybe this helps him know peace.

The sword flies from the chest, trailing gore and dragging his soul behind it. When my sword dances in this way I build up a vortex of ghosts, who are trapped by the blade and transferred along its length into my groping hole. Feeling glee as I suck the dead, I dent a head. The blow is so solid that the skull breaks in the perfect outline of the intruding foot; when I recoil and attempt retraction, the foot stays in the man's skull, my toe claws wiggling in his gray matter. It throws me off just enough to make me stumble, my foot clearing in an eruption of chunks. But that creates enough time for the last of their number to react—react by falling to his knees and praying to me in a rush of hysterical babble. Sparing him does not interest me and seconds later his decapitated head rolls at my feet, then feels the rude insertion of my questing tongue as I take my sweet and sexy time with him.

The few survivors of my assault thrash off through the brush, careening over the rocky soil directly into the sights of others who wish to kill them. Most notably the Hind that I can already hear making its way towards the column. I have no wish to encounter this creature in any way, as its rocket pods could easily tear me apart. I beat a hasty retreat to the temple.

I have a nice slit trench that I bolt up, noting gratefully the sounds of the Hind attacking the lower slopes. I pause and look back, seeing the bug-like machine flash through a gap in the pine and then bob high and away from the slope, its load erupting behind in a roar of napalm. I can feel rather than hear the thin and piping sounds of men being burned alive. It makes my pussy wet.

Then comes a surprising sight, as a sole Iraqi soldier moves into view, in the clearing below my now ruined and smoking temple. He darts rock-to-rock, his clothing charred, his helmet gone, but still doggedly intent on completing his mission. My capture, my death, or his.

I enter the temple from below and take a position in the center of the complex, where I sit back and wait. He approaches through a hole one of their missiles has blown in the wall, and he fearfully begins to examine the temples rubble-strewn interior. Alarmed by the amount of bones and the voluminous silence, he becomes more and more frightened, and his grip increases on the handle of his weapon. He approaches the low and murky corridor that leads to my den. I am exactly aware of his every movement as he draws near and I feel his increasing fear. I raise the level of my breathing to just the point where he might be able to imagine that he hears it, increasing his apprehension to an even more palatable level.

He moves to the threshold of the door, long since removed, and moves into the chamber where I wait above him, folded into a nook of stone. His weapon traces a slow circle about the room, lit only by cracks of sunshine through the broken walls.

He is a young man, dark-eyed with finely-formed features and a thick, manly mustache. His eyes dart intently about, at one point looking directly at me. He stops and freezes, and I pull a thong which releases a load of ossified bones onto him in a sepulcherous torrent. His weapon explodes through the clutch of the crypt, spraying bony chunk. I drop upon the beautiful wretch and in a glimmering arc hack the end of his weapon off in a brief flurry of sparks.

I stand before him and allow him to look at me.

He is Assad, and in the years to come he will be my lover. We will wade through rivers of blood and cum until the day that he is finally buried alive by the beasts of the infidel, with his fine Arabian cock inside of me.

"Allah save me," he gasps. "Save me from this spawn of the devil!" He fumbles with his sidearm and raises a Beretta in my direction. As he does, I raise my finger, lick it, and stick it in the muzzle of the gun, fixing my gaze upon his in a parastolic grip.

"I surrender." I say.

So once again fortune had changed for me, this time due more to boredom than anything else. It had been years of sad and sordid seclusion as I sought to destroy any vestige of humanity I'd had managed to gain during all those pleasant years with Gabby in the south of France. Now, having accomplished that through my decade-long pseudo-canine blood feast, I was ready to re-enter the world of mechanized death without a shred of conscience or remorse. I had heard of the war to the south and yearned once again for the banshee song of the rocket, the sweet stink of rotting flesh wafting across the battlefield, and the grinding of the metal claw as it sought purchase in living meat. I again sought others of my kind, and a rebirthing of the mission for which I'd been whelped (whatever that was).

And I needed another thing—a fat cock all up inside of me.

I stare at Gab's breast as it protrudes from the nightshirt she is wearing and wonder why it excites me anymore that the sight of a fire hydrant.

She is sleeping and she is lovely, even though she is getting older and it must be obvious to her that I am not. But why is she lovely, or why is her face, if it had been corroded with maggots, not?

The sight of the shape of the lower half of her generous breast fills me with lust, contentment, and joy. Of course, part of this is the fact that she is my girlfriend, because if she were not my sex partner then the sight of her breasts might fill me with lust, hatred and confusion. I think dogs are confused—or why would they spend so much time humping legs?

Had I been programmed to react this way? Why else would animals react in certain manners to the shape or coloring of plumage, the particular strut or odor exuded in the pursuit of sex? Because they were made that way. If we didn't have certain clues and stimuli as to the depositing of our seed, we'd never get laid.

But how did these clues get there? Were we programmed by biology, as the scientists claimed? By God, as the mealy—mouthed priests would tell you? Or, in my case anyway, by an eldritch being which existed in the blighted ways of the underworld, creating endless life in a quest to destroy it? How could I know? Was there a reason for what I felt when I stared at her jutting breast, or . . .

Was it something left over from *what I had once been*, something so strong that it could not be erased?

I had been programmed to enjoy violence. Why else would I do the things that I had done? I recalled a night in Stalingrad, so many years ago . . .

"Ursula, show us that trick again," bellows the drunken Batyuk, clad as usual only in his stained underwear.

We are in the whorehouse, which consists of a basement beneath a bombed-out building. Some blackened stairs lead into its fetid depths, and here several women (and I use the term loosely), have set up shop. These are old whores, camp followers of whatever army is nearby, and they have had literally thousands of penises inside of them, not necessarily all at once. They know how to hide a pregnancy, how to kill their own children, and how to turn a collection of grimy mattresses in the middle of a war zone into a profitable business, of which my filthy friends and myself are regular customers. It is the one place in the whole horrid city that we enjoy a truce with the Germans—they get the place two nights a week. They would leave us beer and we would not kill them.

The old vitrola warbles forth distorted tunes as the evening degenerates into another drunken debauch. It's been a busy night; one of the girls has been flat on her back for over five hours and Elsie, the youngest of the group (though through her mask of make-up, grime, and dried semen you would never know it) is passed out. That does not stop my friends, however, as two soldiers hump her with considerable vigor. Their exposed asses gleam whitely against their dark uniforms. Bombardments continue, planes pass overhead on missions of destruction, yet we ignore these distractions to focus on Ursula's "trick."

"What will I get, that I should do my trick, hmmm, babushka?" says the drunken old slut.

"What will you get, why, I'll give you money, or how about these gold fillings I have been prying out of dead Germans' teeth?" spits my colleague in carnage, holding out a dirty fistful of yellowish lumps.

"As I recall, my murderous Mongolian," I interject, "you pried those teeth out of German soldiers that were still alive."

The whore looks at me with the same uneasy glare that she always gives me. I scare her and her girls but I always paid well. After my first few sexual experiences (I had *hurt* those girls) I have been content to come here and drink, my second favorite pastime after killing people. And tonight I have drunk easily a gallon of vodka.

"Give that bottle to me," she says, motioning to an empty container of bootleg Popov. She sets it on the rough surface of the table in front of her, then rises unsteadily to her feet, arms spread like a high-wire specialist. Her show is no less spectacular, as she slowly begins to lower her cock-widened maw upon the helpless bottle, engulfing its mass in the cavernous depths of her suck-hole (mouth). It is both disgusting and stimulating, and the humping soldiers rolls off their inert prey in order to view the spectacle. Barking with each inch as they disappear, Batyuk is fully invigorated by the bottle-swallowing prostitute who now has the whole thing wedged in her face. She lifts her head from the table, bringing the bottle with it, its outlines clearly visible through her expanded throat. A drunken cheer erupts.

Programming! Violence! I smash her on the side of her throat with my bottle, breaking both in a shower of razor-sharp shards. Her throat is ripped open on my follow-through, as both flesh and glass merge in an expanding cone of blood.

It's funny!

She falls back to the floor, flailing at her wound, a horrid gurgling bubbling out of her dying face. The sound, the feeling, the experience is simply too tempting to resist, and I take such great pleasure in the suffering of others. Her friends scream and attack me, pummeling my bulk with ineffectual blows. I beat them senseless in a drunken rage, while Batyuk roars with laughter. The other men stumble out, hurriedly gathering their weapons and whatever booze they can grab. Only Batyuk can bear my presence, being the basest of humans and glad that he can collect his fillings from the dead whore's pocket.

"She's still warm," he mumbles, searching her mouth for fillings, "I'm gonna get her again." And then he fucks her.

Another thing we would sometimes do is chinfucking, which means fucking them in the chin.

We bear her corpse up to the street and dump it into a stinking hole, where unseen things lurk, just beyond sight, and scuttle away from the dead woman that thuds into their midst, only to soon be drawn towards her, first with curiosity and then with slavering jaw and claw. Over the space of hours they dismember her and bear the leaking bits below.

This is where the Quioid, the lowliest flesh-bearers, congregate and wait for fresh influxes of raw material. They feed upon and curry favor from the more powerful creatures with these bits. Short, wiry and foul-smelling, these creatures are the most loathsome bottom-feeders on my Father's food chain. They could be dangerous if assembled in great numbers, but generally they are too quarrelsome and stupid to unite on anything.

This is why I can't do things like take beautiful women out to dinner. I never know when I might ram my salad fork into her enchanting eye. I have been programmed to be an asshole, and a murderous one at that.

It seemed to be my strongest sense, the urge to destroy. But I also knew that I was capable of great love. Sometimes when speaking with someone, anyone, I would be suddenly overwhelmed with a desire to lay a big slobbery kiss on his or her smacker. I feel like it takes all my strength just to stop myself from putting them in a sloppy lip-lock. I could kiss or kill you, and no one could trust me anymore than I could trust myself. It was why I isolated myself, or joined armies. In one environment I couldn't hurt anyone, and in the other I was expected to.

But those years with Gabby had been different. Left alone and without a war, I had changed. I had reprogrammed myself. My natural instincts had taken over. It could, and would, happen again. But so many would have to die before I once again grew weary of the killing.

***

I am chained to a pole in the courtyard of the al-Rashid prison, the largest in the city limits of Baghdad. Since my capture I have been here, enduring punishment for my crimes against the state.

I knew I would be tortured but I did not know how bad it would get. If I had, then I might have stayed up in the hills. But I was quite the celebrity, and I was given very special treatment. It was not as bad as the pain I had endured at the hands of what I had to assume were members of the Mossad, the Israeli secret police. Their pain had been cleverer, as if they understood more of my physiological state and its reaction to the punishment, where my nerve centers were and such. But the Iraqis were far more blunt—they would saw off my arm and beat me with it, or wail on me with hurtful lengths of electric cable. Uday would whack me mercilessly and I would take it with as much stoicism as possible. I would stare him straight in the eye as he worked himself into a tizzy. He took quite an interest in me, and had my face shaved. I was stripped and hung by chains to a wall. They hosed me down to remove the filth that encased and to a certain extent protected my body. My lean form featured a beautiful pair of breasts that Uday would stare at while others beat me. He would rub himself and breathe heavily.

Here are some of the other things that they did to me—

I am bound naked to a gas heater. They turn up the heat. Though I could break my bonds with ease, I allow my genitals to be singed.

Electric connectors are attached through my pussy lips, which are shocked until I release bloody cum.

Molten glass is poured into my rectum.

I am made to wedge my head in between two wooden planks, which they nail my ears to.

I am stripped and covered in honey. Then I am lowered by my thumbs into a room filled with insects.

All that and so much more. And they filmed every minute of it.

They studied me with their doctors. And Uday's erection was often visible through the black military jumpsuit that he wore. I think he was beginning to like me.

But the Iraqi tabloids screamed for my blood. I was a captured Kurdish war hero and my execution was scheduled.

They began to show amazement at my resistance to torture. They had sawed my leg off, and I had not bled overmuch. I was left in the cell with my leg. When they had left I put my leg back on. It was not a perfect fit but I was still strong from my latest battle feast. When they came back I was up and around. Uday came back to personally saw my leg off. When he got there I was fingering myself and rubbing my breasts, moaning softly. My shaved and naked body had a peculiar effect on him. He got very agitated and ordered his men out of the room. Then he jacked off on me in a frenzied rush. I begged him to commute my sentence so I could help them in their fight against the Iranians, a war that was just kicking into gear. Uday was still a kid at this point, just beginning to come to grips with his sexuality. He was the first person who saw me as a woman, and he was also the first person to jack off in front of me, like he did that day.

"I will ponder your breasts—I mean words," he said as he fumbled out of the chamber, zipping up his cum-spattered flight suit.

It was then that they got very interested in me. Uday opposed my execution and favored continued experiments. But orders came from Saddam himself that I was to be shot immediately. I was dragged from my cell in the middle of the night and taken outside.

"For crimes against the Iraqi people, and our great leader, Saddam Hussein, you have been sentenced to death!" screams the officer, sweat exploding from his dark face. "Do you have any last words?"

"I repent for my crimes! I love our glorious leader, and dedicate my life to him! All glory to Saddam! Allah Akbar!"

The squad lines up to fire. The order to ready, and then aim, is given. I stare into the barrels of eight AKs, and wonder what I will come back as this time. I had little doubt that I would return.

Suddenly one of the barrels moves abruptly to the right. The soldier behind the gun shoots the officer in the head, before the order to fire can be given. He slowly sinks to the floor, spouting blood as the squad stands about confusedly in various directions. My savior stares at me, and I stare back, and allow my first smile in years to grace my face.

It is Assad. The young soldier whom I had allowed to capture me. Who has been assigned to my security detail and who has watched my transformation from untamed hill-thing to the shaved and chained sex goddess that Uday has made me into. Then a group of Uday's men arrive in a jumble of suits and arrest everyone except me, who they leave chained to the pole.

Uday enters.

"Fucking Iranian masterbators!" he screams while jacking off.

I'm glad to have not been shot multiple times. I could survive it but it would hurt like hell. And it could possibly scar me, and I was beginning to understand that I liked my new form and the effect the shape of my breasts had on men. It touched programming within the humans, and elicited reactions they could not control. My newfound sexuality would become a powerful weapon.

I lounge in the air-conditioned comfort of the underground train and smoke a Marlboro. Saddam will not be pleased that his son has murdered the party guest. The man had been an old friend of the president, and had known his favor. But this was family. Uday would drink and take drugs for days, then have an emotional collapse at some expensive Baghdad rehab clinic. His father would shun him for a time and then forgive him for his horrific act. Blame would be generated around the victim—somehow he had deserved to be hacked and shot to pieces. As the veil of delusion was more tightly drawn, the fictitious crimes of the victim would grow to the point where it was revealed that Uday had thwarted an assassination attempt against a President that was not even there. He was a hero.

Signal lights pulsed across my composed features as the train slides into the bay area that leads to Saddam's chambers. I knew that tonight he would be there, staring at battle maps of the Iranian front, desperately trying to come up with a way to break the stalemate of a conflict that had taken the flavor of WW I trench warfare.

I enjoyed it. My unit was assigned to one of the most active sectors and saw a lot of action. The "Khomenis," as we called them, attacked often. They didn't show a lot of finesse either. Their standard attack mode was to run screaming in a huge mass of men directly at us. They had little training but inexhaustible numbers. Sometimes it was as easy as depressing the button of a machine gun. You really didn't even need to aim. And this constant stream of mangled corpses-in-waiting, and the energy they released upon their violent ends, suited my necrotic feastings very well. I was content, if a little lazy.

I feel my clit twitch as I don the cotton gloves required when meeting with the president. He is a germ freak and constantly worried that he would be infected with some murderous CIA-concocted bug. But actually at that time the CIA is helping him to destroy Iranians. Soon he will take advantage of this alliance by attacking it. That Exocet missile that smashed into the U.S.S. Stark was no accident. He also makes everyone change his or her socks before you can see him. And you never get back your old ones. Maybe he has a sock fetish. It wouldn't surprise me, as he seems to be immune to my sexual predadations and with the musk that I exude that is difficult for any man. Unless he enjoys jacking off into dirty socks more than being with a woman (even a Whargoul woman with a fake mustache).

We pass into the bunker area through an elaborate system of strongpoints and guards. All of these men in the inner circle are related to the president's family in one way or another. It is one of the ways that Saddam stays in control—he keeps it in the family. That may have meant intermarriage in certain cases, and also might explain the behavior of Uday, which is certainly that of a madman. It is all very interesting to ponder but does impress me too much. The bottom line is what impressed me, and the Husseins of the Tikriti clan certainly have a big bottom . . . line.

Now we are but one chamber away from the president. I am surrounded by superbly dressed bodyguards in Pierre Cardin suits, made bulky by the profusion of automatic weapons beneath the expensive fabric. These men are ostensibly my bodyguards but are ready to attack me in a moment's notice, even though I have fucked several of them. They shuffle about, bumping brawny shoulders, their impassive faces betraying sweat, even with the benefit of the excellent Italian air conditioner. On the other side of the door our party is being scrutinized through the video monitor, and Saddam has been known to murder anyone coming into his presence without the benefit of immaculate grooming.

"There's a fly in here," I think as the door closes with a satisfying swoosh.

Saddam is facing the opposite direction, looking at a giant bank of TV screens displaying a variety of images. On several we can see the scene of the banquet I had just left. The party has cleared out and a crew of paramedics is loading the stiff off the bloody floor and onto a gurney. The band is still playing as apparently no one has ordered them to stop. Saddam watches this intently, bobbing his head in time to the music, which comes over the video feed in tinny noodlings. We stand there, stock-still and speechless until we are recognized. But he betrays no hint of even being aware of our presence as he continues to listen to the music.

Several hours pass. Saddam watches until the last lawn chair is folded up. Still the band plays on. And all the while the sound of that damn fly continues with a maddening vibration. I put my brain on autopilot—this could be a long night. The men around me are swaying from fatigue and boredom. But something has to give and it finally does. The band, after considerable debate, finally quits. They begin to pack up their instruments. As they do so, Saddam leans forwards and whispers into a tiny microphone. Within seconds masked security men burst into the party area. They arrest the band members in a violent manner, smashing their instruments and bloodying the men. Then Saddam abruptly spins his chair towards us, a gun in his hand.

"So. There was a fly in here," he says in his usual expressionless manner, shooting the unfortunate insect out of the sky with a thundering report.

That finally breaks the ice. Saddam motions me to sit down across the desk from him as the security men shuffle out. Behind Saddam I can already see band members being tortured in horrible little rooms.

"What do you know of this?" he says, motioning with an almost imperceptible movement of his hand as the imagery on the screens abruptly shifts. The bank of 64 televisions combine to make one giant image, an image of a blood-drenched figure waving a gore-flecked broadsword and brandishing a great shield. But the edges between the screens I find somewhat distracting to the comprehension of the image as a whole, especially considering that we were a scant 12 feet away from the display. I say this to him and he makes no move in reaction, but within seconds, with the undetectable hum of hidden hydraulics, the entire wall of TVs slides back to reveal one single immense TV, at least 128 feet across.

"The Japanese," Saddam murmurs.

And there it is again. The footage has been shot upon a battlefield on the front—I recognize the natural flora of the area. The ground is marshy and loose, typical of some of our more northern positions. The sky is black with smoke, and the ground choked with corpses, all lying in increasingly stiff attitudes of death. At the center of the destruction is a conflagration of whirling steel and flesh, chemical and soil.

At first I can't tell much about the figure because of the confusion surrounding it. But it is dressed in pre-medieval armor, lets say 800 A.D. A Viking in the classic sense, horned helmet and all. And those scholars are wrong—they did have horns on their helmets, the larger the better, even if that meant going through grog-house doors sideways.

Unfortunately, the Viking with the coal-red eyes kills the camera crew and the imagery shifts to a long shot of the thing, which kneels with his broadsword on a now silent battle plain. It screams at the sky, features drawn and skeletal, teeth chattering with the force of its ancient voice.

Now tanks attack him. With his great shield raised on high, he absorbs several shells. The projectiles arc towards it—they are drawn to it. The eldritch shield protects him from the hail of hate poured towards its owner. He rushes the tanks and attacks them with his sword, slicing into the hulls like they are butter, until the machines explode.

Now there are ten smaller screens that have appeared at the bottom of the screen, at first showing only the large image, then a set of different ones that filtered in across the screen. They were:

A man eating a women's pussy. Actually *eating* it.

A man being attacked by rats.

Midget-wrestling.

A middle-aged woman sleeping in a bed, surrounded by armed guards.

Saddam and I sitting here.

The guards outside.

A view of the view screen which I took to be a shot through Saddam's eyes (neural implants).

A man (Uday) changing into women's clothing.

A man has his guts nailed to a pole. Then a tiger is released into the room.

Men fisting children.

A woman fucking a man.

Saddam turns to me.

"Can you destroy it?" and his lips don't move.

Uday bursts into the room, dressed like a woman.

"Fuck me!" he screams.

He runs at me shrieking, and I slap him across the face with a blow that lays him against the wall. I quickly disrobe him and throw him at his father's feet. Then I return to my chair.

"Yes," I say to Saddam, who is now smiling broadly.

Just another day at the palace.

It was called the Seirka, translated—"the Wraith." Wraith meaning an undead spirit of vengeance. But I knew more; due to the ageless hours I had spent studying the encrypted walls of the sub-tunnels beneath my old tomb-home in the Kurdish hills. Jeez, I had had so many pads. And that had been a good one. Those walls had told me much about the local legends. Like the Persian Emperor who had favored Nordic strongmen for his personal bodyguards. One, a hulking brute named Olec, was falsely accused by the King's son, who was jealous because he thought Olec was banging his sister (whom *he* was banging). Olec was put to death, but before he died he swore a curse upon the family that he would return from the dead to kill the Persian king. No doubt the whole thing had been caused by the constant tinkerings of my Father, striving for entertainment and power at the expense of your race. Now the creature was back from the dead in what I could only assume to be an attempt to draw me into the open. They knew I couldn't resist a good fight.

Olec was alive and wreaking a bitter harvest on the Iraqi front, slicing hither and thither, but making steady progress towards what looked like Baghdad, and the Persian king within. And I knew how to stop him.

Two days later I am standing nude in a ditch. Blinders have been set up around me so the rest of the regiment cannot see into the area. It's dark and they are not paying attention to anything except the sirens howling, warning of an impending attack from the Seirka. I can hear the rasping cry of the thing through the din of the shells that are the only thing that slow it down, besides actually taking the time to hack the hell out of people.

My trench is full of captured Iranians all screaming at my arrival. Stories of my prowess have preceded me. There is not a single Khomeni who has not heard the rumors of the blood fiend that fights with the forces of Saddam. Now they meet me in the flesh. I am nude, and my generous breasts jut forward with vigor and strength. The captives stare at me, hard with the view of their impending deaths and my beautiful body. I approach the mewling mass of men with my scimitar held out, my clit vibrating against the penis-stub in a most exciting fashion. They begin to drop to their knees and scream for their gods. But their gods have deserted them as my sword buries itself in a bowed head.

I kill them one by one until their mass of flesh becomes one writhing mass of severed musculature, pumping its living ichor into the soil—the brown soil that had given home to the organ which had spat me out into water. The blood feeds the earth. It feeds the maw and I am a more local projection of that maw, taking my fill first from the victims but still dutifully filling the sloshing coffers of the beast that is my creator. I am his filthy minion.

So I slaughter them all as my commanders excuse themselves. I fall onto the victims and hump their mass, an ululating muscle of coitus, my membranes flooding with venom. I hear his call and obey, sucking my gratitude, baring my genitals in a furnace of exposure. And as I feed, I stare at the blurred dawn, the crimson reckoning beyond all ken. And in my motion I feel the motion of the world.

Soon, they have passed unto me their force. And I have breathed the life of dawn. I have kissed creation and come away whole. And I come from the trench and am surrounded by specialists who wrap me in the swaddling shrouds of war. They want me to go and kill and I don't kill too many of them as I pass with the force and hatred of my being, such a thing as I am, totally borne to my devotion. Suffused with their hurt, I rise to the hate and bear down upon my target.

He is two miles away, involved with a tank battalion. His only love is that of destruction. He has the ability to make magazines ignite, and the force to blot out all. And still, my allies drive towards him in a dream that somehow they can kill him and absorb his life. They cannot, but they can supply their corpses to the inferno, in order to distract him from my approach.

The whole area has been plastered with so much smoke that I am blind in the ocular sense. But I feel his hatred in a way that transcends the ages that separate us. And I think he feels it as well as I bear down upon him with the vengeance of the centuries. My hand is so tightly wrapped about the hilt of my sword that my knuckles jut out like burial mounds. My being is bolting across the sand, his form illuminated by the burning tanks, and the burning people who spill out of them. The keening wail of those who roast pipes my ears with the rush of the wind. And Olec sees me, turning with his ancient sword. Oh, bloody Olec, I return to send you to a deserved rest. My body heaves, as my muscles ignite and light my explosion of flesh that spurts from my arm like a mass of snakes, seeking purchase in his moldy undead flesh. Tendrils of mutation leap from me as his form rises 20 feet away, bellowing and shaking his sword at the sky. I avoid his shield and attack through flesh. His shield gives him power of aversion against the projectiles that seek to rend his hide. But against my questing feed-tubes he is unprepared. The flailing octopus limb reaches into his guard, slips behind his shield, and burrows into the forearm that holds it. It infuses tiny spines into his arm. They release venom, weakening his flesh. At that point, the Seirka is doomed. Its feeble undead mind is able to grasp this, and at that moment, peering through the Viking's eyes, my master catches his first glimpse of me in many years.

With my body extended into that of my foe, I deliver a crushing blow to his shield, bringing forth a shower of sparks as I inflate my fleshy tendril invasion. It tears his arm off at the socket with a dry and crunchy sound, accompanied by shrieks of undead disbelief. The arm, holding the shield, is thrown through the air, maggots trailing from its torn end, tracked by the baleful eyes of the Seirka who cannot believe I just ripped his arm off.

The creature stands, swaying slightly, holding its ancient broadsword in its remaining hand. It voices a rasping cry to the fates which have deserted it and then charges at me. I leap to his assault with my own, and we rain poundage upon each other. The snap of his blows was enough to tempt any man into the furnace which shone through his eyes. But I fight him to a standstill throughout the swirling night, until the sky begins to accept the dawn.

I cut into his defense, wanting to finish it before dawn. I take his leg, and then I take another leg. He howls his annoyance as I cut off his withered head. 2000 years was a long time to spend in a tomb plotting eternal vengeance, only to have it rudely revoked by a demon more powerful than you and all your centuries-old hate. His bits continue to grasp and kick and so I fight several weakened opponents. The bits try to crawl back to their host and reconnect, but I kick them away. Soldiers run up and place the struggling limbs in separate metal containers, though several men are strangled in the process. I grab the wriggling and limbless trunk and we return to the lines. We take the parts into an underground bunker where a giant kettle awaits us. Soon all of the bits except the chest are bubbling away. The chest, which has finally stopped moving, is split open as the remains of the corpse are boiled into a stinking mush. The internal organs, shrunken and useless, are tossed in the pot. The bones are then removed and smashed up, then returned to the soup. It blorbs along, driving all from the room, save me.

I eat it, along with a whole mess of Metamucil, or at least its Arabic equivalent. Soon I squat above what is left of the moldy corpse, coaxing the rest of him out of my ass. My bowels erupt and I am filling the emptied trunk with vicious, reeking shit. It's like giving birth, at least in that it takes hours. After I'm done I wipe with a large towel and sew up the incision. Next, we encase it in a heavy leather bag and wrap it in chains. Then it's a quick transfer to a waiting Hind. We lumber into the air and fly to a nearby SCUD battery. The creature's remains are loaded into the warhead and then fired at Teheran.

Gabby and I are sitting on the porch. It's a beautiful sunset. Far in the distance we can see the glittering diamonds of the Mediterranean as a robust-yet-gentle wind caresses our food. This is our first real "date." I mean, we had had sex for money several times, but my resources were not unlimited. It was financially prudent to try to fuck her for free. But it was more than that. I was interested in her as a companion. I was lonely, and the dreams were starting to come back, the horrible dreams of burning flesh and blazing machines.

"I don't like sex," she says, a piece of toast hanging from her lip.

"You don't like sex? You're a whore!"

"Shut up you pig, just because I'm a whore doesn't mean that I enjoy it."

"People should always enjoy their work. You spend so much time there, if you don't enjoy it, then you are in danger of not enjoying a significant portion of your life. Besides, you seem to enjoy having sex with me."

"That's different. I'm drunk when I have sex with you."

"So when you are drunk, you get horny," I say, refilling her glass.

"That's right and only then," she says, upending her glass noisily.

"That's a shame. You should experiment more. Loosen up a bit."

"You men always say that. You always say that you should experiment, or that you are the one that can make me enjoy sex. But all you want is to shoot your dirty load and then get back to your drunken friends."

"You know what I think?" I say, scooting just a little closer to her.

"What?" she says, her bottom lip extended valiantly, glistening with booze and spit and lipstick.

"I think you don't want men to touch you because every time that they do they hurt you."

She looks up, the evening sun draping its fading warmth across her lovely face. It is perfectly formed, so saucy in its make-up. She has gone to great length to look especially slutty tonight. Her firm and swelling breasts thrust against the fabric of her blouse, her unspoiled cleavage calling to my face. The smell of a breast, or breasts, and the heart beating against them.

She is beautiful. Well, for a whore. After all, there was that large knife wound which ran down the side of her face. I suppose that is the reason such a beautiful woman is a whore. But there is actually a lot more to it than that. She had received the wound from a jealous suitor who could bear no man to have her if he could not. So her tried to kill her but had only succeeded in maiming. But there are many who say she had deserved it because she had been such a bitch to poor Carlo. And she had killed him. Stabbed him in the neck as he tried to kill her. After courting her for five years. If Carlo had only known that her father had raped her, and that is why she can bear no man. Maybe he would have been a little more patient. But now he is dead and she is a whore.

I try to suppress the sudden image of me raping Nurse Faber. It's a horrid return to a time I had been living to forget. I remember what the Obersturmbannführer had said, how she had been borne below and how I might be allowed to mate with her again. But I flush it. Flush it in the face of the fact that this woman is actually looking at me with something other than terror. A smile spreads across her face, bending her scar. I know I'm getting laid tonight.

"You're sweet," she says, holding out her glass. "Now give me some more wine."

7
EVERYTHING I TOUCH TURNS TO SHIT

How similar is a golf cart to a tank, in the way that they lurk under trees. It's so nice to ride around in either through the beauty of nature, observing the animals and vegetation, feel the cool breeze upon your face, gaze into the azure summer sunset as you make your way down a rutted track, pausing only to wipe out pockets of resistance with your hull-mounted flame-thrower. Well, I guess a golf cart really isn't like that.

"So, Whargoul, what happened to the Obersturmbannführer?"

I have to pause and grimace. The memory of that day is so painful. But I won't be able to avoid the question so I just blurt it out.

"I killed him. Killed him at Kursk, the day Kepler died. I killed him too. Hold on."

I am lining up a 30-meter chip shot into a green guarded by a large side bunker between the hole and me. Cheng watches from the cart as I line up on the ball, check my aim, and then have at. And of course, I hit it way too hard and knock it over the entire green deep into the woods on the other side.

"Who is to say that because you hit it poorly, that you did not also hit it well?" Cheng says from the cart as I fume towards the green. There follows the "cascade effect" where one bad shot leads to another in a rapid series of flails. Soon I am adding an 8 to my card, the dreaded snowman. Of course Cheng rolls in a 20-foot putt for a birdie.

"Who is to say because you made that putt, you also did not make that putt?" I say.

He holds up a finger.

"Nature," he says. He almost pulls it off, but quickly erupts into hysterical laughter.

"I can't believe that shit keeps you immortal," I say.

"I admit my philosophies seem a little dated after meeting a being like yourself. My ideas don't give me my extended life."

"Then what does?"

"I don't know, my friend. But there is no such thing as immortality. Even gods die."

"Or can be killed?" I say, taking out my 5 iron.

"Perhaps. Now tell me about Kursk. We'll go at it step-by-step until we find ourselves there."

I look towards the next hole's tee box. There was a great black lump in my soul that I had yet to face. These memories come out at odd times, like when I am playing golf. Not until I master myself can I hope to shoot good golf, or save humanity.

There is a group of elderly white men teeing off on the short par 3. We have been running into them all day and their oblivious attitude begins to irritate me. The obvious thing to do is to let us play through. I glower at them as Cheng smiles serenely. They tee off one-by-one, hitting a string of poor shots that careen about with the accompanying chorus of lame remarks. Then unbelievably they play on without so much as a nod in our direction. I tune in my ears and close my eyes, forcing the blood in my head to boil up.

"How did a nigger get out here, anyway?" whispers one.

July 12th, 1943. Operation Citadel has been going on for almost two weeks and in that that time, Das Reich had fought hard for the twenty-mile breach that we have torn in the Russian line. But for every defensive line that we breach we find another just beyond it, packed with a seemingly inexhaustible number of men and machines all bent on destroying us. Everyday we kill hundreds, sometimes thousands. We blow up many scores of tanks of which the Soviets seemed to possess a limitless number. Most of the men are at the point of madness, sustaining themselves on schnapps and speed. I am particularly worried about Kepler. He has been awake for days, scribbling away in his book, occasionally looking at me and grunting. His face looks drawn and haggard; his eyes glitter and the features on his once handsome face jerk spasmodically as he feverishly pours himself into whatever it is that he is working on, which he will never show me. He doesn't talk very much but always stays close, observing. When we do speak, the conversations take on the quality of an interview. He wants to know everything he can about my origins and memories.

Again we find ourselves on the forward edge of a great assault wedge. All night they have been bringing up tanks of every variety, forming them into vast wedges of steel. We are brought up behind these machines in our half-tracks. Before the dawn, a huge barrage begins. Rocket launchers and artillery of all shapes and sizes began to rend the skies above us, challenging the dawn with their own fire. We cheer as locomotives thunder across the sky, causing havoc in the Soviet positions. The Russians begin to return fire in a valiant attempt to silence the German guns. In some cases it is successful, and a fierce artillery duel erupts. As the dawn begins to break we mount up, just as the first flights of Stukas streak in to wreak untold carnage in the enemy sectors. The horizon boils with their bombs; it is our last sight before we are locked in our rolling coffin. We lurch forward and I search my pockets for cigarettes, finding none. I bum one from Kepler, whose face is gleaming with sweat as he scribbles madly, eyes darting about the half-tracks cramped interior as if already seeking escape.

I strike a match just as a shell crashes into our vehicle. The blast punches us backwards in a great slamming of bodies and gear. One man is killed by another's rifle—it's sticking in his eye. We roll out of the stricken transport as flames shoot out of the front of the vehicle. The men inside are burning alive with a chorus of high-pitched, yelping screams. We try to help them but the heat is too intense. I grab Kepler and the rest of the squad and we run from the scene, towards a passing Pz IV. We manage to flag it down and mount our infantry on the rear hull. The sky above is rent with flame and shells as we roll towards a small series of hills that the lead tanks are just beginning to crest. As they do so a horrendous barrage drops upon them. One of the tanks explodes outright with an immense *KLUNG*, its turret, momentarily weightless, swirling into the air. The tanks around it scuttle about like confused bugs, snouts questing, set against a wall of black smoke which rises from the valley beyond—a valley that unbeknownst to us is crawling with a sea of Soviet tanks, streaming like rats towards our tanks cresting the hill. The first T-34's, Soviet infantry riding them in dense packs, burst out of the smoke bank a mere 100-meters away from our battle-line, which we have just joined.

We spill off the rear deck and leap into a shell hole, watching in growing horror as tank after tank emerges from the clouds. We open up with our small arms, peeling the men from the hulls with bursts of lead. Our tanks take similar action, and rattle MG fire against the surging Soviet battle line. The main guns open up and the effect is instantaneous and catastrophic. At such ranges it is impossible to miss. I watch as a Tiger fires its 88mm main gun at a T-34/85 a mere 50 meters away. The shell rips through the turret entirely, passing out the back of the tank and exploding on the face of the tank directly behind the first one which explodes in crimson disaster. But it's impossible to stop the surge of Russian metal and flesh that is barreling up the slope. They slam into our positions and are quickly amongst the panzers, cranking their turrets around and firing at point-blank range, tearing up the ground around our haven. In our hole, we stay as low as we can to avoid the spattering steel which rips the air above us, as the noise of battle becomes one sustained roar of hatred. Kepler's face is white with terror, his eyes bulging from his sockets as the ground rocks around us with the violence of the tank battle.

Then he jumps up, screaming something at me that is impossible to understand. He waves madly past me and I turn to see a T-34 burst into view over the lip of our hole. The monster rears up above us like a tidal wave, blotting out the sun, and we leap for life as the front of the tank falls like the sky. I can't get away and it lands on me.

The front right tread catches me on the pelvis and pushes me into the ground. I try to flatten out with the force but it crushes me—crushes my pelvis, my lower organs and my legs. The driver guns it and the treads chew me for a good 20 feet, finally spitting me out like a bloody rag.

I don't pass out but go into something like shock. I lie there in the mud, staring at my entrails strung out in glistening ribbons. Bits of my clothing, smashed equipment, and mangled hunks of flesh litter the trail of my passage. I lay there, noting sluggishly that I can no longer breathe or hear. Almost all of my guts have been torn out. And I think maybe this is what can make me die.

My vision blackened as I sunk into the soil. I'll die, and no one will miss me. Maybe Kepler would. He was my friend, even though he had been acting strangely since discovering what I was. We talked of things together, and protected him. I could see his face above me, bending to me, weeping over my sundered form, trying to push my guts back into place. And in this dream I see my own hands come to him and grasp him by the throat.

I watch my actions as a disconnected observer as I kill my friend. I turn his madly struggling body over in my arms and attack the back of his head with my questing tongue. He is strong, and very much in possession of the materials I require to re-make my body. And I take these things.

The old men have been on the green for 20 minutes and I'm getting pissed. Without a single acknowledgment of our presence they have been three and four-putting with aggravating leisure. They are trying to piss me off and it's working.

"So you murdered your best friend to continue your own life?" Cheng asks.

"Yes, and I felt really bad about it. After I came to, I went kind of crazy. I guess you could have called it grief. I'd never felt it to that extent. I couldn't accept what I had done. I went mad with self-hate."

"What did you do with this feeling?"

"What I'm about to do is drive this golf ball into that guy's head."

Hitting off the tee was the best part of my game, and I fantasize about the results of my violence. The ball flies on a low trajectory, burning towards the green where the old racist fuckers are finally picking up their balls. With a resounding "crack" the ball strikes one of the baldies in the side off the head, knocking him to his ass as a bloody torrent blorps from his skull. The ball drops to the surface of the green within five feet of the hole. I calmly walk to the green and line up my putt, knocking it in for a birdie. To make this daydream a reality is deliciously tempting.

"Control your violence and use the energy elsewhere."

I clear my mind, breathing deeply as the spasm passes, feeling a rush of conflicting emotion. The urge to hurt others has been the strongest and most consistent feature of my life. And for some reason hanging around with this wrinkly old man, playing this stupid game, brought a calm to my soul that I had never felt. I wait with my club in hand until the oldies are done with their flail-fest. Then I calmly address the ball, feeling the glorious sun on my skin and the leather in my grip. Can this silly game really be an outlet for the murder that is my essence? Can this old man really help me to save my soul?

Can I trade golf for dope?

I knock the ball a good 20-meters past the green, deeply into the woods. Cheng smiles blissfully.

"Good, good . . . no one died," he says.

Maybe he can save my soul, but we have a hell of a lot of work to do on my golf game.

***

I reel in my guts and wait for them to settle in more or less the same place. It takes about an hour until the pain has generally subsided and I can begin to heal again. During this time the battle continues to rage around me. My hole changes hands several times, and I feed from these bloody hand-to-hand episodes. Within two hours, I'm feeling well enough to get up and move and I wait for a quiet moment to do so. When I do, I see the drained and mangled corpse of my friend lying at my feet.

For a long while there is just numbness that overwhelms me. I feel physically assailed and I stumble as if I have received a blow. As the realization of what I have done settles upon me, I sink to my knees and hold the corpse of my friend. Great sobs wrack my meat-cage as I learn that Whargoul can cry.

For a long time I just sit there with him, drool running from my mouth and onto his tattered uniform. Then slowly, I muster the courage to remove his journal from his tunic. Slumping away from the corpse, I open the black leather jacketed journal, immediately coming to a page with a portrait of myself staring back at me from the pages of his sacred tome. He really had been an excellent artist, and his style echoed the dark expressionist sentiment of painters like Dix or Nolde. I guess that's why he had tasted so good. The book is packed with his drawings and they are almost all of me—me attacking a pillbox; me drinking a bottle of wine; me staring at a far-off target, a pair of field glasses in my hands. There are notes as well, many pages of disturbingly precise notes, written in his crisp and almost microscopic hand. Notes where he describes my abilities and behavior, and his personal commentary on appalling things which he had witnessed. This is his legacy, to be passed down to the centuries. The proof of the Whargoul's profane existence. I am not a spirit that will be forgotten.

So, filled with a soul-deadening guilt, I place Kepler in the shell hole and kneel beside him, noticing for the first time the thousands of wildflowers which are the only thing that outnumber the Russians. They grow up and around him; bloody flowers are on his face. I reflect on the beauty and the horror, the juxtaposition that was a quality of Kepler's drawings. I sit there and explore the pages, forgetting the battle which is re-forming around me.

"Hands up!" a voice barks from behind me.

I have been very bad today. I have shamed myself in front of my infernal court. I let a tank sneak up on me. I killed my only friend and ate his soul. And now I was about to be captured. I do put my hands up, and also I begin to scream. Standing there, my skin is a mass of gristled paste. It writhes upon my frame. My hands explode into several questing tendrils of rocketing flesh, which stretches as taut as piano wire in half a heartbeat, rooted deeply in their beings. The flesh of my face pulps with agonizing life as my mouthed tenta-claws rip through bone in their search for the enabling fluid of mastery. I suck.

I leave Kepler behind and run towards a passing T-34, ripping open its large upper hatch. The commander looks up in terror as he is shot in the head. I snake into the vehicle. Firing at and killing the other crew members, I quickly feed until bursting, and then dump the bodies out of the tank. Settling into the driver's seat, I turn the tank about and drive towards the main mass of Soviet infantry which is coming up the slope. During my necrotic reveries the Soviet armored strike has managed to push the Germans back a couple of hundred meters, dislodging them from the hill we had so recently acquired. But for now the two combatants have released their death grip on each other, and have reeled apart to re-group and attack again. The troops are hustling up the hill, shouldering their anti-tank rifles and hoisting up their pants, sweating and puffing in the bright July sun. My tank slews from its path directly into theirs, smushing into their midst with crushing abandon. They scatter but I pursue, oblivious to the shells which bounce off the hull of my monster. I fire the machine-gun, driving them away, chasing and destroying their flesh which melts at the touch of my heated breath.

Then a larger explosion rocks the tank, setting the rear compartments aflame. I have been hit by a German shell from behind, and only have seconds to escape the entire tank going up in a scalding inferno. I writhe to the escape hatch and force my body through it, rolling off the hull and onto the bloody grass. The infantry has run off for the most part, but several are still firing at me. I look back towards the German lines and see again the snouts of the metal beasts protruding above the ridge—the Germans have succeeded in retrieving the ridge and again their panzers stand proudly upon it. From this position, they rake the valley before them with fire—the advancing Russian columns are caught in the open and annihilated. I throw myself into the ground as the Germans lambaste the landscape. But the Soviets do not know the meaning of the word defeat, or even pain. The Germans had been taught that their opponents are less than human; ever since they have come to Russia they have learned on a daily basis that actually quite the opposite is true. The average Russian, when wounded, will not cry out. He can dig through stone and survive by eating dirt. After having close to a hundred tanks destroyed in this sector alone, the Russians can still manage another attack with a hundred more, which come churning up the slope in a maelstrom of dust. Soldiers are clinging to the tanks hulls, and this time they can enjoy a longer ride due to the lack of opposing German infantry. They grind closer to my hidden position, and I flatten myself deeper into the ground to avoid being raked with lead. I hear the German tank guns behind me cracking, and see the horrific results as Soviet tanks burst into flaming conflagrations of shredding configurations. Charred flesh rains down around me as I strive to become one with the earth. But then a sound reaches my ears through the cacophony of war's glorious carnage—a harsh, metallic voice that brings back memories of death and a dream of a vengeance unfulfilled—the voice of Necrosov, ordering his followers, the Voiden into battle.

I look up from my self-imposed tomb and see the form of my

rival not more than thirty meters away, crouching behind the blazing hulk of a T-34/ 85. In that moment I lose it. It all comes back upon me; my murder at his hands, my murder of Kepler, the realization of the horror of my birth and life, the predicament of my present position, all that was me comes rushing in like a diseased tide, enveloping my being like a dirty rug and filling me with the broken hope that by killing my rival I can somehow erase my pain.

Oh, Necrosov! How the fortunes of war have thrown us together again. Maybe fate shall ordain that one day we will be boiled together in the collective flesh-pot, so that our beings will be turned into one even more murderous and indestructible scourge of humankind. In a way we are brothers, issued forth from the same diseased cunt that had doubtless spat out so many other killers of our ilk. Come to me killer, so I may murder you!

I run across the short expanse of mangled soil that separates us. I have changed much since my last encounter with him and his squads, but they had only glimpsed me for a moment anyway. I'd like to think that he knows who I am as I fly at him, arms telescoping into blades, blades which carve his flesh until they meet the steel beneath. It is as I suspected. Necrosov's multi-limbed assistant, the one who had installed the rocket launcher into his arm, had also installed a metal exo-skeleton, which now stymied my blows. So shocked is he by the rapid filet of his meat that he merely gapes at me. His great metal jaw clangs open, yet no sound issues forth other than the escaping of some greasy steam. I have cloven a foot deep into each of his shoulders and we stare into each other's twisted faces.

"It's me, brother, your womb-mate. Let's go visit Daddy."

"You're not worthy, yet," he says in a rush of gears. "When it's time, you'll be summoned. Until then you just aaaaAAAAAA!!!!"

His face issues a verbal blow that is considerably more powerful than anything that I could muster. His machinations are deep and terrible, amplified by steel and wire, plastic and brain-juice. It blows off some off my clothes and sends me sprawling. He follows it with a satchel charge which I pluck out of the air and send sailing towards a group of Voiden who are just preparing to fire. It explodes in their midst with a scarlet roar, sizzling them. I leap into the explosion as soon as the main force has passed over me, moving through their life-fume and landing on the other side. Momentarily shielded by the dense smoke and escaping souls, I scramble to a crouch and search about for a weapon as my adversary sends a volley of bullets after me.

My natural shape has returned and I lack the power for any more full-scale transformations, like dicks to cunts or arms to saws. I need power and I need it quickly.

The Soviets are again assaulting up the slope towards the panzers. My adversary has momentarily lost track of me and I leap into a fissure of sundered earth, burrowing into it like a mole, elongating and telescoping my fingers into feeding tubes which snake up the slope, questing pseudo-pods, seeking purchase in pulpified flesh. And there is no lack of it as the Soviet supermen throw themselves into the breach. The machines and men are hopelessly entangled with each other and the venue of advance is severely limited due to the amount of blazing vehicles and piles of mutilated corpses. Their blood and ism oozes from their sundered bodies, their lives escape them and pass into mine with a sickening sound. I bloat on death's harvest.

Necrosov has moved away from me, going for the German lines, mindful of his orders. But the Germans have supporting infantry now and they send an annihilating fire into the massed Soviet ranks. As numerous as the Russians are they cannot take this punishment for long. Their assault is crushed, even with the power of Necrosov and his Voiden. They retreat.

I sense rather than really know this. I am too involved in my feeding process and the application of the power that I am amassing. My body begins to heave and warp, great fleshy ridges bubbling up out of my back. I form in my mind a vision of horror—a great bug-thing, with a huge and slobbering central maw, around which are arranged the appendages which both propel the creature and serve as the meat cleavers. It hacks its prey into slobbery chunks, swallowing them whole, equipment and all. The thing rises out of its pit, its course and horned hide bubbling with venom, a singular eye searching for more victims. Its me in my most ambitious mutation yet, and I surge into the waves of soldiers that had been seeking escape from the terror of battle, only to find their deaths in an infinitely more perverse manner. My threshing cleavers rise and fall, throwing great gouts of spew to the heavens. I suck men into my gullet with the power of my breath; they are drawn to it. Many think that they have died already, merely at the sight of me. I rear up, now as big as a small bungalow, and leave the last vestiges of humanity far behind. I am a whirling, surging juggernaut of obliteration, and they pour fire into me, but I have gained so much power that it has little effect as huge hunks of my body are ripped away. The holes produced by this violence grow gullets and teeth, forming new maws that I force more meat into, killing hundreds as I absolve myself in the communion of death.

Necrosov beholds this in growing horror. Never before has he seen such a blatant display of necrotic power and he wonders about his place. My Father had promised him that he was the favored son, that he would win the right to lead the army of the apocalypse that would herald the age of the LoiGoi. But now he thinks he has been misled—that the world was populated by other creatures like him yet different, all fighting each other, seeking to curry my Father's favor. So he attacks to rid himself of his rival once and for all.

His troops lay into me with every ounce of firepower that they possess, to no avail. I am too strong, and I feel the very earth funneling power into me, as if my Father were somehow watching this performance from his subterranean abode (as I am sure he was), and, amused by the spectacle, had decided to intervene on my behalf. I have now become the mouthed and weeping eye, in that my entire body is one great eyeball with a champing gob in place of a pupil. I don't see anything anyway; I feel the presence of energy and am drawn unerringly towards it. Above, the Germans pour a murderous fire into the backs of the Soviets, while from below they are stopped by me. Giant spines protrude from my central mass at all angles and upon these spines are draped the impaled corpses of my making, inserted with suck-tubes that leave these undead just enough energy to fire their weapons at their friends. So many have died on this slope today and my technique is flawless! I am the perfect murder machine and I begin whirling, hovering four feet off the ground, creating a vortex that sucks men of all passions to their agonizing dooms.

Perhaps if the Germans could see a little more clearly they would not have given the order to advance, but from their vantage point the scene is one of such confusion it is difficult to see the house-sized hell beast which has just slaughtered an entire company. My thoughts are no longer of earthly vengeance or the besting of my rival. I crave godhood and care nothing for what side my prey might be allied with. As the German assault waves come down the slope I am all too willing to stack their corpses in my soul-mill, the wasteful parts of their beings already pouring out of my warty ass.

"Whargoul! Stop!" I hear a voice within my brain. Looking up the slope I see the armored car of the Obersturmbannführer amongst the wreckage of the original German battle line.

"You have done enough! If you consume too much, you run the risk of destroying yourself."

For him, it is an unfortunate choice of words, for that idea appeals to me more than anything else. I surge up the slope towards my commander, who realizes too late my intent, which is to suck dry the most potent power source in the area. I can feel the feed-sack that is Necrosov moving away from me, but he holds no interest—he's a steak but I'm going for lobster. The Obersturmbannführer opens up with his main weapon—a plasma gun disguised as a dual 20mm. This weapon can hurt me and does—it pumps out venom that melts my flesh in an acidic smear. I slowly begin to lose my monstrous configuration, and regain my previous form. But the impetus of my charge is too great to resist. I fling myself upon the hull of the vehicle, plunging my hack-arms through its armored sides and then with a final surge I rip them into the very being of my current patron.

The energy released is incredible, passing into me in an electric rush of power that floods out of him and crackles into me. My appendages rip deeply into his unseen flesh and meet in the middle. You can't really say I kill him; it's more like I *steal* him, like I would years later to Captain Crinkle. I take everything of value and then pour myself into the interior of his machine, which I have taken a fancy to. It is not at all like the interior of similar models. Instead, the inner hull is coated with a fleshy paste connecting to a central mass of gray muscle with no visible sensory organs, unless they were the stalks which issued from the thing I had just killed. Its outer skin sits in the corner, ready to be slipped on if leaving the vehicle became necessary.

Having just sucked the power of a demigod my being is finally sated. I remove the leaking pus-sac that had been, until recently, my commanding officer, dumping it onto the gore-choked ruin of a landscape with a wet plop. His "skin-suit" follows. Then I settle onto the stalk which rises from the floor of the machine and let the pods attach themselves to various parts of my body. I am suffused with a sense of well being, and information about what is occurring outside floods into my crowded gray matter. It is a simple thing to order my machine to back away from the grayish blob and hose it with plasma, just to be sure of its death.

The battle is over. Appalled by the sights of slaughter, the humans have gone back to their holes to try to forget these things, so that they can live again. As for me, I have fully accepted my new form and the evil that it gives. Every time that I tried to find a drop of humanity in the black well that was my soul I was disappointed, and those that had put their faith in me were rewarded with death. But I would remember Kepler through the legacy he had left me.

***

I sit in the golf cart and weep. I am so sorry, my friend.

When we don't play golf we go back to Tiki-BoBo's House of Pleasure. Here Cheng has ensconced himself on the top floor of a five-story brownstone which has four floors of whores beneath it. The whole scene reminds me a lot of the brothels in Frankfurt—basically old hotels or rooming houses where the girls just hang out in doorways, beckoning you to come in. Except with me. They would shriek and retreat into their cum-reeking rooms at the sight of the horribly scarred SS Obersturmbannführer.

Here, however, the women were much nicer to me. I was more attractive—a good-looking black guy with a perfect physique. Way better than a walking cadaver. And most importantly, I had Cheng's stamp of approval. He was my master, and I was his ward, and nobody fucked with me.

Cheng and I sit on the roof and stare uptown. My part of the city seems fairly quiet. There are no convoys of fire engines and armored units streaming towards the areas where havoc usually beckons. It's almost as if when I stay away from my neighborhood, peace breaks out.

"I have been put in a position where I can recognize and sometimes befriend beings who are beyond human. I don't know why I was chosen for this task. Many years ago I was a simple philosopher."

"Simple?" I snort, having spent many hours trying to decipher his ancient manuscripts and contemporary adaptations of his wisdom. It was all very confusing to an ignorant Whargoul like me.

"There have been many others like you in the sense that they possessed power beyond reason. As far as I can tell I am here to try to guide them away from the power that brought them to be."

"Powers like my Father?"

"Yes. Your creator. You were made to inspire the humans to

kill each other. At the same time you have been programmed to be obsessed with sex. You have a constant need to mate, and create new life. You have gone through your life both destroying life and creating it."

"Wait a minute. Creating it?" For some reason I had felt there would be no consequences to my continual rutting.

"Yes. You have sired many children."

"What! When? Who?" Or more importantly, "How?"

"I think even you know the answer to that question. I can't say I know where you came from, but I know that your seed mixes with the human female egg quite nicely."

"What has become of my children?" I say, fighting a growing sense of panic. I didn't need a mutant bastard smashing down my door with a submachine gun, screaming for child support.

"The women that you have impregnated are taken below into the hives of the flesh sculptors. The fetuses are removed and are used to power new life forms. They are not allowed to develop into fully-realized beings."

My face scrunches up with a bevy of conflicting emotions. How would you feel if you had found out in the space of a few minutes that not only had you been a father several times over, but your children had all been murdered.

"You know well the power that dwells within the soul of a child. You have killed many yourself."

I look up at him sharply, remembering the taste of Baby Kiesha's brain. Cheng never changed the inflection of his voice, whether he was helping me hit my 2-iron or telling me that I was a baby-eating mutant alien with a Father several miles across. We sit for a long time in silence as I ponder ridiculous fate.

"There is so much I don't understand, and so much that I don't remember. So much I don't want to remember. I tried to erase my mind with drugs and alcohol, but it doesn't work for long. The visions are beginning to crowd my mind again."

"You must confront these visions. You must draw them from yourself and master the fear that they contain. Your creator is calling to you, sending you these thoughts. The drugs you think are helping you are actually making you more susceptible to the control the LoiGoi is attempting to assert over you. You must control yourself without using drugs or violence."

"But I like drugs and violence!" I say, totally exasperated.

"And a life of misery it has been, not to mention the pain you have meted out to countless humans. Not long ago the thought of you even playing golf would have been ridiculous. But today not only did you break 100, but also you did not murder that racist old man. It is time for you to change."

It's true. I haven't shot junk or felt the urges for weeks, ever since I started hanging out with Cheng.

"How do you do that?" I ask.

"Honestly my friend, I do not know. I only know that when I was upon my deathbed some 2000 years ago, I did not die. Instead I entered a dream state where I saw the future of this world laid clear to me. I saw the nature of the struggles to be and identities of the players to come. I think I even met you then. You see, I have known you many times before. You have dreams sometimes where you see yourself in bodies that you do not recognize, do you not?"

"Yes, yes, all the time. Me hacking and killing with the Roman legions, fighting Celts and Gaul's, flying a Sopwith Camel, lining up with Napoleon. I'm sure I was there."

"Yes. You have lived for thousands of years. And in many of those years, I was your friend, fulfilling my purpose, keeping an eye on you and others like you. For whatever reason, the gods have chosen me to observe this war and if possible affect its outcome for the benefit of nature, the only true power. I know much but there is still much that escapes me. Like where you and your kin come from. What the ultimate goal is. And how you can be stopped before this world is destroyed."

"Okay. Well, here are a couple of guesses. We are an alien race bent on making earth or own personal buffet table. My Father creates murderers in order to lead the humans to slaughter. The murderers also fight each other in an attempt to gain Daddy's favor, y'know, be the favorite son and maybe get a fat inheritance. And the only way to stop it is by chopping off the head."

"But before then, we must finish your story. We must find all that we can in your past so that when you confront the LoiGoi he will not be able to use it against you. He will try to drag you over with the weight of your crimes. You must destroy your own past before you can attack the future."

And there were many black pages left in my infernal story, pages I had not dared to look at. But it was pointless to delay any further. I had to purge myself of the blackness before I could step into the light. I felt that I was getting close, but I instinctively felt that the last memories were going to be the hardest ones to deal with. That's why they were the final ones, because they were so submerged in the pit of my being. I had to draw them forth, face what I had done, and move on. If I could do it, then I might be able to save the human race. If I could not then I would be fated to destroy it.

The Native Americans had arguably been more mistreated than the blacks. Or the Irish, South Americans, or Asians. Some of these cultures were able to better adapt to the rigors and ass-kissing of the American machine better than the others. Some showed nothing but contempt and a total unwillingness to do anything other than fuck with whitey at any possible moment. Like when black people walk across the road in front of your car and give you that "come on and hit me" look. They don't really want to get hit, they are just happy that they have done something to fuck up your white-assed day. Of course you don't see the Asians doing that. They want to hurry up and get to the corner store they run in the middle of a black neighborhood so they can charge black people 2.89 for a loaf of Wonder Bread, then take all the money which they had gouged out of the blacks, and go shopping at Super-Fresh.

The blacks wanted to fuck shit up. They were the warriors, and my Father had invaded their gene pool long ago. He knew, determined as they were to fuck themselves into perpetuation, that they would produce many strong sons, who when they went missing, would not be so easily missed. These sons were conveyed below, and copied, replicated, cloned, whatever . . . it was like no science ever known to man other than on the receiving end. They kept what they needed and discarded the rest. The savagery, the aggression, the coordination, they kept those things. The sympathy, the understanding, the compassion, they got rid of that. And they had to instill obedience. And that came hard. Large sections of pinkish matter clogged fleshy drains. There was no need for that in a warrior. From the blacks, the LoiGoi found the perfect soldier to buff out the ranks of his infernal army.

In the Native Americans he found his heavy artillery. The U.S. government had strangled the "Indians" to the point of extinction. It was only the outcry of the liberal press that saved them from being exterminated. The reservations they had been given in return for their sacrifice was a paltry trade, a ghost of the glory of their past. Perhaps martyrdom was better, and many braves died to prove that, leaving a legacy of guilt upon their living ancestors. This feeling would boil up on occasion, like at Wounded Knee and the place in Canada where they wanted to build a golf course on Native holy ground. And when they did assault the braves holding the fort, they shot their own guy and tried to blame it on the natives. Just like with Koresh, who, by the way, is still very much alive, alive in the lower regions, bubbling in a vat of life-sustaining ichors. Ahh, poor David! Just when he thought that everything was over, his dream existence of having the pick of the litter and dying in a blaze of glory on his way to meet the maker—well, that just was not to be. Instead the floor opened up (I'm sure he thought it was the ATF) and out came a great and clutching tentacle to drag him through the caverns of the underearth where fleshy devices were pressed against his. How his eyes bulged as they stared through the thickened crystal at the workings of the flesh sculptors as they created new life from death, occasionally moving over to his tank to change the mix of chemicals sluicing into his brain.

But the natives. The Apaches were the most aggressive in many ways. They had the legacy of Geronimo to guide them, a name that still scared schoolchildren one hundred years after his death. They were pissed and they were poor and they were about ready to POP! So, fearing a total insurrection in the reservations, the government did something so dumb that you almost couldn't believe it. Yeah Mr. Indian, I know we invaded your country, and raped your women, killed your Buffalo and made you live on these stinking reservations, and we'd like to make it up to you. So here's a gambling casino!

That's right, they legalized gambling on a lot of the reservations. I guess they thought all the Natives would do was get drunk at the bar (they always were susceptible to booze). But those dumb Injuns had learned a lot from their captors in the many years of subjugation. They know that when an enemy has you by the balls that the best thing to do is play possum, lay back and observe for weakness. And that's just what they did. They learned how to be capitalists. And when they finally got those casinos they sure knew how to make money off of them. SO MUCH money that the government got immediately concerned and tried to stop it. But it was a lot harder to rip up a contract than it had been in the days of Custer. So they just kept banking, because they were saving up for something special.

The government had been initially worried about the Italian Mafia moving in on the Native-Americans casinos and trying to bring in drugs and prostitution. But the accepted rationale was that the Mafia had its hands full elsewhere and besides, who wanted to fuck with a bunch of drunk Injuns? But as soon as the declared incomes for these places started coming in, and they were substantial, people started showing real interest. If this was the declared income, then what was the undeclared one? Before you knew it every Sleazy P. Martini wanna-be was sliding into town, looking for a cut. And they would get it. Right across the throat.

Because the Apaches had new friends now. The Russian Mafia never had any qualms about working with the natives, supplying them with guns, drugs, and most importantly protection from all the other parasites that were out to get a bite. They hated the U.S., whom they blamed for the economic collapse of their beloved Mother Russia. And of course, the Native Americans had no love for the hosts that had stolen their land, lives, and honor. They thirsted for vengeance of the most horrific kind.

They wanted a nuclear weapon, and the Russians got it for them.

The deal was complicated and laborious. And very expensive. Buy-offs were made at the highest levels. Luckily, the gambling coffers of the native gods were stuffed full of much wampum. The weapon was from Russia, when a group of disgruntled officers, disgusted at not having been paid for months, highjacked a truckload of nuclear devices. They were purchased for a billion dollars apiece by a group of Argentineans who also happened to be Nazis. And they were happy to sell a nuke to the natives. After all, they, with the help of the Japanese, were planning on invading the U.S. after the race war had taken firm hold. They were massing on the Texas border in giant underground bunkers. We couldn't stop illegal aliens from crossing that border, and we were never gonna stop the Wehrmacht.

So now the natives had a nuke and they didn't know what to do with it. The leaders of many tribes came together to discuss the matter. The majority of the elders favored using the weapon to hold the U.S Government hostage. They would present evidence that the device was real, and threaten to use it on an unspecified target unless the natives were returned a reasonable portion of their homelands. It seemed a good plan until several voices started to dissent. They wanted to use the bomb to nuke New York City. It had long been a symbol of just how badly the Natives had been duped. The richest city in the world had been obtained for a handful of beads and glass. So lets take it back by reducing it to radioactive slag. More voices began to join in with support for the mad idea. It made no sense, several argued. A tremendous act of spite was all that it amounted to. And it would solve nothing, grant no new rights. It would make the Natives the most hated group of people in the U.S. The Army would come and destroy the reservations. But everybody finally agreed to it as my Father's tentacles had grown up everybody's butts. The questing tendrils implanted new thoughts in old minds until people couldn't believe what they believed.

In Tiki-Bobo's House of Pleasure, much was forgiven. It was a place to come and purge one's soul. Men would strip naked and lounge in front of great fires. Women would writhe about, copulating frequently with the customers and each other. In the lower chambers was my cell, "The Howling Room," the place I stayed in screaming agony as my soul was re-awoken.

It was the room. The room of my torment as I relived my life. The life of an ageless slaughterer. Cheng would coach these memories from me. Sometimes I grew violent. This necessitated the lower chamber, so I could not escape and run amok in the street.

The meditations helped, the back rubs and soothing teas. The Whargoul got into herbal medicine. By my balls, I was becoming a hippy. And the endless sex provided by a bevy of gorgeous Asians (not a tit-job in the bunch) didn't hurt a bit. Still, it was a painful process. Because I'd been so very wrong.

So I was hanging here all the time. And that meant my dog had to live here too. Maug had been growing increasingly jealous of my thriving friendship with Cheng and my constant humping of the entire brothel. I wasn't being a very attentive pet owner. We never took our traditional runs out to the countryside anymore. But it was getting dangerous for blacks to travel outside of the cities. So he retreated to his world, the sewers. The subterranean world beneath

Manhattan was his stomping ground and his knowledge of this place was far greater than mine.

So I stayed there, and sweated it out. And in those weeks just before the war broke out, I learned a lot about myself. All the blocks were shattered. I was able to meet and master myself. I saw the worst in me and knew I could then find the best. Lying in my bunker in Harlem, jacked on heroin, strapped to my cot, surrounded by guns and assaulted by the pure hatred which emanated from the neighborhood was not the way to deal with my problems. Cheng supplied me with the perfect environment in which to reveal my soul. He listened without judgment. He gave me the strength to face the guilt of what I'd done, and the determination to do what I must.

One night, about two weeks before the Super Bowl, I had my most intense recanting, a story I will soon tell. Afterwards I had passed out in sheer exhaustion. That is when they came. They came and killed everyone in Tiki-Bobo's House. All the beautiful whores, all dead.

I find Cheng on the first floor. They have crucified him, a bemused look on his purpled and bloated face. He's been tortured badly and the variety and nature of his wounds are ingenious. Most importantly, his belly has been split open and his noodle removed. The empty sack of his body flaps like a piece of thick cloth or perhaps a husk of fruit. The noodle, a ropy and gelatinous mass, lies coiled in a glistening heap. One end of it leads to a jagged hole in the floor where a stinking vapor wafts up. It disappears into the depths, beckoning me to follow. But I recoil from the now-fouled thing and rush out of the place of death. I can't find my dog, but I can't find his body either. I burst into the street which is echoing with the urgent cries of sirens converging on this location. I leap into the Riv and peel out in a smoking arc, hurtling the car down the yawning canyons until I enter the old neighborhood. I dump the car a few blocks away and finally make it into my bunker, where I immediately blow my fucking head off.

8
ENDING IT

Beneath the earth of Poland, I hurtle along in the flesh-tube. I am encased in it now, traveling through hot rock. I feel my body being stabbed repeatedly with some sort of injection which soon renders me unconscious. In this way, I am brought to the flesh hive.

When I am spat out they have again remade me. And this time I am wondrous to behold. I have been purged and healed. My skin is smooth and white, my hair fair and blond. My features are cool, stern and dignified, a face younger than its years yet betraying no sign of immaturity.

I had inherited another man's life. A man who had been a great hero of the Reich, whose name and picture were in every newsreel and magazine. A man who had received his Iron Cross from Adolf Hitler and had danced with Rommel's wife. A man swathed in glory that was on the verge of his greatest assignment, one that supposedly stood a chance of knocking the Americans and British out of the fight.

Unfortunately, I had murdered him. And thus his carefully constructed persona had been destroyed. That was an event that my Father had not prepared for and he saw a need to replace his useful tool.

It took awhile, but he managed it. And thus I received my new being, the one I would retain until the day that Mossad blew Gabby and me to bloody bits. It was probably my favorite form, and it certainly was the one that I inhabited the longest.

My mission was the great Ardennes offensive, and I would command a special Kampfgruppe of the finest machines and cruelest of men. My unit had been known in Russia as "The Blowtorch Brigade," due to our propensity for reducing entire villages and all of their inhabitants to ashes. Now I had assumed command, and the unit was the armored spearhead of the attack. The mission was to break through the American lines, sowing terror and confusion in the rear areas. We would drive as far and as fast as we could, through the densely forested and under-defended center sector of the Allied lines. There were certain objectives that had to be taken, and of course I would try to do so. But I was much more excited with the sheer killing potential of the hulking death machine at which I sat at the head. My men could see my confidence—morale soared. Once again the German army was on the offensive from the mind of a fleshy construct animated by an alien mind. And the men just loved it, as they loved me.

I was the Obersturmbannführer.

The attack, code-named "Watch on the Rhine" so as to dupe Allied intelligence, was scheduled to begin on Dec. 16, 1944. The barrage began at 5:30 a.m. and it was an impressive sight that I watched from the cupola of my command tank, a Pz V Rockets, 88's, mortars, and every conceivable caliber of artillery began to saturate the American line. The ground shook with wrath and the trees lost their shrouds of snow. Even giant railway guns had been brought up, hurling their 14-inch projectiles at the enemy with rumbling hatred, tearing across the sky with the force of a runaway comet. The symphony of Mars played itself out to our unrivaled awe. My men cheered in raw exultation, as the Americans got plastered.

The Americans. This was the closest I had ever been to them. I had never even killed one before. They had a reputation for being poor soldiers, not as tough as the Russians, not even in the same league as the Brits, lazy, drunk, and they were ready to break apart under our merciless onslaught. The only thing they really had going for them was their seemingly endless stock of raw materials which resulted in things like overwhelming air support. This hopefully would be negated by the crummy weather into which we would make our attack-"Hitler Weather," they called it. I looked forward to killing them.

Ahh, a flashback . . . the flesh hive, inflating me with stolen life as my tissue is stripped away and then re-made. And my Father's bulbous eye, so vast, staring up from the depths like an unholy octopus. I shudder and look at my hands. Different hands than what I had had, but still working with the same intent. Mechanized death on the grandest of scales.

The barrage continues as the men smoke their cigarettes and cheer. About 10 miles away, a 150-mm round falls to earth. It strikes a house which had stood for over a hundred years. This house has seen the armies of Napoleon, Frederic, the Kaiser, and many more. During this time many people, all generations from the same family, had lived in the building for various periods of their lives. People, precious people and all of their precious stuff. When some people died, the others would keep the best stuff and throw the rest away. Some things would get put into the attic, others things would end up on the walls. The family had produced artists, and their work filled up a lot of space. Some was good, some not so, but they put up their work anyway. The family had produced warriors, and their banners hung proudly. There were great forgotten boxes filled with their letters. All these people had clothes, books, kitchen utensils, and a myriad of other things. They had been packing this abode full of stuff for years! And of course, there were the people themselves. Remarkably complex beings made up of bones, organs, and electric impulses known as thoughts and feelings. So much careful planning, so many decisions on what to keep and what to chuck out, so much evolution, so many ideas, so much life, all blown to shit in the space of a heartbeat.

The column winds back into the woods like a giant metal snake, ready to uncoil with its destructive purpose. Smoke begins to drift about us and I check my watch, engraved by a family I had never had.

"On your graduation day. We are proud. Mother and Father."

And I didn't even know what they looked like. I'd never been to school, though I had destroyed more than a few, sometimes with the students still in them.

"Herr Ober—there is a message from OKW," says my radio operator from the depths of the tank.

"Thank you, Hans," I say as I put on my radio set. For a moment there is nothing but silence, then slobbering sounds come across the wire. This is followed by an increasingly louder series of grunts and moans, set against a backdrop of continual squishing. I listen and occasionally nod, my crew staring at my impassive face with looks of gleeful anticipation. The message ends with what sounds like a long and painful fart. Then the line goes dead.

I receive no more orders from the high command. My men's eyes are still glued to my face, but none of them dare to speak. I look from face to face, noting weakness and strength, imagining how they would look with the stamp of terror, exhaustion and bloodlust, emotions they would be feeling soon.

"Hans—put me on the radio net." He does so and soon my voice is being relayed to the entire unit.

"It is time for the attack. Time to let slip the dogs of war, and hold the reins loosely. All elements forward. Heil Hitler!"

We move.

But our breakthrough does not come easily. For much of the first day we get caught in giant traffic jams. The winding and snow-covered roads of the Ardennes continually hamper my column's attempts to move. Finally, I abandon my command tank and transfer to a Kubelwagon, roving up and down the column, exhorting my men and machines to move. I shoot horses, blow up trees, beat people. I am possessed of an inhuman energy to get to the killing. I need to feed badly. At one point we encounter a stretch of road that has not been cleared of the German mines which litter its length. I have no patience in waiting for the mine detectors that would divine the lurking canisters of death—instead I order my tanks into the minefield to set them off. I lose several machines and a few men but precious time is saved. Finally, around midnight, my exhausted men reach the village of Lanzerath. They rest the night as I prowl naked through the woods, searching for my first American. But I can't find any. I return to town, put my uniform back on and allow my men to sleep for one more hour, and then mount up. We move onto our next objective—the town of Honsfeld. Straggler American units have been pouring into it from other shattered sectors and I anticipate a great killing. We have been attacking for over 24 hours and have met no real resistance other than our own troops clogging up the roads. The only Americans I have seen are dead ones. Aside from the uniforms they look like most other corpses.

We approach the tangle of buildings under cover of darkness, meeting no resistance. Feeling no trace of hesitance, I order my units into the town. I have never commanded a group of men bigger than a squad, which is usually no bigger than 12 men. Now I have thousands of men and hundreds of machines under my command, and because of the imprinting into my mind of the Obersturmbannführer's experience I can command them just as capably as he could. We assault the village and the sounds of small-arms fire begins to crackle ahead of me. I leap back into my tank and drive to the front of the attack, my adrenaline surging, smashing through houses and scattering personal effects across the bloody snow. A couple bazooka rounds bounce off our hull as we smush our way into the village square. But once again we are disappointed—the Americans are surrendering en masse. But they are . . . the enemy.

And they look terrified, surrounded by my SS men who have guns trained on them as they loot their rivals of interesting possessions. I walk up to the mass of men. The Americans, while alive, look better fed than my own troops. Though white faced in the glow of the burning buildings, they do not have that hollow-cheeked look that so many men of the Wehrmacht have; I guess somebody feeds them.

"Who is the commander here?" I bark, speaking (perfect) English.

"I am, sir," says a stocky American in his early thirties, stepping forward with his hands in the air.

"Captain. I am Obersturmbannführer Pieper of the 1st SS Division. I need information regarding the disposition of U.S. forces in this area, especially in the vicinity of Bullingen. I expect your full cooperation. In a moment we will adjourn to the comfort of that church over there. I will have your men placed in that barn. If you do not tell me everything that I need to know, then I will burn your men alive."

His men gasp, my men snicker. He stares back at me, his face livid with hate and fear.

"I'll talk. Just don't hurt my men."

"DON'T TELL ME WHAT TO DO!" I scream, slapping him across the face with a blow that sends a shower of blood and teeth from his ruined mouth.

"Move him to the church. Get these men in that barn. Then form up for assault."

We take the senseless Captain to the basement of the barn and strap him into an ancient chair. I have the protesting priest taken out back and shot, even as he offers to suck off the entire company. Then I order my men from the room. Quickly stripping, I again slap the Captain, but this time with my limp dick, which by the way is not as large as it used to be. It feels good so I massage it until it's big and fat. Outside I hear a light American barrage striking the town as slowly the Captain regains his senses.

"Captain Huggins," I say, reading from his dog tags. "Wake up and smell the mold crusted upon my ancient penis."

He does wake and the sight of me, naked before him, immediately sends him wild with terror. He surges against his bonds, but only succeeds in crashing sideways to the floor. His head impacts with a hollow thud but he does not lose consciousness.

"What the fuck is wrong with you?" he gasps.

But I am far too involved with myself to respond, as I jack my cock into a state of twitching ecstasy, feeling my love blob slowly and exquisitely drip its way down my aching penile shaft. I work it quickly, flooding my nub and releasing a torrent of molten goo squarely into his incredulous face. Bucking and moaning, I encase his head in my seminal excretion as he tries to breathe through the cum-bubble. Leaving him to shake the slop off his face, I remove a cat o' nine tails from a black leather bag. The handle is shaped like a dildo; I got it from Goering. He was a stinkin'-ass Prussian faggot who loved to ram pieces of expensive art up his ass. I sit the chair upright again and face the terrified American.

"If you promise to speak the truth, I will wipe that cum off your face." Being far from normal cum, it's starting to eat into his flesh.

He does and I do. I don't need to go into elaborate details as it doesn't require much to get him to open up as wide as a whale's vagina. He is a sentimentalist and all it takes for me to get what I need is to threaten his men with a hateful death.

There is a big gas dump north of here, and it is guarded by a mixed group of engineers and stragglers. Not much to stop my SS troopers, and we need that gas.

"I thank you, Captain, for that information. And I also applaud your resistance to my living cum-blanket. But I find that I have changed my mind regarding the disposal of your men. You see, I am an alien beast who feeds on the energies released by war. My primary feeding source is about 20 cc's of the brain juice located within your cortex."

I throw up my hands, still covered in black leather and blood, fresh from that morning's fisting session in the turret of my command tank. I knew the inner hull was spattered with shitty clods, which I had forbidden my crew to clean up. That wouldn't stop me from achieving total victory. You see, I knew that the Germans were building the atomic bomb, and they had the V-2 to send it shrieking into the middle of the enemy capital. I wished to strap myself to the nosecone and absorb thousands of screaming dead. I knew that women had babies but saw nothing wrong with fucking a man or an animal. We were all animals, no matter what pussy we might have come from.

But enough fun. I have an army to destroy. Quickly, I drive my nipples into the American's eyes, forgetting that I had promised not to kill him. Oh, that's right, I didn't forget. It's too late, the nipples are already deeply imbedded in his face as his body jerks and writhes beneath my mammalian assault. I suck him dry with my teat-straws and leave his drained corpse next to a stack of dusty bibles. This chamber also holds a rude cot on which the priest used to molest choirboys. I can still see the traces his molten man-jelly. The world is full of faggots!

Kill the prisoners! Burn the barn! Slaughter the civilians! Distribute more speed to the men and mount up—we are attacking!

I am with Assad on the Kuwaiti front.

There they were, the perfect armored juggernaut. The Americans had learned their lessons from the battle manuals of the SS, and they had learned them well. They came with maximum force at a localized weak point. Our position had started the war in good shape, but had steadily eroded since then. Everyday we faced the constant hammerings of the B-52's—'whispering death," as the Viet Cong had called them. Then came the close air support—F-16's, A-10's (one of which I would fly in a couple of days, stolen from Captain Crinkle), helicopters, even massive "Puff" gunships that chewed up great swaths of dirt and any men unlucky enough to be caught by the metal storm. One by one our real (and fake) tanks were destroyed. Then they began to work over the bunkers containing the men. We were truly at the mercy of the gods.

I spent this time in the lowest level of my command post, bathing in the Italian air-conditioner, smoking hashish and opium, drinking heavily and getting fucked by Assad. And now as the wave of death approached, I felt the first stirrings of fear in my gut. For too long had I been living like a bloated savage, swarthy and unrepentant. My last battle had been years ago, and that had been unpleasant. The Kurds had been rising on the border of the territory over which the Iranians and us had been fighting. I suggested we use poison gas. Saddam had approved and we killed over 100,000 people by spraying it from our helicopters onto their villages. But on the downside it rendered their corpses unsuitable for harvesting. Their souls left quickly and their meat was tainted. The poison swallowed them up and it also infected the land. We couldn't move in to steal their stuff for days. Not that they had much worth taking. But soldiers like to loot the dead, and take pictures.

Maybe it was payback time. I'd certainly killed enough Americans. At Malmedy, for instance, when I'd been young and lean. There had been no doubt as to the victor, and even in defeat I found glee, as me and the remnants of Kampfgruppe Pieper stumbled out of the pocket we had dug into their lines, leaving our shattered and wrecked vehicles strewn across the Belgian countryside, me feeling as a god. To think that these men would still follow me after all they had seen from me!

Like at Malmedy where we capture a large contingent of American artillerymen. They are terrified and we herd them into a field where they stand with their arms raised. When I give the order to fire, I tell my men to fire low, as only to wound. When the prisoners have been reduced to an immobile and moaning mass, I order my men to mount up again as I worm my way into the field and out of my clothing. I send my body out in the rudest emulation of what my Father had shown to me—similar to what I had done at Kursk but with more of a rending of form. My being is thrown out like a blanket, and when it has re-made itself I have again assumed a sac-like shape, from which extend the feeding tubes which grind their way through the flesh of my victims. Never have I had so many freshly wounded in one place before, and I glut myself on their beings as the network of tissue becomes a thousand questing mouths. The wounded men cry out in horror and agony, and pathetically try to crawl away through the snow. As if being machine-gunned by the SS wasn't bad enough—now they have to contend with a necrotic changeling who feeds off the images of loved ones conjured in the corridors of a dying mind.

I lap and suck, my howls filling the frozen air as the bloody snow surrounds me like a vortex. And as my body grows, so does my mind. It begins to reach out into forbidden places, forgotten times and other planes, other realities. Worlds of boiling mud where mile-long creatures thrive. They know they could leave their world, and live upon the excretions of the skin of another being, this one as big as a thousand suns, or as small as a dot in the mote of the eye of a god. A dot that is a lake, a great lake of desecrated waste, teeming with fat chunky slab, cracked and steaming. And the things that live there—the first one, Old Cranny by name, with a head eight times the size of his goatish, gleaming body, eyes lurking beneath crusted domes of intricately woven bone. Below this is a X-shaped hole; into this tissue oozes, though flatly across the skin. Sprouting from the top edge of its maw is a long line of miniature arms, all clutching different weapons, though the one aspect they all share is that they are only of crushing varieties, and all imbued with a variety of expungent hexes and banes. Ringing these are elongated spines; these are its torment as they point inward. The creature moves across a sea of excrement, leaving a wake broken through the once-molten slab, as it moves towards its nemesis, the Pustulator, a living mountain of shit with two baby arms, which are correctly scaled but mightily swollen. A mile-wide eye juts from its octapoid head assemblage, which sports its hideous maw. From there, I see that the sea of shit pours from its mouth. I do not witness the conflict that follows, but quickly rush back into myself in the crisp winter air of the forests of Europe primeval.

I stand, all senses trembling, assimilating the power I have gained. I am a good half-a-foot taller and much thicker in general, my muscles standing out in straining ridges as steam emanates from my yearning body. Blood streaks my hide in jagged rivulets as I breathe in the carnage of my making. All around me are the dead, their drained corpses stiff and grotesque as they clutch at the earth, seemingly trying to claw their way into it. Some have escaped into a nearby wood and I let them go, relishing the red haze that dissipates into me. A loud *CLUNG!* breaks the spell and I snap my attention to the road which runs parallel to the field of death. Here, my column has ground to a halt and one of my mighty King Tigers has collided with a half-track. Half the Kampfgruppe is standing in shocked and muted silence, staring at the gut-draped landscape of the crimson whirl. Pinks and purples and mangled sludge slurp up into my throbbing calves. I totter above the carnage, glaring back, tongue thick and rigid, unable to voice my desires. Then a strange noise begins to rise above the dense pines of the Ardennes landscape. A far-off wailing, and the sound of rushing wind. My own cry joins that of the new machine as it cleaves the atmosphere—a formation of triangular aircraft with black crosses on their wingtips, moving at incredible speed. These are the new jet planes we have been hearing about. I herd my men onto their tanks with great threatening gestures and soon we are in column again. I ride atop a King Tigers hull, holding a heavy MG with a full crate of ammo. We encounter an Allied roadblock and light it up with heavy fire. My tracers home in and set off some shells. I can see men running through the woods and I fire at them, noting the American tank destroyer coming up through the trees. I yell to the tank commander, and the great 88 mm. gun crashes out a blazing bolt, igniting the branches as the shell passes like a torpedo through the underbrush. It strikes the gunshield of the turretless vehicle, ripping through it and detonating on the other side. We roll on, machine-gunning the fleeing survivors and driving over their corpses. They pop.

But now, here on the sifting sand of the Kuwaiti desert it is my turn, and as they say payback is a bitch. I'm too big with my tits hanging out. This is the time of the abomination, the time I was a pseudo-woman with the fake pussy that doesn't act like one, but feels good to fuck. There is something wrong about the whole thing and it has to end. Lost in my grim reverie, I watch as the Americans envelop my frontal positions with waves of fire from their armored horde. Maybe it is time for me to die. I don't like dying—it hurts. But sometimes you just need a change. I had the option of regenerative suicide, something no human could have. But I never know for sure if I will come back or not. As I observe my wailing men being herded into a restrictive section of trench, I grow aroused. Assad presses hard up against my ass.

"Holy shit…" he mumbles.

Soon, my forward battalion has been flanked on both wings. Across its front is a solid line of American machines, in some places four-deep, sweeping the trenches with sheets of fire, forcing the men within to cower into the darkest bottoms of their holes, as any attempt at counter-fire is ruthlessly suppressed. Then the Americans bring up M-1's and Bradleys fitted with great bulldozer blades. On an attack half-a-mile wide, they move right up to the of the edge of the men-filled pit, some raising their rifles above the lip of the trench, improvised white flags (underwear) attached to their bayonets. But the bulldozers care not; on they come, braving the occasional RPG whilst spraying death, keeping our heads down and attacking the earth which we thought was our savior. But they turned it against us, dug it up and poured it on our heads. I watch as they bury my men alive then grind the dirt down. The impact on morale is immediate. We are Saddam's cannon fodder legions and we have been doomed to die. If only I hadn't fucked Cat Stevens.

First comes bombs, then shells. Then raking cannon, MG, and Gatling gun fire. I do my best to help by ordering my remaining units, some several thousand strong, to fall back to the last ring of trenches surrounding and leading to the command bunker. This is an order which makes no sense other than to help the Americans in their quest to destroy us all, although my units are happy to oblige when faced with the blistering array of American technology, which frequently misfires. But overkill is the theme, and it works, and the same calamitous sequence which has swallowed my lead units begins to be enacted on me and the surviving elements of my army.

And I let it happen. I don't lift a finger, don't fire a shot. I just sit there and watch it happen, as I gather my men and call prayers to Allah, packing the men thickly about me, their legendary commander, the undying one, the flame of Islam. They are ready to die as well, though they don't want to. But it is a testimony to the effectiveness of my Creator's will that they are still ready to surrender their lives. We cower, as I crush Assad to my side, whispering to him soothingly as his lips tug at my nipples. Other men, overcoming their fear of me through the abeyance of lust, crawl towards me. I am smothered in hairy Arabic men who lick off my clothes. We mush into a big fucking mass of spurting cum and flailing limbs. Men abandon religion for sex as they are buried alive. Living slabs of protoplasmic flame crease the sky, rent by burning bolts as the walls begin to crumble around us. I feel the waves of escaping life, shuddering the soil, echoing into me. My greatest suck, the obliteration of my being, another shot of the molten bolt that is the passage of my life, poised like a clutching cleaver to the saving of your souls. Thank you, Uncle Sam.

And from there, came I here.

***

Firing madly from my Harlem blockhouse with an M-60, I am weathering the assault of what could be any number of factions or units, though so far I have identified National Guard, SWAT, and regular army troops, which are separated on racial lines and all fighting each other. Then there are the "rebel" units, more independent than anything else. These units are myriad, fielding B.A., Native, and gang fighters.

The fighting had raged through the area for three days straight. Since I had destroyed the messenger of my Father I had not been threatened from below, so I had been able to expend all of my skill at repelling the series of assaults which had been made on my building, which stood up like a sore thumb in the path of the advancing armies. I rejected the advances of all comers with cunningly accurate bursts of automatic fire. Rebel stingers were keeping aircraft from close assault, so attacks were usually ground-oriented affairs preceded with mortar barrages. They had beat the hell out of my fort but I still held out, retreating to the sub-tunnel at the bottom of the elevator shaft with Maug the wonder-dog panting at my side, his hide slick with blood. He kept my tunnels free of vermin as I attended to matters above.

Night in wasted Harlem. The place is blown to shit. Flares are popping in the air, keeping the place fucking lit. Jackals are calling from the shadows, chanting a war song, to excite the throng. To keep it going on, as the souls flush to the bottom of the well. How long can it go on? Until everybody is in hell.

They bring up a 150 mm. Sheridan and point it at my house. It's an awful gun, essentially unchanged in a one hundred years of war development. They used these things a lot in Vietnam and this one had been gathering dust in a National Guard armory since Desert Storm. Its short barrel and excellent mobility make it a perfect choice to rip the front of my fort off in a devastating hail of burning murder. All those hours spent toiling on my walls has saved my ass for weeks but finally one cacophonous projectile has sundered my haven. Spinning into the back wall with spine-shattering force, I am rendered senseless. During these precious moments, the crew of the tormentor reloads their filthy weapon and sends another shell crashing towards me. This time their aim is off and the shell passes through the area they have just destroyed. It plows into a row of perforated tenements, sending splintered wood and shredded flesh careening through the murk.

A disturbance in the rubble next to me denotes the presence of Maug, shaking off a cloud of dust with some annoyance. He bounds towards me as I raise myself painfully from the floor, noting the fact that the entire front wall has disappeared and my battle van is on fire. Only the TV remains, running off the generator, still spitting out lies as it dangles from a cord through a hole in the ceiling. From there, I stare into the eyes of my dog and read his thoughts on the matter.

"Boss, its time to get the fuck out of here."

I agree, and we stumble into the escape tunnel just as another shell reduces my proud ghetto-castle to a shattered outhouse. Into the underworld we go, the noise of the battle dimming behind us, until we come to a series of increasingly wet passages leading to a great central reservoir area. This part of New York's vast sewer system is over a hundred and fifty years old, and no one comes here anymore. It is ancient and crusted with rime, like the mazes beneath Constantinople. It's the perfect place for my boat, just a little more than a canoe, but really a nice vessel which I had spent some time and effort building myself. With my faithful dog at the bow, I bid fond adieu to the surface world and steer my course into the nighted depths towards the moment unknown.

We paddled along, a boy and his dog, my head brushing the ceiling. Maug would die if he came with me. Everyone else I had known was dead. I had killed some of them, inadvertently caused the deaths of others. Death by association. There was no salvation for a soul as tainted as mine. My crimes were simply too vast. But there was a time to start the healing. Not of my soul but of everyone else's. I could kill the wrong. But not my dog. Oh no, not my dog. My dog would live.

I pull up next to a tunnel and send Maug up it. Of course he obeys unhesitatingly and dashes out of sight. I pause, torn for a moment, and then stroke powerfully away from the tunnel, leaving him.

The sewer is already showing corpses from the trickle-down. New York is being transformed from below. The water is getting thicker and I don't let up until I'm taken by a sudden downward current and tossed into a lower chamber. Rusted grates reveal other areas of pouring murk regulated by stepped stone. Water, blood, and bits of flesh pour in from all angles as my canoe begins to founder. How quickly they did come. Already changing, burrowing through earth with a thousand gluttonous tendrils. I go deeper as Maug's mournful howls fade behind me. As usual I'm a heartless son-of-a-bitch.

It's a long way to where I'm going and I'm in a hurry. I know other creatures are using these tunnels but I don't fear them.

Driving with the current, I move into the lowest levels I have yet explored, deeper into the hole than I have ever gone, until I know that I could never find my way back. Deeper until I drop with a viscous *plop!* into the last chamber where my boat will fit. An area where the stench of decay wafts so powerfully that it almost makes a Whargoul swoon. Fully packed with decaying bodies the chamber is fed by eight shafts, all of which provide the matter which fills this pit. The harvest shafts are below the surface, slowly sucking out the waste though the chamber never empties. Now content with the reek of the flesh, I sit in silence, enjoying my boat.

Dead eyes glare, still I am at rest. Most of the stuff is unrecognizable, mutilated flesh, yet still I am content. I haven't brought any weapons, but I have the hunk of pulsing crystal, pried from the staff of the wraith my Father had sent to collect me. I remove it from my ass and stare at the galaxy within it. A series of endless mirrors, all betraying a different scene. And me featured within them, shaping and unfolding in a procession of arrays. Lust, war, hate, and power are all there. So are my sins. Everything that I have been is unfolding. All that I have told you—then I know that it was all true. And then I know fear. Because I begin to remember the part that I have forgotten, and as I begin to remember it, I realize the biggest thing I have ever wanted in my life, is to forget this part.

The non-combatants were the biggest victims of the mad scheme. Their worlds were ruined, houses destroyed, toilet off, no food, dead son, dead family. No one was unaffected by the rending claw, and the wounds never healed. Hate bred hate which was celebrated through the ages. Oh, the incredible splendor of the military parade! The ribbons, and champing mares, and proud old men with tentacles up their butts. Men who, at the end of a busy day, lay down in a gauze box, while twittering servants pumped fluids into their bodies. All of this came from something.

Like a train full of humans, terrorized, displaced, held guilty for the ills of society. A convenient scapegoat or a lump of coal? Crated like cargo, they, as I, draw closer to the camp. There is no mistaking that you are drawing closer to the end. It smolders on the horizon much the same way as Stalingrad would when its furnace was at full blaze. But when approached by the subterranean route, I know that most of the victims go below. It takes so much energy to run an operation like this, and the walls heave with it. Sometimes they are of solid stone; sometimes they seem more fleshy, dripping with great bulbs of forming pus. Often, a thin yet indestructible membrane of resinous tissue will restrain molten magma. And always, I will catch phantom glimpses of unseen things scuttling away from the edge of my sight.

Now the flesh raft has left me and I move at my own pace, yet ever downwards. My way is strewn with a gut-garland until the innards become part of the walls. The tunnel clamps upon me with all its length, pinioning me in a suffocating embrace, squishing me into the audience chamber of my Father.

Above, the train has arrived, and the first wave of fodder is chosen. The rest will be worked to the point of death, and then consumed. About half go straight to the showers. They are stripped, whipped, shaven, and driven by vicious dogs. Some are fucked. Some are fucked by dogs. Some fuck dogs . . . but I digress.

Naked and humiliated, they stand huddled together under the nozzles, sobbing, screaming, some praying, some smashing at the scarred steel doors. Then the sound begins, a great deep groaning, like the sound of your hungry belly but a million-fold vaster. It is the opening of the abyss, and it comes from below.

The floor drops out of the shower room, revealing to those within a bottomless pit ringed with muscle, adorned with tooth and spike, belching with noxious fume. They drop into it with a chorus of despairing shrieks which fade into the groaning depths. Some manage to leap off the shoulders of their fellows and desperately grasp the dangling nozzles, only to be shot from the doorways by the laughing guards. Sometimes thinner tentacles will rise from the depths and wrap a toothy tongue around a kicking leg. These are dragged below. All that remain are the suitcases and these are burned. The chimneys at Auschwitz work day and night, burning clothes and luggage. The stench comes from the many unburied dead in the fields and within the camp itself. That does not sit well with the Germanic sense of order but the truth is that no Germans work here anymore. Some of the creatures that run the camp may have once been Germans, but they are no longer even human.

Gas is no longer needed.

Now before my maker I fall to my knees in supplication, attempting to understand the writhing mass that is He, the Creator, my Father. The closest thing your world has to a god.

The viewing-chamber is several miles across, and his being takes up fully half of the place. And it is only one small part of him, a continuous wall of pulsing, oozing, contorted tissue shaping and reshaping itself in a infinite multitude of feasting organs and champing maws, exploding up, out of, and into the pus-choked sea like some horrific paddlewheel. Every organ, every limb, every possible mutation of every possible configuration of flesh is represented in an ever-changing rotation of form. Eyeballs bulge and give way to a harvest of gesticulating arms and penises; which surge, in turn, to a devouring maw that floods forth with the vomit of God, which in turn brings forth another set of impossible life. What ripples like cilia is a sea of legs and fingers, all out of scale and jerking across the surface of this grisly canvas in which can only be agony. Entire generations of families are spat forth, dangled through stinging clouds of urine and smiting insects, only to be obliterated as they are sucked again into the flesh-wheel. And not only the form of the human being is exploited here—all forms of life are sucked in and despoiled, devoured and regurgitated. Huge crab claws dwarf inverted whale cunts, which spew forth with a wretched ichor loosed from the unseen and then seen bowels of some great, mutated insect. Herds of bloated buffalo stampede through bottomless planes of shit as the LoiGoi struggles to define itself, dislodging chunks of loose matter which cling to the walls and ceiling, quivering with confused life, oozing, groaning, and then dropping back as the entire chamber turns upside down, all this re-assimilated into the greater mass of the LoiGoi. His tentacles and questing pseudo-pods, his yearning and multi-segmented feeding stalks stretch forth from his squirming central mass through an uncountable collection of holes and chambers, disappearing into the hollowed earth, towards whatever distant slaughter from which he drains his lamprey-like existence. A hole like a giant mouth, surrounded by a collection of bearded men whose brains drip from their ears, opens with a great sucking sound, spitting out the latest shower stall-full of cattle to be consumed in the hatred that is the LoiGoi's hunger and need—to thrive on the misery of others.

I am confronted with the undeniable proof of the existence of my creator and ruler of this world. I am of him, and he has called me home. I watch the spectacle in weeping horror, knowing full well that I have contributed to its making, that my efforts has assured his domination, and that his death will be mine. Boiling madness grips me with paralysis as I loll in a pool of clinging, foaming slime at the belly of the beast, a belly that splits in a mile-wide explosion of obscene jelly and scalding suppurations, sprouting out a coiling meat-rope with a great toothy anus on one end, an anus that could have been a vagina, as long as the vagina had eyes and horns. It's a slimed opening that rears up on high above me for one brief and endless moment, the last tableau before my new transmosis as it slams down upon me, engulfing me and stripping away the lairs of my being, chewing me into pulp and remaking my form, to spit me out again to the surface of your earth as the latest version of one of his most faithful murderers. And so had Pieper been reborn, to wreak the havoc upon the surface world that was my Father's plan.

In my boat on the seething sea of liquefied flesh I tear my eyes away from the crystal, staring blankly at the mass of twisted and decomposing flesh which surrounds and threatens to engulf my craft, tucked here in the lowest corner of the known world. It was true, all of it. All of my worst suspicions were confirmed. My Father was a world destroyer, and one day he would destroy me as well. All this death, all this hate, and the killing that it led to, all of it was a pattern of behavior that was normal to creatures like the LoiGoi. You couldn't even call him good or evil, he simply was.

He had drifted through space for a million years, shunned by his kind, until he had found this place. He had found the humans here, and judging them to be of good stock, he had burrowed deep below the surface of their world, sending out the feelers that would grasp and control them, and which one day would lead them to the brink of oblivion, the prepice upon which we stood today.

From far away comes the sound of grinding boulders and

screaming cows, bursting floodwalls and whispering cobwebs. The sea begins to heave, scattering droplets of reeking disease, spattering upturned jowls with necrotic load. The boat begins to move, propelling me sluggishly forward, displaying the caked walls and their secrets in a merry-go-round parade of rot. Slowly we begin to tip inwards, towards the center of the vortex. It's like an immense toilet is being flushed, and as we drop into the gurgling depths I laugh, though a flowering of wormy growths erupts from my thighs. For this time my Father would not find me a willing supplicant.

I drop into the lowest of levels, swallowed whole and moving inside the tremulous and heaving corridors that are my Father's bowels. Passing through the thickly gelatinous and sometimes transparent passageways, I observe the great hive chambers where thousands of flesh-sculptors work diligently on the abominations that are the realizations in flesh of my Father's will, created to be spat out upon the surface of the world. These creator-creatures are much like the arm-thing that I had encountered in the chambers beneath the temple of Necrosov. They note my passage with twittering approval, waving their clawed and instrument-bearing appendages, hissing and mewling with gaping and slickly glistening maws, mouthing to each other the obscene comments which only they could bring themselves to understand.

For I had been invited here, drawn below to fulfill the purpose for which I had been created. I was to lead the army of the apocalypse in the final war of this blighted world. But I could see beyond the plan that was designed to complement me for years of diligent service. I knew that upon the completion of my mission—the resultant devastation of the surface world and all the life that walked upon it, then my usefulness would be at an end. I would be consumed again, my body broken into bits that would give my Father the power to break free of the planet that was both his home and his prison. He would leave behind only ravaged chunks of debris that would travel the universe for eternity, mute testimony to the struggle that had engulfed and ultimately annihilated this world. And my Father would drift again into the void, empowered, yet still ravenous, searching for another world to consume in his quest for what he ultimately desired—the destruction and consumption of all reality, to remake it again in the form of his choosing.

How I could know all this, I was not sure, but for all appearances I came to my Father as a willing and obedient slave. I came to accept a commission, but really I faced a choice. The fact that my Father did not know this was my only chance of defeating him. If only I could find the strength within me to resist his will.

But before I could face this, which promised to be the defining moment of my life, I had to prove my worth one last time. For during the years of my service on the surface world, others had struggled for the same master. Created by my Father, they sought to curry his favor by mindlessly obeying his will, by murdering millions in the name of a god who had none. Some of these creatures I had met, some I had destroyed. Some had attempted to destroy me. Many others I had never met, and they had slaughtered and been slaughtered in the never-ending wheel of war. Now, on the day before the apocalypse, there were only two left. They had to fight, and one had to destroy and consume the other before he could be emblazoned with the rank of high executioner. My Father would watch this battle with interest and amusement, and provide the tools necessary for its implementation. And I knew full well the name of my rival.

Necrosov.

"How are you, my brother?" I say to him, as we face each other across a vast and murky chamber that will shift and form itself into whatever battlefield my Father deems appropriate.

"I am well," he blares back at me, his voice cracking with bile. "And I congratulate you on getting this far. It is a shame to have worked so hard, only to meet your death on the doorstep."

He's changed, as have I. Flesh covers all of what I suspect to be a fully metallic exoskeleton, full of hidden weaponry. I briefly regret not bringing a weapon, then just as quickly forget it as the world whirls into the comforting-yet-cramped confines of a bunker dug into the western wall of the corpse-generating machine that was Verdun. World War One, what fun. But there is considerable comfort in the filthy hole that we call our home. It is much better than slowly bleeding to death in a reservoir of mud like so many others are doing this evening.

We regard each other across the stained and pitted table. He pours me a cup of dark wine.

"You don't deserve this, you know," he says, as outside far-off artillery rumbles. "You disappeared for years, and there was good killing to be had. You hang around with whores and an old fool who fills your head with shit. You play golf . . . pathetic."

"Golf is cool."

Another blast shatters the night, this time closer to us. We both look to the roof.

"The blacks, the whites, all the races, they are all trying to kill each other. One of us will rise from the depths, to lead them to the point where they can finish the job once and for all. So—a last drink before we kill each other," he growls, as his eyes burn hatefully into mine.

"What shall we drink to?"

"To our Creator, and the wonderful world He has made for us."

"A world you won't be enjoying much longer," I say, a leering smile curling across my thick lips.

He chuckles and we raise the cups. Necrosov whips out an unseen pistol and tries to shoot me in the face. I manage to get a hand up and the bullet tears into my palm. I burst forward, bulling the table into him as he fires the pistol repeatedly. My fingers elongate and sharpen, tearing into his chest, ripping and slicing the flesh and exposing the gleaming metal beneath his skin. He ignites his boot jets and blasts off through the ceiling in a flurry of flame and splintering wood. He flies back to his lines, trailing a comet and followed by my coarse epithets. I order a series of assaults across the hell of no-man's land. The fighting rages for days in a pointless and agonizing manner. When all of our forces have been consumed, we go to meet each other in a field so thick with decomposing corpses that you can walk across it for miles and never touch the ground. Years later, they will build a monument here, a great and colossal piece of brick and mortar inscribed with uncountable names. A real eyesore, and they built it that way on purpose.

As the blood sinks into the mud so do we, dropping out of one time and into another. We are both ape-like creatures, fighting over a particularly bountiful tract of hunting real estate, both tribe leaders responsible for the feeding of an entire clan. The clans are based in cave complexes which are passed down through generations of the same family or change hands as the result of fighting. If the leaders are killed, the rest of the tribe is eaten except for the young women. We fight everyday at the watering hole that is on the edge of the hunting area.

We are young and fresh at this point, reveling in the most primal form of our beings. Necrosov is unspoiled by the savages of the wars and wounds he will grow into. The scars of endless surgeries and transformations have yet to road-map his bestial frame. His body gleams with sweat and spit as we eye each other across the expanse of the watering hole, glittering in the sun, showing off for the girls behind us. It is fun to be a kid again.

Large clubs are the weapons of choice. Our fight involves lots of screaming and yelling, splashing water all over the place and rushing to the brink of bone-crunching violence, only to shrink away from its edge. It's as if we know that if we kill each other that it will set off an eternity of pain. We, the warriors in their earliest form, are reluctant to bestow our curse upon the world. But then the women withhold sex from us, demanding we make an end of it.

So, the next day I smash him upside the head with all the force that I can muster, knocking a handful of teeth into the bloody water. His tribe bears off his inert body—I'm already getting fucked in the mud.

But he's not dead. He can't die, and our contest, at this point, can have no victor. We are putting on a show for a limitless audience of one immense being. The curtain rises on the next spectacle of carnage. While our tribe lies drunk and insensate next to the dying embers of our cave's fire, our rivals set fire to huge boughs of dried twigs they have gathered and placed around the entrance to our dwelling. The choking fumes billow in upon our sleeping forms and cause immediate panic amongst us. A wall of living flame blocks our only escape route. The only choice is to rush headlong through it—unless we do this the tribe will be suffocated. But no one will take the chance except me. I grab a thick sleeping skin from the floor and quickly urinate on it, forcing out my pee in a painful stream. I then drape it around my shoulders, imploring all to follow as they stare at me with wild and uncomprehending eyes.

"You idiots wouldn't last a day in Stalingrad," I scream, assailed by a memory of a future past. I rush through the flames in an instant, dropping and rolling to extinguish any flame which may be clinging to me. Shrugging off the pelt, I am immediately assaulted by a horde of club-wielding tribesmen who beat me to death, as the rest of my clan is burned alive. This one goes to Necrosov.

But there would be another transmosis and another chance to avenge my latest destruction. We fought in the court of Vamier Tomb, Lord of the Realm that you would one day call Atlantis, though they called it Talingar. The people were harsh and warlike, and their empire in its developing years was dedicated to the subjugation of the entire world. Vamier was a cruel warlord that I had served for many years, slowly working my way up through the ranks of various units, earning a reputation as a cold-hearted and ruthless warrior, fearless in the embrace of death yet not lacking in the lust for life, and adept at hypnotizing chickens. One day there was a great ceremony in the Hall of Hatred to affirm my position as leader of the Sho'kai, an elite group known for their berserking battle-lust. I had endured and undergone the ritual scarification and genital mutilation which marked my passage into this order. A collection of ears circumnavigated my neck and shoulders several times, and I had acquired the nickname "Babyraper," for my activities within the bowels of the newly born. All that remained between me and the assumption of my command was the ritual of acceptance. My deeds would be spoken in front of the unit and any who expressed doubt in my abilities would have the opportunity to try to best me in battle for the right of leadership.

The list of my atrocities had taken hours to read but my unit held iron discipline throughout the entire process. They knew full well that they would be rewarded with seven nights of debauchery in appreciation of the patience they now exhibited. The streets would flow red with wine and blood as the warrior classes hurled themselves upon the city in a frenzied orgy of humping and drunken lunacy. During this time no one could deny any warrior's request and as a result families had been smuggling their wives, daughters, and pets out of the city for days.

Ur the Intoner, a multi-tentacled bulb of flesh who rose through the floor as the only visible part of a much larger creature, finally reaches the end of the list. Not a snicker had risen from my men, even as the details of the frozen midget episode were revealed. For my part, I had been hanging by my balls for over three hours.

"Let these deeds be recorded as most foul, and through his love of the murk, let this being attain new status. Let his scrotum be released, and let him assume his command, or speak your grievance against him now, knowing that false words will feed the gibbering hounds of hell."

"I will speak!" comes a booming voice with which I am all too familiar.

Necrosov, clad in the raiment of a Tolgar (the same rank that I occupied and sought to elevate myself from), strides forward with unbridled aggression towards the Throne of Swords, which our leader is impaled upon, within "The Symbol." All of my rank have the right to impede my progress through trial by arms if they felt that they could defeat me in individual combat. Necrosov, who is not called Necrosov but goes by the name of Cromis, feels he has that skill and therefore that right.

The illusion of our battle is so complete that I have lost all memory of my later life. Each conflict generated by the mind of the LoiGoi is so perfect in every detail that I believe in them utterly, as does my rival.

Kneeling before the great throne, Cromis presents his case to our hollow lord (such it is said about our master who never appears anywhere without his fully encasing plate armor). Vamier hears his plea. Cromis is strong. Cromis is loyal. Cromis is a rampant butt-pirate. Cromis will kill me and gain my power, and in doing so the Master will enjoy an even more powerful servant than if the two of us walked the same earth. And the master, bound by rituals even stronger than he is, must agree. And so our battle continues.

We are stripped naked and placed upon a great lead disc, suspended by huge steel chains above a pit of flaming coal. We are each handed a cruel knife with which to gut each other with. With a blare of trumpets and a cheer of approval, we attack.

My opponent is cagey. He has waited and planned for this usurpation for years, waiting for me to come to this plateau of my development in order to intervene when I was at my weakest, blood streaming from my loins, my scrotum pierced and mangled. So I indulge him in his plan, feigning exhaustion and making no offensive moves. Letting him think that it's working thus far, I slowly draw him in as we circle about on the disc, which is growing increasingly more hot and uncomfortable. Ordinarily I would increase the density of the soles of my feet, but in this earlier form of myself I cannot attain the state of transmutation.

I don't watch his eyes, but always his blade. His eyes cannot kill me but his knife can, and I wait for his rush with the patience of the hunter, sensing that the ambush I planned was unsuspected. But suddenly I become the victim.

He throws his knife in a curved and quick motion that he has practiced for years. A quick and little movement yet propelled with an amazing amount of force. It is done at eye-level, so for the barest fraction of an instant the knife appears to be in the same place even though it is drawing closer to me. When I realize his stratagem, it is too late. But even then I have not grasped the fullness of his plan. The knife covers the space between us in a flickering instance. All I can do is twist my body so the knife imbeds itself in my shoulder rather than my throat. But why would he throw away his weapon? The answer is immediately obvious as he bulls into me, attempting to drive me off the edge of the disc into the fire beyond. My weapon arm is paralyzed from making a downwards thrust into his back by the wound he has inflicted upon me. I have but one chance. I let myself be pushed back at great speed towards the edge of the disc, but at the same time lock my good hand deeply into the tangle of dark hair that sits atop his head. As we pass the edge I thrust my knife sideways, the only range of motion that my arm will allow. I wedge it into the middle one of the links of the great chains that suspend our arena. Too late he realizes he is caught. As we go over the edge, my body pivots around the knife's sketchy purchase within the link—Cromis, propelled by my strenuous pulling of his hair, goes right over.

But this split second of violence is not yet over. As he falls he claws madly at my body, seeking any sort of hold which could save him from his fiery fate. His nails rake my stomach and loins, and finally lock around my penis in an iron grip. The force of his motion travels up my aching shaft, through my body, and to the knife in the chain, which is our only link to the safety that the burning disc offers.

Which is stronger, my cock or my blade?

The knife snaps, and we both tumble into the abyss.

We land on the dusty slopes of a rock-strewn landscape, thickly blanketed with pine trees. Around us a great battle rages between the armored legionnaires of the Romans and fur-clad barbarians. But I have little time to observe the details of our latest trial as Necrosov launches himself upon me in another series of slashing attacks with his weapon, a long-bladed spear. I defend myself with my glaive, parrying his mad thrusts while attempting to find an opening and spill his guts in a definitive manner. All around us struggling knots of men slay each other with utmost savagery. Here, in the Teutonburg Forest, the expansion of the Roman Empire will be halted, at least for the time being. Every member of my legion will be slain. But it matters not, for these men are already dead. Their loss has decorated the pages of history books for centuries. But I have a far more personal struggle at hand as I beat back a series of slashing, stabbing thrusts to my midsection. Three times I knock my attacker's spear aside, all the while seeking an opening to reverse the attack. Necrosov, or whatever name he goes by in this time, grunting and sweating, presses his assault. His fourth thrust comes under my glaive at a difficult angle and jabs through the lower part of my breastplate, penetrating through my leather undershirt and into my abdomen. The pain is immediate and intense, shocking in its newness—a pain I have never really felt before. Gasping, I reel away, the spear lodged firmly in my pierced armor, wrenching it out of my adversary's grasp as he loses his footing in the loose soil. A wild-eyed tribesman rears up in my path as I seek to understand what has happened to me. My weapon lashes out and cleaves his face in twain, spattering the pine needle carpet with the droplets of his being. *And no power is transferred into me to heal my wound.*

Panic grips me for a moment as I realize that the rules have changed. As the LoiGoi sends us whirling through time, the parameters change with each confrontation. Now fully cognizant of my future lives and the implications of this battle, I have been stripped of my necrotic abilities of soul-sucking and transmosis. I am essentially only a powerful human, and I can only hope that the same rules apply to my rival, who has grabbed a sword from a dead man's hand and pursues me up the slope. All around us shrieking men lock in their death-throes, as I painfully pull the spear from my side and send it whizzing by Necrosov's head. The wound is not deep but it is bleeding profusely—I can feel the hot liquid streaming down my thighs. But I stand my ground and meet his charge with vigor, blocking a series of cleaving blows that ring like the anvil of Pluto off our shivering swords. Here, in an age not our own, in a fight not of our design, in a body alien and unforgiving, I have never felt so alive. Exulting in my pseudo-humanity I block, hack, slash, and parry, seeking any opening in my opponent's guard. But he gives me none. We stand, locked in the web of weaving steel, each blow shivering through our bodies and into the bloody ground below. Neither one of us will give a step or even an inch. Gradually the outlines of the battlefield begin to melt away around us, the struggles and screams of the victors and the vanquished begin to fade. They are slowly replaced by an infinite blue void, studded with stars, and the great roaring shout of a deep-throated god. We float in this space and rain blows upon each other, slipping through time in an endless profusion of costumes and battlefields. With each blow, our situation changes. I am of the Mongol horde—he is a warrior of the Eastern Marches, then a Viking, then a renegade monk bent on despoiling the Vatican. I am Alaric the Visigoth, he is Valens the Vanquished, burning in a barn as his martial dreams turn upon him. Cucullan and Mushasi. We follow Charlemagne and Pepin, Salidan and Philip. We slay in the name of Jesus and Satan, Mohammed and many other gods and men with names forgotten by time's sad march. Our guises fall from us like rain, only to be replaced by another, and another, and another. Somewhere throughout this struggle, I wound him in his shoulder with a battle-ax. The weapons are changing as well as we march towards the present through the decades of carnage that our master has visited upon this planet. We fight with clubs, then spears, then swords, then guns, then nuclear bombs. Millions are consumed by the legacy we bring and leave behind, and still we hammer each other and the planet beneath us to the edge of futility. Only my opponent's contorted face and hacking arm remain constant as we fight through time, each blow sending showers of plasmic froth from our boiling bodies. Locked in the death struggle, we vaguely notice that we have become one being.

But such things cannot last. Our maker has enjoyed the show, his tour through the endless wars of his making that have led us to the brink of the apocalypse. He has enjoyed watching his two favorite puppies fight against the backdrop of endless hatred. But the final act beckons, and the action that precedes the final act is Necrosov burying his ax in my skull, splitting my upper palette and imbedding it in my lower jaw. At this, time's whirl stops, and I stumble backwards, droplets spraying from the obscenity that was my head. My motion tears the weapon from his grasp, but he is too canny a foe to give me any respite. My senses reel. It's too late. My fingers claw at the shaft of the weapon, trying to drag it from my skull and strike back at my foe. But it's no good. I sink to my knees in a pathetic heap, my eyes trying to form a single vision. Necrosov looms above, steaming and carnal, joints glistening, eye gleaming with a hellish light as he exults in his victory. He is the chosen one. Now the gates of the underworld will open, and the armies of the flesh-sculptor's making will savage the earth, ultimately consuming themselves in the furnace from which they issued. And Necrosov shall lead them, glutted on my strength, invincible in his own. I have failed.

He moves his mouth to the wound, holding the sides of my split skull in each hand. He opens my head like a clam and bends to slake his lust on all that my life has been. All I can do is weep.

Suddenly, there is an explosion of motion and force, a muscled mass that leaps over my back and collides with my rival even as he stands at the altar of his destiny. He is denied, and he falls back with a muffled curse, seeking to extricate the 160-pound combo of fang and claw from his face.

Maug has somehow followed me through the sunless depths of the underearth, wiggling through the wretched walls of filth to fight at my side one final time. Necrosov stumbles and falls heavily, Maug tearing a scarlet ruin through his facial flesh. I realize I have a chance, and I wonder if my Father gave it to me.

I rip the ax out of my head and lurch forward, massing my strength. I can't see my target—I can only sense him struggling ahead of me, bellowing curses, unaware of my approach. Maug's war cry abruptly becomes a shriek of pain as I bring the ax down in a crimson arc that lands full force on the neck of my adversary, severing skin, muscle, steel and bone as his head leaps off his body in a geyser of blood and corruptive juices. I grab him by the shoulders and lift him into the air, emptying his body into the maw of my split skull, which sprouts teeth from the edges. Drinking of his life, I feel his pain. He has suffered so long, just as I have. He has been used, as I have. And he also has sought relief from his pain in the most abominable of ways. But in the end, perhaps he knew that his strength, added to mine, would help me achieve my mission. And maybe in this he found a measure of peace.

As has Maug. Panting heavily, he lies on his side, guts bulging from where my blow has torn him open. As my skull knits together, my vision clears through the red-rimmed haze; I behold the death-throes of my lovely friend, here, in this nighted vault far beneath the surface of a world gone mad. The chamber breathes and expands, revealing its true depth, and the gently glowing, rippling rings of flesh or fat that surround me for miles, packed to bursting with the malignant creatures observant of the ritual.

Maug dies with a final shuddering gasp, and his energy passes into me, as it had with Kepler, and Gabby, and Cheng-Tzu, and anybody else that had ever been close to me. But I smile, as I see the final shadow fade from his eyes. The sacrifice they have given me is the humanity I have tasted, and this has given me the will to pursue what I have searched and striven for, ever since I first dreamt it could be a reality—the chance to destroy the destroyer, to commit demonic patricide, and rid the world of the curse of war.

To kill the arch-devil that unseen tongues named the LoiGoi,

Corpse-Lord of the Hollow Earth, seducer of the humans into the role that had been set for them—that of food . . .

Here comes Daddy.

And when he comes to me he chooses a shape that is simple for me to understand, not the roiling and flabbergasted mass of pulpifying flesh that is one of his true guises. When my Father comes to me, to set me in command of that infernal legion which is arranged around me in the endless chamber, he comes to me in a way that will both soothe and tempt me at the same time. He comes to me as a woman.

It is Nurse Faber, the nurse that I raped and murdered in Russia, the one the Obersturmbannführer said that one day I would be allowed to mate with again. No, wait. I am, no, I was, the Obersturmbannführer. But as she glides closer to me in a serpentine manner which goes far beyond the natural grace of a woman, her outlines begin to flutter and fade. She is Gabby, and then she is my mother from the steppes of Russia. She is the charming Jewess I murdered in the sewers of Warsaw. She is all women, and then none. Finally she is a he, an it, a forty-foot tall insect-like being, clad in intricate plates of overlapping armor that give him the appearance not unlike (yet not like) that of a huge deep-sea fish. Its eyes are white and soulless, lolling in their sockets as they grasp at truth with no meaning. Numerous mandibles and cleaver-like appendages jut from his body at all angles, and a curious stalk of gristly flesh rises from between his eyes, ending in a another eye which weeps a stream of viscous pus. Chittering in an alien tongue, his hide cracks and splits and lets forth with waves of excretions and gasses which bubble up and coalesce into new life, which spring away into the darkness to pursue their hidden tasks. And as he gibbers and shakes above me, I sense that this is the center of his true form.

His body is immense beyond belief, his feed-stalks traversing the tunnels of the hive-world known as Earth, running to every battlefield, every mass-murder, every Joy-Division and death-camp. His body provides the living quarters for legions of his servants who are busy creating the apocalypse army I was apparently destined to lead. I have despaired on how to kill such a creature. Where do you start?

You have to start at the center, and judging by the ecstatic power-rush which I am garnering from his being, that is where I stand. Just beholding him is the most intense of sensations, and my skin crawls with delight. I am next to the greatest depository of brain-juice on the entire planet. There is enough of it to power everything that he has created, and I notice the slimed stalks and tentacles which come off of him and disappear into the floor. He has to control this immense being from somewhere, and it is done from here, his brain. I have been traveling inside of the LoiGoi for some time, and now I have reached the final chamber.

"My Liege," I say with phony reverence, bowing before him, yet knowing in my heart that even at this moment, nay, especially at this moment, that I ran the risk of turning to his side.

Bulging, he looms above me, glaring down with remorseless will. His first words are not understandable in any conventional communicative sense. When he opens his mouth I am assailed by a wave of palatable force and corruption, a surging vortex of depthless hunger. His is an implacable will, his breath like the ice from the tomb of a god. The maw grows larger, and with a vigorous wave of stench I feel myself becoming engulfed in his horny and slimed tongue, sucked asunder. He wraps me in an obscene embrace that I gratefully repel into. Suffused with the power needed to fully recover from my battle, the joy of my Father's love heals me. I am his chosen child, and so many have died to bring me here. He is proud of me, and he shows his love by taking me into his mouth.

"Daddy, oh Daddy, take me into your womb. Let me make it your tomb."

Now is the time for my betrayal. In his necrotic embrace I find my opening. In the strength he gives me I find the strength to attack him. I extend my arms upwards, fusing them together into one stabbing mass which I drive into the roof of his mouth, which splits with a hideous rending crunch, vomitous ichor cascading all over me. Still I drive my murder-pole into his being, piercing his vile braincase and penetrating into its depths. As I reach the core of his being, I explode the shaft outwards into many corkscrewing shafts, ripping into the vaults of his mind and doing as much damage as possible, seeking the feeding juice that will give me the power to destroy him.

I claw frantically, like a rat on a treadmill of flesh. I have made my body as barbed as is possible, to inflict as much damage as I can. It is my only hope, to attack in a totally unexpected and apocalyptic manner so as to mortally wound him with the first blow, delivered at the least-expected moment. I hope to assassinate the beast and in doing so destroy myself and free your world. And as I rake at the jelly of his mind I am immediately aware that my attempt will fail.

There is no resultant power rush, no immediate rebirth. No soul-searing testimonial to the transmittal of mutational power. Instead I feel a shifting of his being, a great sloshing which sends the ichor into other, unreachable parts of his mass. He has immediately detected my betrayal; indeed it never had a chance. It did not even cause him pain, if in fact he could even feel pain. But it annoyed him that this part of his plan had been a failure.

I am spat out of his face like a wad of snot. He has formed two perfect human hands to cradle me in, like you would a precious insect that you were about to drive a pin through. He is acting on his new plan immediately. His form is rapidly growing, and I am borne earthward, smashing through the ceiling, through layers of rock, flesh, and magma, towards the surface worlds.

My Father is pissed. I was to have been his sweetest slave. I was to lead the forces he had created in the final conflict, the conflict that would either exterminate or define them. They were the B.A., they were the Voiden, they were many more. They came driving from the depths of hell in the wake of my father's making. For now, my Father would lead them himself.

I gaze into his face as the last layers peel away. Its surface writhes with life as he strives to remake himself as the destroyer. He will not watch the final battle from the comforts of the underearth. He will lead it, and to do so he must devise a face which will slay all who gaze upon it. And this uncertainty rattles him as a legion of mutants attempt to crawl out of his face all at once. The ugly snouts of tanks protrude from between his grinning teeth; burning pus spatters away in lake-filling quantities as woven armor plating bubbles from his skin, an expanse of waving and toothed tentacles, appendages, and hooves. A giant penis erupts from his chin, spitting venom; knocking creatures away from his face and into the tunnel he leaves behind us, where they join the mass of things following my Father's movement through the earth.

Things were bad in Times Square, but no one could have comprehended just how much worse it was going to get. The carnage was now loose in all the boroughs of New York as various splintered factions fought each other over the city and its spoils, as the National Guard vainly tried to impose order. The regular army was breaking apart, as a major part of the U.S. Army was black, and they had rebelled quickly. There was much bloodshed on the steps of countless armories, and tanks full of drunken men rolled through the streets, blasting expensive shops to hell. In the time I had been underground, which had felt like years but had really been only a few days, the battle of New York had changed from a ghetto block-razing event to a matter of serious contention. The forces opposing the forces seemingly possessed infinite reserves and an increasing amount of heavy weaponry. They came up from below, moving through the sewers and spilling into the lower levels of the colossal towers that defined New York. People had been trying to escape the city for days but that wasn't easy. The landings were under mortar fire and military traffic came first. A bomb went off in the Holland

Tunnel after years of rumor. The government had organized a massive boatlift to get the refugees out of the city, but it didn't work too well. There were monsters in the water now, things that dragged ships down with all aboard screaming for deliverance. And above, in the plush and privileged places of control, gibbering things came through the walls and slaughtered all they found. People tried to flee the populated areas as everything broke down. But the woods were full of devils, slavering things with automatic weapons that wiped out your family and ate the Winnebago. In the city, many buildings were still occupied by hordes of terrified humans who were ill prepared to deal with the onslaught from below. They did their best to barricade their dwellings, but defensive measures invariably only delayed the onset of mutilation, and heightened the flowering of terror. Grinning things which became stronger flayed their flesh, and as the creatures claimed the buildings they became towers of death, spewing RPG and machine-gun fire across the concrete canyons. There was no longer any reason for my Father to conceal his intentions, to trick or goad the humans. Malformed things with cleaver arms marched straight out of the East River directly into combat with whatever lived, whatever emanated the power that they craved. They grabbed weapons. They crewed tanks. Things hadn't gone to hell—hell had come to us.

Times Square had become the focal point for all of midtown's carnage, and had been in a state of perpetual battle for three days straight. Looters, terrorists, soldiers, and hellspawn all converged on this place in order to kill each other. Burning and mangled barricades, festooned with corpses from all the marauding elements, cut the space up into more defensible areas. Wrecked armored vehicles and burnt-out cars littered the playing field like so many broken toys, charred corpses draped across their hulls, roasted flesh black and glistening. There was no three-card Monty tonight, but there was a new game in town—the deadliest game, the game of war. And to aid this quest the sewers spilled murderers, fresh from the flesh-hives that continued to pump out murderous life until the last possible second. Bullets shattered windows, rockets swooshed redly across the void, random vehicles burst into flames and collided with buildings and occasionally a helicopter would come along and chew the place up with its gatling cannon. This would quiet things down for a while but the fighting would soon flare up again. There were no sides anymore, only the confusion of melee as all creatures involved sought, received, or distributed death. But all ceased their ghastly endeavors at the noise of my Father's return.

He holds me cupped in his immense yet childlike hands, me swaddled in snot, protecting me as the top of his being torn through the last layers of asphalt, pipe, and wire, and spills into the street. First there is a crested and warty ridge, followed by voluminous billowings of pig-like flesh, splitting open at various junctures to emit stalk-like feelers and legs. These grind into the pavement with sulfurous cracks, straining with the effort of extricating my Father's central mass from underearth for the first time in a million ages. Then grayish eyestalks squirm aloft, unblinking as they behold the surface world they have come to destroy. The flames around him seem to leap at his presence, and from the ruined streets all manner of malformed creatures leap into the light, capering and twittering their love song to their bloated master, whose pulsing head pushes its way through a mass of rippling and ruined pavement. There is one hideous moment as he takes in his new world and the gaping hole of his mouth splits in the ghastly mockery of a human smile, a torrent of greenish liquid burbling from between tombstone teeth, bubbling down his horned hide and onto the street below where great clouds of steam leap up as the asphalt dissolves. Then a vast amount of his mass pours from the ground and into the air with a deafening roar of hateful triumph, echoing from deep within, shattering glass and picking up the stones of the rubble he has made. His body surges into the sky, a mass of writhing tentacles, joined to heaving masses of decomposing flesh bags, bags which explode with larvae, larvae which rain onto the street below.

With the sound of a million whale farts his swollen corpulent being begins to rear as large as the buildings that surround him, then as big and bigger, his malformed shoulders pushing into the shattered sides of burning blocks, ripping through their facades and sending meaty probes lashing down their corridors.

My Father is out on the town.

And so he rears, exultant, hide crawling with festering regenerative material. He glares at the hate of his making, the shattered glass that was his audience reflecting his incomprehensible visage. Any human that gazes upon him goes automatically insane, and they begin to plunge out of windows or swallow their guns.

Suddenly a vehicle bursts into the mix, careening in from a side street, smashing through a barricade in a fiery burst of debris. Demons cling to the sides, howling, lashing at the skin of the heavy panel van while being assaulted from within by the occupants of the vehicle who are firing madly through the walls. I watch as the vehicle slews about in a great semi-circle, slowly lifting up onto two wheels as the creatures rip the roof back. A flurry of automatic fire erupts from within as the van lands on its side in a shower of sparks, scattering the creatures in flailing bundles. It hits a crater and comes to rest at an angle as the back kicks open. A figure dressed in a red jumpsuit with long black hair, tied back with a red bandana and carrying an AK-47 jumps clear, firing at the things that are already gaining their feet. He knocks them back with well-aimed bursts of lead, then turns and beholds my Father for the first time. I can see his hair turning white as his weapon clatters from his nerveless fingers to the ground. The creatures again rush towards him. He tears his sight away from the surging mass of champing flesh that rears above and produces a small black box with a series of cables, which disappear back into the vehicle. Before he goes down beneath a flailing series of cleaver blows, he manages to turn the key that arms the device, and then hits the *detonate* button with a wild cry just as he is beheaded. The proud Apache death squad has accomplished their mission. And the

Russians didn't gyp them either. The nuke goes off.

It is a ten-megaton device, ground bursting with roughly 600 times the power of the Hiroshima bomb, and it explodes about 100 meters in front of Dad and me. It's a modest bomb by today's standards but nevertheless it is the single most destructive event ever visited upon a populated area of the planet. Times Square melts as we are engulfed in a searing wave of thermonuclear plasma. Like a great expanding soap bubble the beast annihilates all in its path, as the concrete canyons of Manhattan do their best to swallow the blast. But it is to no avail. The blast peels back the stone facades of the glittering towers of Babylon, the flames surging through the expensive offices of the corridors of power, ruining upholstery. The boiling flames of vengeance pour into the richly appointed lobbies, melting carefully crafted corporate logos. Offices where corpulent bosses bent their slutty secretaries over the water cooler simply cease to be.

And the sound. How can you describe the sound of a city collapsing under the weight of a nuclear fireball? And the people within, their screams, the sound of their souls escaping? We will never know how many died in that blast, but they numbered into the millions. It was as if a rift to hell had opened up, as the streets cracked open and released the infernal fire that would cleanse the world. And at the center of the blast, my Father and I lock in the last chapter of the death embrace.

Our bodies have been destroyed. The tremendous destructive power of the nuke is great enough to make our flesh as to nothing. But we cannot die. Though our bodies, mine human in form, monster in being, and his, the indefinable mass, are reduced to slag, our beings cannot be ended. Because here, on the eve of the apocalypse, we enjoy the greatest soul-suck ever known. It was payback time for all those bombs that I had missed. Our beings are stripped to atoms, the only living things able to retain their personalities, their souls, if you will. And these souls become the conduit for the countless other souls which were stripped from their bodies by the death wave. Stripped and sucked into the feeding hole that was the ravenous appetite of both my Father and myself. Pouring into our gaping beings which gobbled this life into an expanding power pool, growing beyond ourselves at unthinkable levels, until thinking itself was no longer needed, so that spontaneous knowledge of all that had ever past was achieved with scarcely an effort.

The obliterated outlines of the stricken city are erased as our exultant forms become one with the fireball and expand towards the heavens where we take our place as gods, hovering over the flaming crater that up until an instant ago had been known as Manhattan. There we continue to suck in the discarded souls of the countless victims of our violence. I can comprehend the form of my Father, far away from me, floating in the fire like an immense embryonic bug, his outlines illuminated by the blast. His true outlines, totally alien and repugnant, sucking with chittering valves all that the race can give him. And I suck too, intoxicated by the sweetness of the souls, trying to gain as much power as I can in hopes that I will be able to grow powerful enough to somehow destroy him. And, curiously detached from the carnage of our making, we enjoy a moment of perfect peace in the center of the vortex of slaughter. I come to look upon and into myself, so that I may know the truth of my being, and understand the mystery that is Whargoul in a way that I never could before.

As the sky-borne strata of the stricken city roils about me in its venomous green and bloated purples, beset by the assault of the red and orange, I see the things which my Father has hidden me from me peeled away one by one. The basic building blocks of my existence are laid bare. And when it is before me, I accept it with the deepest sense of gratification that I have ever known. In that instant my cause is validated, my purpose affirmed, and my mission reforged. I meet the truth of myself, and it fulfills all my dreams.

I see it all replayed, how I was stolen from the steppes of Russia over 50 years ago, stolen from my mother's side, adopted by an other-worldly master, poisoned and pumped with agonizing alien life in an obscene effort to create the ultimate Judas, the race-betrayer. The human that was more than human who would lead his race into oblivion. But a human nonetheless. This basic truth had been hidden so well even Cheng-Tzu had never suspected. Despite the alien filth which had infected my body and damned my soul, I was a human being.

And in that moment of self-realization my Father's plans become undone. It is a moment so profound that he stops his feeding to observe mine. For the newly-gained knowledge of my humanity gives me the ability to suck the cast-off energy of the dead at a greater rate than that of my Father, perhaps because they were were drawn to a like kind. And, sensing this failure, he releases a scream that makes the universe shudder and cringe, alerting his brothers. A fell cry of utter defeat and wailing hopelessness as the plan that has spanned thousands of generations, who dutifully fed their young to the war-machine, meets its failure. For in that moment my power surges beyond that of my Father, and I reach across space to open the dimensional rift which must consume him. He feels the cosmos slip and he begins to be drawn from the world that for so long has been his home. I do not have the power to destroy him, but I can banish him to a corner of the multiverse so remote that he can never threaten Earth again. He has no choice in this matter, for fate has ordained his doom. A doom ordained by me that I shall be victorious, and the affirmation of my humanity makes my cause just. I pass my transparent hand, as big as all of Asia, across the heavens, re-ordering the stars and setting forces in motion that soon I would never understand, but for this one moment of omniscience comprehend as easily as you may know yourself. A rushing of stars heralds the creation of the hole, a folding of space marks its presence. Recognizing his fate he begins to slip into the blackness, stretching and warping as the infinite confines of deep space begin to envelope him. Shrieking his protest he struggles mightily, thrashing the world, slaying as many as he can, seeking to somehow match my unexpected supremacy. I straddle the globe, bundling up his many tentacles and pulling him from the crevasses of the planet with a series of grisly pops, much like a dentist would remove a diseased tooth. Huge sections of the world are annihilated—the destruction visited upon Manhattan spreads across the globe in his last futile strugglings as whole continents are dislodged or drowned. This final ravaging kills billions, and their deaths give me the strength I need to complete my task.

Now his endless hordes realize their Master's fate, and their fearsome countenances cloud with fear and uncertainty as they pause in their butcher's work. Father's lowly minions are drawn to him and his removal, and they begin to leap from the surface of the world, burrowing into his flanks and clustering at his fleeting being. With a last mighty heave I pull the entire writhing mass free of the world, which for so many eons has endured their hate. I ball it up like so much trash.

"This is our planet," I bellow in a voice that can be heard throughout the solar system. "You don't belong here. Now go!"

With a final Herculean spasm, I complete my exorcism. Flopping and flailing, his minions flaking from him like dandruff, he hurtles from the Earth and into the cold hole I have prepared for him. It greedily sucks his soul, if he had such a thing.

Already my power is dissipating, my body changing again. I plunge through the atmosphere, shredding cloud and vapor and almost knocking Air Force One (with the new lady President) out of the sky. I fall back into the ruin of the city, colliding with the crater with the force of a fallen angel. The icy waters of the Atlantic rush in, drowning the nuclear fire; taming the Earth-plasma, and sealing the wound the world has endured.

As the water closes above my head I shut my eyes, unsure of my fate. I feel the portal in the heavens shutting, locking him in limbo, placing him behind a wall from which he can never reach Earth again.

He is gone.

I settle back into the seething pool of nuclear magma that once was Manhattan. My consciousness blots out as my body begins to reform, wracked by the spasms of the rebirth. But I pass through them unaffected, bathing in the feeling of well being that suffuses my body. My journey is nearing its end. As my flesh re-knits itself, so your world begins to heal.

As it has before my new body comes forth from the river, gaining the blighted bank and gazing back on the destruction I have left in my wake.

The city is gone; the land reclaimed by the sea. The entire area from uptown to the southern tip of the island has crumbled into the deep. Great powers have been released by the detonation of the bomb, forces greater than the power that the weapon had contained. The elemental power of Earth has been awakened by the blast, another force that had long struggled against my Father. The boundless destructive energy of the Earth was added to that of the bomb. And the force generated was truly amazing. The Earth has been scooped away in the area that had been Manhattan, leaving a great pothole which quickly filled. The greatest city on Earth has paid the price for its own indulgence. A great blossoming of crimson and azure energy expands above the still frothing surface as debris continues to rain back into the water. I turn my back upon the spectacle and walk away, the heat of the reclaimed city burning across my naked shoulders.

A beat-up pick-up truck has skidded off the road and come to rest in a ditch clogged with corpses. I gingerly step through them until I come to the cab, where I bend to the rear-view mirror to examine my new features.

The face, pleasant, the eyes, twinkling with mirth despite the hells on which they have gazed. The mouth cracks into a familiar smile, a crooked and wry grin which had rewarded many of my ravings. I am younger than he had been, but there was no mistaking the face of my mentor.

I wear the features of a man named Cheng-Tzu.

I walk through the world I have saved and try to feel my place within it. Can there be happiness for me in this world, or what is left of it?

Passing through the ruins of Newark and Jersey City I see few signs of life. Maybe that is a good thing.

Soon I leave the blighted area behind and begin moving through the meadowlands and the forests beyond. New Jersey is actually a beautiful state once you get away from the turnpike. It has a bad reputation that it doesn't really deserve. I had heard there was a creature that lives out here, a horse-headed, bat-winged thing with blue skin that they had actually named a hockey team after. I wondered if the beast had fought for my father or against him, or had chosen to just hide throughout the whole bloody business. The one thing I don't consider was that the creature never existed.

The days I spend in the woods, keeping out of sight, and observing the humans from a distance. The destruction visited upon the planet in those last few moments of my Father's reign is truly mind staggering. An earthquake of unprecedented magnitude had shaken the entire planet, leveling or damaging virtually every structure on the face of the world. Between the war and the quake, over three-quarters of the planet's population had met their doom in the space of a few months, and most of them had died on that last day. The world is covered in unburied corpses and the ruins are filled with those who have been buried alive. Everywhere that I go, I see humans working together to deal with the dead to save those that still live beneath the rubble. In the ruins of a shopping mall I observe a group of humans working frantically to free a trapped child. Disasters of great magnitude often bring together the human race for limited periods of time, and inevitably they settle back into their hateful ways as soon as the short-term consequences of the tragedy are dealt with.

I still retain my super-normal powers. My senses are all still intensely acute, my strength still boundless. Cheng has taught me to control my lust for brain-juice, and for the time being I have no desire to feed upon my brethren. But my stomach calls for something, so I enter the ruins of a deserted small town. Gaining entrance to a convenience store through its shattered front window, I help myself to some food. I load up on canned goods and snack foods. Fashioning myself a makeshift pack out of some pieces of cloth, I shoulder my goods and make my way out of the desolate hamlet, munching on a candy bar and considering my future. I head east down the main road. I had begun to formulate a plan concerning the disposition of my fate, and its implementation required the sea.

Suddenly I hear a buzz behind me—the sound of a car traveling down the road I am on. Turning, I wait until I see the vehicle crest the hill behind me. It is a police car, and its driver spots me immediately. Cutting on his lights, he speeds in my direction.

The cop pulls over next to me in a cloud of dust and flying gravel. The officer, a middle-aged and portly man with a broad face and a multitude of chins, exits the car quickly and crosses around the hood, assailing me with a confused jumble of words and gesticulations.

"Hello! Well hello there! It's good to see someone. Everybody, well everybody that was left alive, and there weren't too many of 'em, well they went up to Emory, up to the armory. The armory at Emory, funny, huh? That's where most people who made it are going, meeting up there to try to find their loved ones or what not. They've got power up there, and food and what have you. Not much point in staying here. But I stayed, in case people came around, looking for family or what have you." He smiles and nods his head like a happy puppy seeking approval.

I stare at him in bewilderment. He grabs my hand and pumps it vigorously.

"I'm sorry, I didn't even introduce myself. My name is Bill, Bill Grainger. I'm the sheriff here, or what's left of here. God, it's good to see somebody. I was just leaving myself. And you are—?"

"My name is Cheng . . . Cheng Tzu. I come from up north. I am making my way to the sea."

"The sea, huh? That's where a lot of those things came from." A visible shudder passes through his frame. He removes a flask from his pocket and quickly swills. It seems to calm him.

"Well, they're gone now. Now we can start over. Well, hop in." Noting my uncomprehending stare, he continues.

"I'm heading that way, at least until the turnpike. I'll give you a lift."

A couple-hundred miles later I take leave of my new friend, along with some of his clothing, baggy yet functional. It had been an enjoyable and informative ride, and I hadn't even killed him.

Since the destruction of New York, it seemed that a kind of spontaneous peace had broken out across the entire planet. All the warring factions had declared an immediate and unconditional peace treaty. Everywhere we went we saw the humans working together to heal the damage wrought by the LoiGoi's war. The human race had been driven to the edge of the abyss, taken a good look, and turned the car around, motoring like mad towards the paradise that now, for the first time, seemed within their reach.

Maybe it had worked. I could only hope that with the removal of my Father, his cohorts, and their hellish manipulations, the curse of war, an idea alien to this world, had been lifted from the Earth. That maybe it had been "the war to end all wars." The Whargoul, discovering the humanity that had been hidden from him, had erased the greatest plague. Now the humans had a chance. There was only one thing left to do to insure that the gift kept giving.

Finding a job that suited my needs was easy. The considerable energy of the people was being poured into the rebuilding of their world. I found employment on a barge which delivered cement to various ports on the east coast. My immense strength and quick wit made me a popular member of the crew, so popular that the captain gave me a cabin onboard. I enjoyed the company of my crewmates and the feeling of the sea beneath me. I had never spent much time on boats but they had always made me smile, when I looked at them chugging or sailing along above the glassy depths from whence I'd come. The depths that were calling me back.

I would sit on the deck for hours, staring into the water, lost within myself. When storms would come, I would stay topside, grasping the rail and howling as the rain and wind would lash my body. At these times I felt more alone than I had ever felt in my entire life. At my birth I had not known any better. I was the Whargoul, the killing machine, reveling in my filthy existence. As I had grown older and learned more about my kin, I had felt that I was part of a vast and complex conspiracy, and this had given me a familial feeling of belonging. Later, I would know love, and would love with a passion reserved for the gods. And through it all I would have friends, friends that unfortunately I would either murder or indirectly cause their deaths. Now with my victory, I had lost all these things. There was no longer any sense of purpose in my life.

Then, there was the fact that I was unsure how long I could control myself. I had no idea if my homicidal rages would return or not. I had to do something, but still I tarried, enjoying the spray of the sea and the heave of the deep, the stars shining brightly and the gulls greeting us at the many ports we visited. The Earth was beautiful, and would be beautiful for eternity. I took a deep satisfaction in that I had helped to restore it to its natural state, a state of peace, perfect peace.

There was just a couple of things left to do. I began to write, to record the details of my life in an anonymous black book very similar to the one that Kepler had spent so much time scribbling madly in. The memories of my manic friend always made me smile, and the details of his death brought me great pain. It was a particularly hard passage to write about, but it went in there, as did every other sordid and violent detail of my life. As I wrote I was frequently appalled at my actions. There could be no redemption for me. My crimes had simply been too great. But at least I had tried, and I took a small measure of comfort in that. And when my book was done, I made my last move.

One calm night upon the Atlantic I go into my cabin and get my gun. The sheriff had given it to me with instructions to throw it into the sea once I got there. The entire planet was in the midst of a colossal unilateral disarmament. The guns, tanks, and bombs were to be melted. The steel was to be used to build a vast hydration plant in the Sahara Desert, which was to be turned into a vast garden to attack the hunger problem that had plagued the African continent for so long. The only thing the humans couldn't figure out was why it had taken them this many years to do something that was so obviously to the benefit of the species. If they only had known.

I go to the bridge where I know the captain is awake, drinking coffee and staring at the sea. Upon my entering the room, he turns to me with a smile. A smile that turns to a look of shocked disbelief when he sees the gun in my hand, a gun pointed at his face.

"Cheng, what the hell?"

"Shut up. Don't talk, or I'll blow your fucking head off."

Others on the bridge scramble back and voice their incredulous protest. I silence them with a menacing gesture towards their beloved captain.

"All of you, shut the fuck up. Don't fuck with me or his brains go everywhere. Do exactly as I say and nobody dies. OK?"

They nod as one. With the new and placid attitude of the human race, I know that they won't be a problem.

"Cheng," says the captain. "You don't need to do this. Put the gun down and we—"

"Shut up !" I scream, buffeting him with a verbal blow that blows his hair up around his head. I feel my hatred, my frustration boiling up out of me, and I struggle to control it. I might have banished my Father from the planet, but I could never banish him from within myself.

"You don't know," I say through gritted teeth. "You don't know anything about me."

I turn to the first mate. "You! Set a new course, due east. Full speed. Do it!"

The course will take us to the middle of the Atlantic, into the deepest waters that this part of the world can offer. It will suit my needs perfectly.

First, I disable the radio and collect all of the cell phones. Then I take the captain down onto the deck and order the crew to form up in front of us. Instructing the first mate, I have him tie a length of stout rope around the captain's neck and then hand me the loose end. Then I have the crew break into the cargo hold and bring up a whole bunch of dry cement, which they begin mixing in large tubs. It takes many hours. These guys aren't masons. Through it all I stand stock still, though I let them bring the Captain a chair. I ignore all the questions, and then finally have him gagged. There is no point in talking now. Too much has happened, too many have died. It is time to make an end of it.

Halfway through the next day I'm encased in a massive blob of curing cement. As per my instructions, only my head and forearms protrude from the mass—one arm holding the gun and one holding the rope. A large iron hook has been set into the cement, and I have the crew attach a cable from the massive winch. I instruct the captain to sit atop the rude construction, reassuring him again that he will be unharmed. Then I am hoisted into the air, swinging crazily above first the deck and then the foaming sea. I wait until the pendulum has ceased its motion, and we hang poised above oblivion. Myself, in my self-made tomb, and the captain sitting atop it. In truth I don't know if this will be the end of the Whargoul. But I can't stay here. A world without war is no place for me.

"If you want to know why I do this, look in my cabin," I scream at the crew lining the rail of the ship, pleading with me not to do this thing that they can not understand. "There is a book there, and the story within it is mine. Let it be a warning to those that would rather forget. Enjoy what has been given to you, and remember me."

There is a timeless moment, as I breath in the surface world for what I pray will be the last time. The shifting sea, the swirling clouds draping the face of the moon, it is almost enough to tempt me from my watery grave. Then the red-rimmed atrocity of my life sweeps across the sky like a cloud of angry bats. I have to go.

"Now release the cable, or I'll blow his fucking head off!"

The cable flies loose. The ball drops towards the surface of the water. I suck in my last breath of the surface world, while releasing the captain. The ball crashes into the depths, taking me to a place where I can never hurt anyone again.

It was done.

The ball hurtles through the depths and finally crashes into the murk at the bottom of the ocean after several minutes. The encasement doesn't crack open as I had feared it might. I was not as deep as I would have liked, but I was deep enough. Deep enough for me to be banished for eternity.

The days passed like mud in my watery tomb. There wasn't much to do. I notice a prodigious amount of life down here and I had no doubt they would soon get interested in me. Bizarre phosphorescent fishes floated by, looking curiously like my Father. Then a horrible thought struck me.

What if being banished from this planet was what my Father had wanted the whole time? What if I had been skillfully manipulated into helping him achieve his goal, escaping the planet that was his prison just as surely as this blob of cement was mine? What if in freeing the Earth from the curse of war, I had doomed the universe to an eternity of suffering? Could it be that I was not the redeemer, but the scapegoat, the Judas, the fool who had cursed all creation?

One will think of these things while imprisoned on the bottom of the sea. It was a depressing notion. But now I had more pressing matters than ruminating on my hopefully imaginary failures.

Crabs were eating my face.

ABOUT THE AUTHOR

Dave Brockie is an artist, writer, and musician hailing from the crumbling southern splendor of Richmond, Virginia. For 25 years he has been best known to the world as Oderus Urungus, bellicose lead singer of the shock metal band GWAR, and lesser known as one of the founders and main artists of Slave Pit Inc., GWAR's legendary underground production company. Here he has been the spearhead for many of the groups side projects, such as the X-Cops and Death Piggy, and has created many of images and costumes used in the 25+ year run of Slave Pit madness. This is his first novel.

www.ODERUS.com

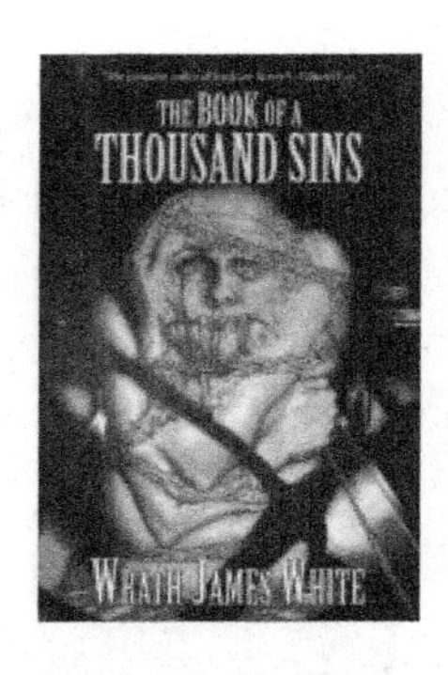

"The Book of a Thousand Sins" Wrath James White - Welcome to a world of Zombie nymphomaniacs, psychopathic deities, voodoo surgery, and murderous priests. Where mutilation sex clubs are in vogue and torture machines are sex toys. No one makes it out alive – not even God himself.

"If Wrath James White doesn't make you cringe, you must be riding in the wrong end of a hearse."

-Jack Ketchum

"Squid Pulp Blues" Jordan Krall - In these three bizarro-noir novellas, the reader is thrown into a world of murderers, drugs made from squid parts, deformed gun-toting veterans, and a mischievous apocalyptic donkey.

"*. . . with SQUID PULP BLUES, [Krall] created a wholly unique terrascape of Ibsen-like naturalism and morbidity; an extravaganza of white-trash urban/noir horror.*"

- Edward Lee

"Apeshit" Carlton Mellick III - Friday the 13th meets Visitor Q. Six hipster teens go to a cabin in the woods inhabited by a deformed killer. An incredibly fucked-up parody of B-horror movies with a bizarro slant

"*The new gold standard in unstoppable fetus-fucking kill-freakomania . . . Genuine all-meat hardcore horror meets unadulterated Bizarro brainwarp strangeness. The results are beyond jaw-dropping, and fill me with pure, unforgivable joy.*" - John Skipp

"Super Fetus" Adam Pepper - Try to abort this fetus and he'll kick your ass!

"*The story of a self-aware fetus whose morally bankrupt mother is desperately trying to abort him. This darkly humorous novella will surely appall and upset a sizable percentage of people who read it . . . In-your-face, allegorical social commentary.*"

- BarnesandNoble.com

THE VERY BEST IN CULT HORROR

deadite
Press

"Rock and Roll Reform School Zombies" Bryan Smith - Sex, Death, and Heavy Metal! The Southern Illinois Music Reeducation Center specializes in "de-metaling" – a treatment to cure teens of their metal loving, devil worshiping ways. A program that subjects its prisoners to sexual abuse, torture, and brain-washing. But tonight things get much worse. Tonight the flesh-eating zombies come . . . *Rock and Roll Reform School Zombies* is Bryan Smith's tribute to "Return of the Living Dead" and "The Decline of Western Civilization Part 2: the Metal Years."

"Necro Sex Machine" Andre Duza - America post apocalypse...a toxic wasteland populated by bloodthirsty scavengers, mutated animals, and roving bands of organized militias wing for control of civilized society's leftovers. Housed in small settlements that pepper the wasteland, the survivors of the third world war struggle to rebuild amidst the scourge of sickness and disease and the constant threat of attack from the horrors that roam beyond their borders. But something much worse has risen from the toxic fog.

"Piecemeal June" Jordan Krall - Kevin lives in a small apartment above a porn shop with his tarot-reading cat, Mithra.She brings him things from outside and one day-brings him an rubber-latex ankle... Later an eyeball, then a foot. After more latex body parts are brought upstairs, Kevin glues them together to form a piecemeal sex doll. But once the last piece is glued into place, the sex doll comes to life. She says her name is June. She comes from another world and is on the run from an evil pornographer and three crab-human hybrid assassins.

"The Vegan Revolution . . . with Zombies" David Agranoff - Thanks to a new miracle drug the cute little pig no longer feels a thing as she is led to the slaughter. The only problem? Once the drug enters the food supply anyone who eats it is infected. From fast food burgers to free-range organic eggs, eating animal products turns people into shambling brain-dead zombies – not even vegetarians are safe!
"*A perfect blend of horror, humor and animal activism.*"
- Gina Ranalli

ERASERHEAD PRESS

"The Kobold Wizard's Dildo of Enlightenment +2" Carlton Mellick III - ARE YOU READY TO PLAY SOME DUNGEONS AND FUCKING DRAGONS? The story of a group of adventurers going through an existential crisis after having discovered that they are really just pre-rolled characters living inside of a classic AD&D role playing game. Featuring: punk rock elf chicks, death metal orcs, porn-addicted beholders, a goblin/halfling love affair, a gnoll orgy, and a magical dildo that holds the secrets of the universe.

"Ass Goblins of Auschwitz" Cameron Pierce - In a land where black snow falls in the shape of swastikas, there's a nightmarish prison camp known as Auschwitz. It is run by a fascist, flatulent race of aliens called the Ass Goblins, who abduct children from the neighboring world of Kidland. Prisoners 999 and 1001 are conjoined twin brothers forced to endure the sadistic tortures of these monsters. While the Ass Goblins become drunk on cider made from fermented children, the twins plot their escape. Forget everything you know about Auschwitz...you're about to be Shit Slaughtered.

"Super Giant Monster Time" Jeff Burk - Aliens are invading the Earth and their ray guns turn people into violent punk rockers. At the same time, the city is being overtaken by giant monsters tougher than Godzilla and Mothra combined. You choose one of three characters to try and survive the end of the world. From cult author Jeff Burk, comes a tribute to those old Choose Your Own Adventure Books from your youth, just with more punks, beer, and city-stomping monsters.

"Night of the Assholes" Kevin L. Donihe - From Wonderland Award Winner Kevin L. Donihe, comes a hilarious tribute to Night of the Living Dead A plague of assholes is infecting the countryside. Normal everyday people are transforming into jerks, snobs, dicks, and douchebags. And they all have only one purpose: to make your life a living hell. The assholes are everywhere. They're picking fights, causing accidents, and even killing people. Six survivors, cut off from the world and surrounded by a sea of assholes, must find a way to last through the night.

"The Emerald Burrito of Oz" John Skipp and Marc Levinthal - ZOMBIE MUNCHKINS! TURD-FLINGING FLATHEADS! EVIL CORPORATE CONSPIRACIES! DELICIOUS MEXICAN FOOD! OZ IS REAL! This loving Bizarro tribute to the great L. Frank Baum is an action-packed, whimsically ultraviolent adventure, featuring your favorite Oz characters as you've never seen 'em before. Let super-hot warrior sweetheart Aurora Quixote Jones take you on a guided tour of surrealist laffs, joy, and mayhem. More fun than a barrel of piss-drunk winged monkeys!

"Rampaging Fuckers of Everything on the Crazy Shitting Planet of the Vomit Atmosphere" Mykle Hansen - With the wit of Christopher Moore, the inventiveness of Terry Gilliam and the rudeness of South Park, comes an award-winning collection of three short novels by a master of satire. Hansen's surreal fiction is ridiculously fun to read. His subversive tales capture the smugness of mainstream culture, as he thrusts his characters into absurd and humorous situations that reveal the defects in the modern social fabric. A must read for fans of weird humor.

"Shatnerquake" Jeff Burk - It's the first ShatnerCon with William Shatner as the guest of honor! But after a failed terrorist attack by Campbellians, a crazy terrorist cult that worships Bruce Campbell, all of the characters ever played by William Shatner are suddenly sucked into our world. Their mission: hunt down and destroy the real William Shatner. Featuring: Captain Kirk, TJ Hooker, Denny Crane, Rescue 911 Shatner, Singer Shatner, Shakespearean Shatner, Twilight Zone Shatner, Cartoon Kirk, Esperanto Shatner, Priceline Shatner, SNL Shatner, and - of course - William Shatner!

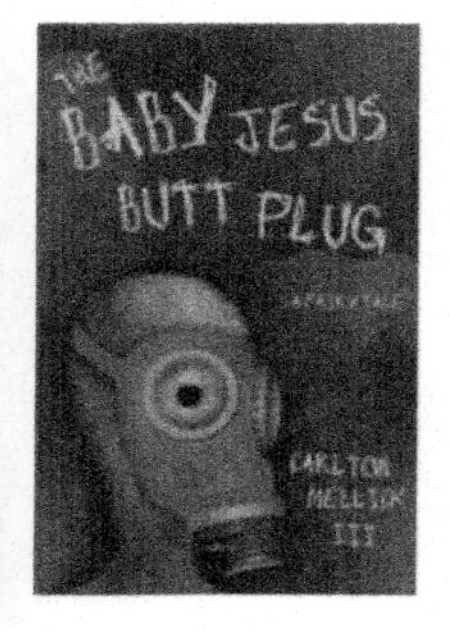

"The Baby Jesus Butt Plug" Carlton Mellick III - WARNING: DO NOT MOLEST THE BABY JESUS! Step into a dark and absurd world where human beings are slaves to corporations, people are photocopied instead of born, and the baby jesus is a very popular anal probe. Presented in the style of a children's fairy tale, *The Baby Jesus Butt Plug* is a short dystopian horror story about a young couple who make the mistake of buying a living clone of the baby jesus to use for anal sex. Once the baby jesus clone turns on them, all hell breaks loose.

AVAILABLE FROM AMAZON.COM

CPSIA information can be obtained at www.ICGtesting.com
Printed in the USA
LVOW04s0328240315

431758LV00026B/510/P

9 781936 383